The Candidate

Brian Shostak

Preface

Reading has always been a part of my life. As far back as I can remember I enjoyed putting myself into another world and experiencing all types of stories. Never in my wildest dreams though did I think I would actually write a book, and I have to admit the process has been fun and challenging. It's amazing what you can come up with after waking up from an exciting dream you have one night.

When I began writing this book I had no idea how it would turn out. At one point I had the book almost completed but didn't like the way it was turning out so I started over. I set out to write a novel that would make someone who doesn't read pick it up and enjoy the story. Then hopefully set them on an adventure to read other books. Finally satisfied with the story and the way it was written, I owe some special people a thank you.

First, thanks to Spencer, Courtney, and Abigail for basically reading the book as I was writing it and telling me that the book stayed interesting throughout. Also for the feedback that helped shaped the story.

I'd also like to acknowledge Susan who gave me early thoughts and feedback on the book and let me know about things I may have not explained well or overlooked or even some things I was questionable on.

A special thanks to Trevor Gray at Gray Digital Ink for designing the cover to my book. Trevor really captured my image on what I wanted and I was blown away by what he submitted. I couldn't picture a better cover for this book. Definitely recommend his graphics talent to anyone that needs it. Visit his website at www.graydigitalink.com

I also want to thank Lori for doing one of the edits on the book for me and fixing most of my grammar, punctuation, etc. I know it must have been awful to endure…. Just kidding. Even though you don't consider yourself a professional per se, I'm grateful that you did this for a self-publishing author. I couldn't have asked for a more qualified and knowledgeable person to do that for me and again, thank you.

Lastly I give my thanks to you. Whether you purchased, borrowed, or illegally obtained (please don't) this book. I hope I have given you a story to enjoy as much as I have enjoyed writing it. One of the challenges I've noticed as a self-publishing author is being able to accept your book the way you write it. Even though my book has gone through many edits, it may not be perfect as far as grammar and other things go, but I hope you enjoy it and you continue to read and put yourself into new and exciting stories.

Table of Contents

Prologue

Above Earth in the blackness of space sat a mysterious ship. It was orbiting the Earth and had been after arriving a few days ago. On board was a crew of a highly intelligent race that had just discovered the Earth and was sent to study as much as they could just for a few days. The ship then moved from the dark side of the planet back to the light side in what seemed like seconds.

A slim, tall, and translucent figure with lean muscle, dark short hair, and eyes that were as black as space itself, leans back from what looks like a holographic lens pointed down at the Earth and asks another figure, "Do you think this planet will create life like our own eventually?" The other figure who wore a sort of suit that signified he was the captain of the ship stood at the large window of the ship overlooking Earth, hands behind his back. He looked once at the male that asked him this question and then back out at the Earth. "It is possible. Our home world began similar to this one. But to say that they would eventually evolve into us is something not even I can predict. Plus, even if they did, there would be no knowing how different they would be from us. We may not call them glowans."

On a holoscreen just above the window there were images of what the glowan was looking at through the lens. There were large creatures taller than some of the buildings back on the home planet with sharp teeth. The captain watched as these creatures would attack and eat other creatures of similar appearance. He walked away from the window and sat down on a chair that overlooked his crew that controlled different parts of the ship. Each one of these figures had the same type of skin texture. You can see light pass through them but you couldn't see anything on the insides of their bodies, almost like they had a glow about them.

Some of the glowans had long, dark hair and the others had short dark hair. Besides other obvious features, this was a way to tell the males from the females.

"Notify home base that we have found a planet similar to ours that has life on it. Ask them what the next steps are," the captain instructed one of the fellow glowans sitting at what looked like a communication console. The male glowan relayed the message then acknowledged he understood the next directions. He turned back around to face the captain and said, "Home base would like us to return to be debriefed of our findings. No mention of a return date." The captain stood up and walked back to the large window. Sadness overwhelmed him. He was the one who found this planet and the life on it. When this planet starts to evolve and produce life, possibly like him and the rest of the glowans, he might not be here to see it. He may be long dead by then. "Set a course for home," he said.

Circling back around, he retreated toward the depths of the ship onto a deck called 'travelling.' Anytime the glowans had to travel they would have to sit in a seat that would place them in an invisible cocoon of sorts. When the captain and the rest of the crew were all finally in their seats and secured, he ordered, to what seemed like the ship itself, "begin travel" and the ship turned away from the Earth, opened a sort of black hole in space itself, and traveled through it leaving Earth light years behind.

Chapter 1

There was a figure lying in a tub of clear liquid. Not moving. Not breathing. Completely motionless. Another figure that looked similar in appearance, with longer hair and female anatomy, walked over to the tub, pressed a button, and the liquid started to drain. When it reached the bottom, the glowan inside the pool coughed twice bringing up the liquid that was in his lungs and, being that it was the glowan's first time in this liquid, a little bit of blood.

"How long was I in for?" the figure asked in a deep voice. The other figure replied, "Just over a year." This figure had long black hair and started to smile before she then said, "You're lucky I didn't leave you in there longer Marctus. We could all benefit from your absence." Marctus got up and started stretching his back, legs, and arms, then said back to the other figure, "But if that happened you wouldn't be able to stare at me all the time, Valee." Valee blushed at this comment because it was true. She had secretly admired him ever since she met him a year ago when he had been brought in to begin the testing.

Valee walked over to another figure with the same features as Marctus, short black hair, black eyes, tall and lean, and said, "Captain, Marctus is your last qualifier. His time in sleep was one year, four days." The captain acknowledged her and knew that for him to last over a year in the liquid meant that he could last as long as needed for the mission ahead. "Thank you, Valee. Would you please gather Marctus and the rest of the qualifying candidates and have them meet me in Dock E please?" Valee acknowledged him at first and as she was walking away she turned back around, "Sir, you said E right? No one is allowed in E unless Admiral Schur allows...."

"I am aware of who is allowed in there, Valee, thank you," the captain said as he cut her off mid-sentence. Valee then advanced with a fast walk, grabbed Marctus by the arm and left the deck. "What was that about?" Marctus asked. "Just so you know, no one is ever allowed in Dock E. It's supposedly the dock where all secrets are held for future missions. So, if I were you, I would pay attention and mind your tone." Valee then shoved him into a glass room that was located before the actual door to Dock E. In there with Marctus were 19 other glowans. He didn't know any of them. From looking around at them he noticed there were ten males including him and ten females.

Just as Marctus was going to ask if anyone knew what was going on, the glass around them turned a dark black. Marctus could no longer see Valee standing on the other side. All he could see were the lights that outlined the door into Dock E. Minutes passed. Then, the door opened. They saw a large room with nothing in it. Empty. No windows. No tables. No chairs. Nothing. They all walked inside the room, looking confused. As the last glowan entered, a male, the door quickly closed causing them all to jump. The room itself now turned a pitch black. Marctus held his hand in front of him and couldn't even see his fingers. The glowing effect of their bodies was extinguished by the darkness. Then, all of a sudden in the middle of the room, floating in midair, a big, circular object appeared. It was spinning slowly. Marctus and the rest of the glowans walked toward the spinning sphere. When he got closer it looked almost like the planet they live on, except the land—

Marctus' thoughts were cut off as another door opened across from them and the Captain, along with the Admiral, was walking toward them. Marctus had never met nor even seen the Admiral. He had only heard of him in books from school. The 20 selected glowans stood and watched as the two figures approached.

Finally, stopping just in front of the sphere, the Admiral gave a huge grin, held his hand out toward the sphere and said, "I present to you the first planet we've found to contain life: Earth."

Chapter 2

Marctus and the other glowans all looked at the Earth with the same curious expression. Some of them had their jaws hanging open. They all watched the planet turn. Marctus walked around it looking at the amount of water the planet had as well as a huge mountain range on one of the continents. He noticed the clouds and weather formations on the planet. He was simply fascinated by it. It was so similar, yet so different when compared to their planet.

The Admiral waved his hand and the image of the Earth disappeared and was replaced with an image of a forested area. "The Captain here was the first of our species -- along with his crew -- to find Earth in the early stages of life there." As the Admiral said this, the image moved and was actually a video of a tall creature with arms that were very disproportionate to its body. The creature was running. Fast. Chasing what looked like smaller versions of itself. Eventually, it was able to lower its ginormous head and grab one in its mouth. It cut the smaller creature clean in half. The scene then changed to another video showing creatures similar in texture but with very long necks standing in an open field that was encircled by forest. They would walk up to the edge of the trees that were as tall or taller than they were and eat the leaves from them. They didn't have sharp teeth like the first creatures did.

"These early stages of life existed when we were at our peak of technology. After the captain returned to give us these videos and other data, he requested to be put into a timeless sleep until such time as we could return here when intelligent life should be blooming." Another male glowan standing a few feet from Marctus blurted out, "How long ago was that exactly?" The admiral smiled and motioned for the captain to respond. "Well

Birgue, that was 145 million years ago." At this statement the whole room started whispering. Everyone was talking to each other. All asking the same question, how was this possible?

As far as Marctus was concerned, no one had ever been able to stay in timeless sleep for more than a few million years. After that time it seemed as if the body no longer reacted to the Silpo, the liquid substance used for timeless sleep. Back when Marctus was going through his first years of school, the teachers taught them about the substance that was (as much as they knew) unique to their planet. Marctus only knew a few people who were actually alive millions of years ago. Each of their bodies could only last so long in the Silpo, that when your time was up, you would awaken immediately and would never be able to use the substance again.

Most people would wait until they were about 30 years old then would opt to use the Silpo to see how long they could get into the future. Some would last seconds and some years. It was all dependent on the body. But now no one is really doing it anymore. Mainly because the technology the glowans have created is at a peak. Because of this peak, no one sees any point in 'living longer' to see new technology or new developments.

The captain then said, "With the Silpo, as you know, we are able to put ourselves into a timeless sleep and how long we can last completely depends on our bodies. Some of us a few seconds some of us a few million years, and some of us not at all. Upon arriving back home, I wanted to be put into a pod and sleep as long as I could because I wanted to be here when we would find out more about Earth and the life there. So taking the risk that I may only last a few seconds, I went into the Silpo. When I woke up, I felt like I had just climbed in it a few seconds ago. I was worried it didn't work. But upon waking up, I noticed there was a new admiral in charge. I was then briefed by the admiral here about what has transpired all these years which, up until recently, nothing really interesting happened on Earth. On our home planet the only things that changed were positions of power and leadership and things of similar nature, but I wasn't really interested in that."

He walked around the room watching the huge creatures and continued to speak, "It was a few years after I woke up things started to get interesting. Forty-five years ago the current life on Earth was starting to venture into space."

The whole room started whispering again around Marctus. He was about to ask a question when the admiral raised a hand to silence the whispering going around the room. After a moment he said, "The captain is the only one to last longer than a few million years. The crew he found this planet with is long gone. So we are lucky that his body was able to sustain itself up until a few years ago. While he's been sleeping we have been monitoring the planet from one of our drones currently in orbit there. The footage we get back is always interesting and we can get an estimate of how advanced they are becoming by viewing it." The admiral waved his hand and another video image appeared. Marctus and the rest of the glowans again gazed open mouthed at what they were watching.

They were looking at a race very similar to themselves but with only small differences. Some of the figures were larger than others, had different skin tones, different hair, different eyes, and the major difference was they didn't seem to pass light through their body like a glowan did. The video changed again to an image of a cliff side. Standing in a small area was a group of figures holding metal circles and sharp metal sticks. They stood in a formation as a huge army charged them and, as soon as the two groups clashed, the smaller group came out victorious. Marctus watched astonished as the smaller group didn't lose a single member in the fighting. The video then changed again to a desert setting. There were tons of figures climbing ladders hauling stones to place one on top of the other. Marctus watched as the video fast forwarded showing the stones they placed eventually took the form of a pyramid.

"From looking at recent video we know that they call themselves humans. The previous videos were from the early years of this race. Their technology is not much different from the early years of our race. The videos you saw are from two different time periods, from two different places on this planet. For time's sake, we are going to skip up until recently. From studying them all these years, they have turned into a violent race, also not much different than us." The admiral then waved his hand once more and a scene opened looking at a beach with a long white metal object that was yards away. Marctus and the rest of the candidates watched as the long white metal object started lifting off from the ground leaving a trail of fire and smoke as it climbed toward the sky. It looked as if it was going to come right into the room. Then the feed cut out.

"This is the last thing we have received from the drone we had. That object you saw is similar to what we first used in our first space flights. They call it a rocket. It launches the smaller piece that you saw on top out into space to orbit the Earth, or, that's what the purpose of this one was. However, upon takeoff, it crashed into our probe and we lost video feed. We received this video about a year ago in their year of 2014 they call it. It was at this time we decided to start the planning for the mission you have been selected for."

"So, what has happened since then?" one of the female glowans asked. The captain spoke this time with certainty in his voice, "Well, Lilan, we are pretty sure they are not much more advanced. They have only been able to land on their moon thus far and that was 45 years ago and, like the admiral said, when we started taking interest." Then, a question came to Marctus. Why were they here learning about this? Why us? Why do we need to know this about these humans? "So what exactly does all this have to do with us?" Marctus asked. The admiral looked at Marctus with a confused look on his face. He was thinking to himself, how could this candidate not understand the importance of learning about these humans? Learn about what they do, why they do it, and what other differences there are from us to them? "Everything," he said.

"And why did it take 145 million years for us to finally decide to learn about this?" Marctus also blurted out.

The admiral looked at him and said, "We wanted to see how the planet evolved, the events that occurred and anything else that happened up until humans evolved. We again didn't know if something like this would happen, so we simply watched all these years, and all these years we have been trying to find other planets with life. But to no avail. Unfortunately, the way we move through space is that we have to physically travel somewhere first, only then can we open the worm hole to get there in a matter of minutes."

The admiral paused and then continued, "This is how we have been getting pretty much instant video feed, by sending a drone to and from Earth every few years to see if anything is new. After the first hundred thousand years we didn't send a drone again until millions of years later. At that time we saw the first evolutions of the human race. From there we monitored them daily just to study them. Again, Marctus, we didn't really see anything worth doing up until recently when they landed on their own moon. Now we have something to do, a mission with a purpose. This mission will be given to you in due time."

Chapter 3

The admiral waved his hand once more and the Earth disappeared. Then, from the floor, a table rose and on the table was what looked like Silpo in a small bowl. Marctus walked over with the other candidates and they gathered around the table still facing the admiral and the captain who stood on the other side. The captain and admiral both rolled up their sleeves and drew from their pocket a small device in the shape of a small rod. The rod was just a little bigger than their middle finger. Faster than the candidates could comprehend, the captain and admiral sent a light shooting out of the rods toward each of their forearms, producing a cut down the length of it. The laser was no bigger than the size of Marctus' hand. The captain let blood from his arm drip over the Silpo for a minute while the admiral let his arm drip blood a little longer. When they were done, they both flipped the rod around and shone another type of light on the cut which healed almost instantly.

"We will explain these devices at another time. For now, pay close attention," the admiral said before taking a sip out of the bowl containing the Silpo. After he took a sip the captain then took one as well. After the captain put the bowl back down, Marctus saw the captain go limp but remained standing upright but saw the admiral fall to the floor unconscious. Just as Marctus got over to the admiral lying on the floor, the captain spoke, "Don't touch him he's fine. Or should I say, I'm fine." Marctus and the rest of the candidates all stared at the captain confused. Marctus said, "What's going on?" Some of the other candidates nodded wondering the same thing.

"This is Admiral Schur. I am simply controlling everything about Captain Reath from my body while lying unconscious." This was definitely not Silpo. Marctus started to think if he ever heard of anything like this in school or even just in talking to friends. He couldn't come up with anything. How could he have forgotten something as important as this? "Admiral Schur, I don't remember learning anything about this particular function of Silpo. I thought you could only go into a timeless sleep using it," a candidate named Reol said.

"That is correct Reol. Silpo is only used for timeless sleep. This form of Silpo, however, is modified." The captain then walked over to the remainder of the Silpo that was in the bowl and poured it out onto the table. The candidates immediately stepped back so as not to get hit with the splash of it falling onto the table, but when the Silpo hit the table, it simply stopped. Like it was a heavy boulder falling onto the table.

The candidates all stepped closer to examine the table and to see why the Silpo was not running off of the table. It had the same watery texture as Silpo but it simply would not move unless forced. Marctus touched it with his finger and his finger went ice cold. It definitely didn't feel like Silpo. Silpo had a warming temperature to it, not ice cold. Other than the temperature difference and the fact that it didn't flow wherever it could, Marctus couldn't see any other differences.

"Now obviously there are secrets that we cannot show you. However, given the recent circumstances and what our mission will be, you will be briefed on a few things." The captain waved a hand and the table with the bowl and modified Silpo disappeared. In the middle of the room a spaceship appeared. Marctus looked at it and didn't recognize it, nor did any of the other candidates it seemed.

The ship Marctus and the rest of the candidates were looking at in the middle of the room didn't look anything like the other ships Marctus had learned about. It looked like an abstract piece of art with all the angled plates to ricochet off of asteroids, but it had the look of a space ship. The weirdest feature was that it looked almost invisible. If you stood in front of the ship you could see it perfectly. But when Marctus tried to walk around it, he no longer saw it. He could see the edge of the angled plates, but the rest of it seemed invisible. As Marctus walked back to the front of the ship, the captain said, "Let me go back to my body and we will talk about this ship." With that, the captain looked like he shivered, and was back to his normal self. Meanwhile, the admiral was getting up off the floor.

Chapter 4

"How did you break the connection?" one of the female candidates asked.

"That explanation will come at another time," the admiral said firmly. He waved his hand and another type of ship Marctus knew as a Viper, appeared next to the new one. The new ship was significantly larger than the Viper due to the fact that the Viper was more of a fighter ship and the new ship was obviously meant to hold a large crew and maybe even some Vipers or smaller ships on board. "This ship is called 'The Stalker.' It is the only ship of its kind and it is Top Secret. Is that understood?"

"Yes, Admiral," all the candidates replied.

"You will be briefed on the purpose of this ship at another time. Now, I'm sure a lot of you are wondering what exactly you are doing here and what all these things we have talked about and the things I've showed you have to do with you select few." The admiral waved his hand again and the picture of the Earth reappeared in all its beauty.

Admiral Schur nodded at Captain Reath and the captain began to speak, "I will be the captain of this ship. With me will be a crew and yourselves. Our destination is Earth. Your purpose will be explained once we get there. If you choose not to go then please inform myself or Admiral Schur and we will get you removed from the mission. Please let us know now."

The room was quiet. Everyone wanted to go. Marctus especially wanted to go. He wondered if they were going to do some spying on Earth and maybe even get to visit the planet. Maybe even make peace with the humans and bring them to their world and interact with them. Marctus noticed one candidate named Lilan raise her hand but the captain and admiral did not see her before the captain waived his hand once more.

A door on the far side of the room opened. "You have 24 hours. Do anything you wish to do. Meet at the ship bay at 6 PM sharp. Do not bring anything with you. You are dismissed." Even though Marctus learned and saw a ton of information and secrets, he left feeling empty. Yeah, they showed them new technology and showed them a planet that has intelligent life, but one thing burned in his mind: why were they going there? If it was something simple, why didn't they just tell them during the time they were all in there? Marctus got a bad feeling about this mission but hoped his instincts were wrong.

Chapter 5

"I still don't understand why we didn't tell them the purpose of the mission, Admiral. What if, when we get there, they decide they don't want to do it?" the captain said nervously and also kind of angrily as he sat down in front of the Admiral's desk. Looking around he saw a lot of pictures of the admiral with other military personnel, standing in front of Gliders, old models of ancient Gliders from the first era when they were built. Also behind the admiral sat a shelf with numerous awards.

"Because, Captain, unfortunately for them, they don't have an option to back out. Out of the thousands and thousands of people we tested, they were the only ones that passed the Silpo test. If they choose to back out, they will be executed."

"But Admiral—"

"Is that understood, Captain Reath?" the admiral glared at him, daring him to continue his line of questioning.

"Yes, Admiral, I understand the reason for the mission but I don't agree with how we are going about it and I think we should tell them the whole mission. Not just the part they are there for..."

"Well, you won't have to worry about it. You will have a team of our top biological scientists on board to do the hard job. Your job is the simple one. I am expecting that you will explain the guidelines and rules for this mission to the candidates in the previously discussed matter and will not reveal the most important part until I have given word to do so."

"Yes Admiral. As for the Silpo test, you believe the modified Silpo will work with their bodies for as long as we need it to?" Captain Reath then asked.

"Yes. If they all lasted over a year in it, Dr. Symborg told me that the modified Silpo will work. It doesn't have a 'time limit' per se. As long as they can last over a year in the original Silpo…they will be fine. It should not alter the mission or affect it in anyway," the admiral said and then dismissed the captain.

Chapter 6

Marctus was at the ship bay 10 minutes early as well as everyone else. Everybody seemed eager to learn more about what they'd be doing. Marctus wondered how many of his fellow candidates said goodbye to their parents. He sort of regretted it now but he thought that if he said goodbye, he would never see them again. He hadn't seen them in over a year after being forcefully taken from his home and put into timeless sleep. Last night when he left the facility and saw his parents for the first time in over a year, they hugged and kissed him but he didn't tell them about where he would be going the following night. So he skipped saying goodbye after what he thought was never even a hello. He had eaten breakfast alone and then spent the day with his friends saying his goodbyes and promised to tell them all about it when he returned.

When 6 PM hit, the door they were waiting outside of opened and Valee was there. Marctus wondered if she would be going with them to Earth and what her possible role might be when they were there. Would it be different than his? But, then again, Marctus didn't even know what his role would be.

"Please follow me candidates, the captain is waiting for you," she said.

The candidates all followed her through the door and into a large hallway. On the walls of the hallway were pictures of all the past space explorers from the beginning of the space program. Marctus recognized a few of them, especially the one of Gurt Heifu who was the man that found out how to travel at the speed of light safely and to establish the wormhole connection.

After walking for what seemed like hours, they approached the captain outside a large door. He was standing with two other males each holding a deadly energy rifle just outside the door. Valee left through a side door and the captain began to speak.

"I'm supposed to ask again if there is anyone that wants to back out. Please speak up now."

To Marctus' surprise, one of the female candidates spoke up, "I'd like to resign, sir. I do not want to leave my family." The captain turned to one of the guys with the guns and nodded.

"Thure will escort you out." The guy on the left grabbed the candidate by the arm and led her down the hallway.

"Shall we continue?" the captain asked. He turned and the door opened into a hangar where a Glider ship was sitting. Just as they entered through the door, Marctus could have sworn he heard the high pitched sound of the energy gun going off but, as he turned to look, the door was shut.

"Wait here." The captain and the other glowan with the gun walked toward the ship sitting in the middle of the huge, wide open hangar. Marctus watched as the captain spoke with who he assumed was the pilot sitting outside the ship examining it. Marctus admired the triangle shape of the Glider. It did not look anything like the Stalker or even the Viper. It was a ship entirely of its own. He saw the pilot nod and he walked toward the back of the Glider, up the entry ramp. As the captain returned to the group of candidates he spoke swiftly,

"We will be taking this Glider to the mother ship. Do not talk on the ship. Do not ask questions. Do not do anything but sit and wait. Is that understood?" All of the candidates nodded.

"Good. Follow me."

He led them toward the Glider, which Marctus had never seen up close. He had known it was big, perhaps as long as one of the mini skyscrapers in every city. It was one of the main ships that took people from the planet to the mother ship. In reality any ship could but being that they had a group of about 20 glowans, the Glider would be suitable. Marctus and the rest of the candidates all walked up the entry ramp and into the huge hallway of the ship. Doors lined the hallway of the ship leading to different quarters and traveling rooms. Turning left at the end they entered one of the main sitting areas where the captain instructed them all to sit down. The captain then left through another door leaving the glowan guard with the gun there with them.

After a few moments a voice filled the room and seemed to come from the walls of the ship. "We are headed toward the mother ship. This is your last chance to leave. Please let Hairt know now." Obviously the guy with the gun was Hairt, and he looked at each of them in turn. No one said anything and he clicked a button on the wall.

"Good. We'll arrive at the mother ship in just a few minutes." And the voice faded.

Chapter 7

The Glider had no windows (except for the windows in the control room of the ship) so Marctus couldn't see the mother ship as they approached it. He thought maybe the new Stalker ship would have windows so, when they left, he would be able to see it. The captain's voice came through the walls again, "When we land, stay where you are and wait for me to personally escort you off."

After a few minutes the Glider landed with a thump into what could only be one of the many hangars of the mother ship. Marctus and the other candidates waited for the captain while Hairt watched them all closely.

After a minute or two, the captain appeared and motioned for them all to follow. One by one they got up and followed Captain Reath down the ramp, off the ship and into the open hangar. As they came down the ramp, Marctus watched Birgue fall right in front of him. Marctus tried to hold in laughter as he helped him to his feet.

"Thanks," Birgue told him laughing at himself and Marctus nodded at him, still trying not to laugh. As they looked around the hangar, Marctus did a complete turnaround. The hangar he was in was ginormous. He counted at least 20 Gliders parked on landing pads being re-energized and some of them having damage repaired. There were workers driving Floaters around to get to and from doorways, ship to ship, wherever you needed to be transported. Just as Marctus was done examining the room, a Floater stopped in front of them.

"Everyone get in. This is taking us to our quarters for the evening."

The captain got in last, said "Mission E Quarters" and the Floater began to move on its way. As they passed by several Gliders with other glowans working on them, he wondered where the other ships, and even the Stalker, were being held as he wanted to see them as well.

"Captain Reath, will we be able to walk around the ship and explore before we leave?" one of the candidates asked before Marctus got the chance.

"No, we are going to be busy explaining more mission details to you, eating and getting some rest before we leave morning after next." The captain looked around, like he was anticipating someone to start complaining about not being able to explore the mother ship. Surprisingly, no one said anything.

The Floater went through a couple doors that led to smaller hallways and eventually stopped in front of a door with the letter E glowing on the door. Everyone got out and entered the door into a small room which had two doors on the far side. One said Males and the other Females. Marctus followed the Males through the male door and saw ten beds against the wall in a long room. Also in the room was a bathroom through a door halfway into the room, and then a lounge area where the recent news broadcast was displayed on the holoscreen above the couches.

Marctus almost forgot that the captain was behind him and jumped when he began to speak,

"You may do whatever you like in here until tomorrow morning. I highly suggest you eat and sleep rather than stay up and think about wandering outside these doors. I promise you that if you do, you will not come back." They all nodded that they understood and the captain left.

"So who wants to go exploring?" one of the glowans named Zeed asked. "I don't see why we wouldn't be able to come back here." He started walking toward the door, listening to see if the captain had left the area yet.

"I wouldn't. Back when that girl wanted to leave to be with her family, I could've sworn I heard them shoot her just before the door closed." Marctus looked over at Birgue who said this. He then knew the shooting must have happened if he wasn't the only person who heard it.

"No way, man. They wouldn't kill us for not wanting to go, or just because we go exploring. I'll be back in five minutes." With that said, he left the room. After five minutes, he wasn't back yet. After an hour, while everyone else was eating, they heard the door open and turned to see the guy had returned. Only he was sweating like he'd been running for a long time and had blood on him. Marctus couldn't tell if it was his blood or someone else's.

"Everyone," he started panting, catching his breath. "We…need to leave…now…somehow…someway. I just saw…," What he saw Marctus and the other candidates never found out. At that moment, a fountain of blood exploded from his mouth, ears, eyes and nose and the candidate fell over dead. The captain walked in the room holding a small energy gun, saw the bloody glowan on the floor and signaled to someone outside the door. That person came in and grabbed the body and hauled it off.

The captain shut the door and turned to the rest of the male candidates. "As I said before, if you leave this room you wouldn't be coming back. Do not leave this room without my personal escort."

"What happened to him, Captain?" A glowan named Sul asked.

"He disobeyed an order and suffered the consequences is what happened. Keep that in mind." The captain left the room with the door silently closing behind him.

"Does anyone else feel like they're not telling us something about this mission?" Birgue asked.

"I think they're not telling us a lot of things. Not yet at least. I think by telling us now they think it will leak and spread, and they don't want that." Marctus said.

"Yeah, but to kill someone over it? This mission must be something different than anything they've ever done before."

Marctus turned and walked to an empty bed, lay down and closed his eyes. He thought about what the other candidate could have seen that would get him killed. He couldn't think of anything other than it was something about the mission. Maybe Birgue was right. They were going to tell us when we were all alone by Earth as to not leak anything. Either way, Marctus felt a chill come over his body just before he drifted off to sleep.

Chapter 8

"Why has no one been in here yet?" Birgue asked. Marctus really got to know him on the Floater when they were shaken awake and basically dragged out of the room to be transported to another room with 20 chairs facing a view screen. Birgue had almost run away not wanting to come. He said he had a terrible feeling about this mission and wanted no part of it, but he decided to come anyway. Then he and Birgue talked about things they were both interested in and decided that they would stick together through this whole mission. Marctus felt good to have a friend with him now.

"No idea. Probably just taking their sweet time since we really have no other choice but to sit here," Marctus said. Just as he said it, the door opened and the captain walked in alone, which was unusual since he had been accompanied by at least one armed guard since they saw him back on the planet.

He walked around to the front of the room, faced the candidates and snapped on the holoscreen. A bright blue light filled the room and then the blue light seemed to flood into the holoscreen and created a three dimensional image of Earth.

"Today we will briefly discuss our mission and go over some items that will be used during our mission. Let's start with the humans." As he finished speaking, the screen changed to an image of a male and female human, each naked. Marctus noticed that, unlike the glowans, the male and female had different hair color and eye color, but the skin color was the same color.

The captain rotated his hand and the image rotated to show their backs.

"As you can see, they are very similar to us in appearance. Same sex organs. Same body shape." He then walked to the door he had entered through and opened it to let another figure in. This figure was wearing a uniform that Marctus knew was associated with medical personnel, specifically surgical doctors. The male doctor walked to the front of the room with the captain and faced the candidates.

"This is Doctor Symborg. He can further explain the anatomy of the humans, as I have little knowledge of what lies under the skin." The captain stepped aside. The doctor tapped on his wrist and a new image appeared on the screen.

"Hello candidates! As the captain told you, I am Dr. Symborg and I will be accompanying you on your mission to Earth, along with a select few medical doctors." The image that appeared was an image of a human body that was cut open with the organs floating alongside the body.

"You're probably wondering how we have this information on the humans when you were just informed of their existence hours ago. When we first lost contact with the drone orbiting Earth, we sent a team there to abduct a male and female human and return the specimens as quickly as possible. Upon their delivery, we cloned them and killed the originals as to study their physiology."

The candidates all sat listening closely to the doctor, interested in what he had to say. Marctus personally thought this was disgusting. The doctor flicked his wrist and the human was now standing in front of a bright light.

"As you can see, their skin is not as transparent as ours. We simply glow around the edges depending on the light shown on us, whereas the humans don't do so at all."

He then zoomed in to where Marctus and the rest of the candidates could see into the male human's mouth.

"They have the same number of teeth as us and the same gum structure."

He zoomed back out of the mouth and next focused on the human's skeleton.

"The bone structure is exactly the same as ours as well, same number of bones, same everything."

The doctor then brought up the image of the organs as removed from the body seen earlier.

"The only difference between us really is the eyes, hair and skin complexion. However, this is data from only two humans. We need many more examples to fully understand our difference which is why you'll—"

"That's enough Doctor," Captain Reath interrupted. "We are not yet to that part of the briefing."

"Of course, Captain my apologies. I simply got ahead of myself. Candidates that is all I have for you right now. We will be talking more once we get to Earth." The doctor then hurried from the room.

The only question that Marctus had through the whole presentation was why did they clone the humans? Is a clone as human as a human is? Just as Marctus was about to ask the captain that very question, a human walked into the room. All of the candidates stood up out of their chairs like there were a nasty creature crawling around under their feet. One of the female candidates actually screamed. The human male that Marctus saw on the view screen was standing in front of the candidates next to the captain.

"Hello candidates!" It said. Marctus and the rest of the candidates simply stared, transfixed, and unable to speak. Marctus didn't know what he could even say. He, nor the rest of the candidates, had any idea what this was all about or what was going on.

"This is Doctor Symborg. I am controlling this clone using the modified Silpo you learned about earlier." Doctor Symborg, or the human, or whatever, started jumping up and down, running around the room, and was even touching some of the candidates which caused them to jump a little.

The captain then motioned for the human to stop and spoke, "Part of our main goal is that you will be controlling a human clone of your own. For what purpose you will find out when we get to Earth but, as for now,…this knowledge will suffice."

The human then pulled from its back pocket a small energy gun and pointed it at the candidates.

"Who would like to shoot me?"

The candidates all sat there dumbstruck. Marctus didn't even know what to say. The human knew they were all astonished to the point of not speaking and therefore decided to do it himself.

"Alright then, allow me."

With that, he turned the gun toward his head, and fired. The humans head then seemed to cave in on itself and then explode sending blood everywhere. The body collapsed instantly with blood pooling underneath the body.

A few minutes passed as the candidates all stared at the body on the floor, trying to understand what just happened. Then the door opened and Doctor Symborg walked in with other doctors who took the body and left.

"So what did you all think?" asked the doctor.

"What just happened?" a candidate asked.

"I was controlling the human via the modified Silpo. Once the clone died, I simply woke back up in the other room. The clones will allow us to examine up close what the humans do on a day to day basis and who we can experiment on and abduct next. We can also—"

"Doctor, you are saying way too much for right now" the captain said barely containing his temper. "We are not to inform them of anything else until we get to Earth"

"I apologize again, sir. I will be leaving and see you all on the ship."

The doctor left and the captain put a new image on the holoscreen that looked like a small silver rod that Marctus recognized from the initial meeting with the admiral. It was the same type of rod that he and the doctor had used to cut their arms open over the modified Silpo,

"This is a unique tool. We call it Adapt." The captain took the rod and held it in his hand and then, in an instant, it changed into the small energy gun they saw the doctor use moments ago, then back into the rod again. Then it changed into a disc shape and hovered in the air for a moment. As it hovered, the view screen showed the candidates. Then when the disc dropped into the captain's hand and changed back into a rod, the view screen went blank again.

"Let's talk about this for a minute," the captain said.

Chapter 9

Captain Reath walked around the room and handed each of the candidates an Adapt. Upon receiving his, Marctus held it in his hand and stared at it thinking how he could transform it into the flying disc camera thing. He turned it over in his hand repeatedly and nothing happened.

"So how do you get this thing to change into something is what you are all probably asking, right?" Captain Reath walked back to the front of the room and held his Adapt up, which instantly turned into a small one-handed energy gun.

"All you need to do is look at the Adapt. Picture in your mind what you want it to be and it will transform." As he finished saying this it transformed back into the main small rod shape.

Marctus pictured a nice big steak to eat but the Adapt did not change. All around him people were looking at their Adapt, thinking of what they wanted it to change into. Some of the candidates even looked like they were going to pass out from staring at it so intently.

"As you can see, it will not transform to anything and everything. It can only transform into a few unique set of tools." Captain Reath held up his hand and the Adapt turned into the disc shaped camera again.

"The four tools that the Adapt can change into are for one, the small handgun I showed you earlier which is *very* powerful. One shot into someone will blow up their heart and send blood out of their body or, as you just saw, a shot in the head will have their head collapse in on itself then explode. That's also how all of our energy guns work, in case you did not know." The captain then changed the rod into the small laser cutter he had used earlier with the admiral to cut open their arms.

"This tool will cut through anything and everything. But be aware that the strength of the rod can cut through your entire body if you do not use it right." The captain then seemed to withdraw the laser and the rod turned into a blue square pad no bigger than his hand.

"This tool is a healing tool. It will heal every wound you can think of." The captain very quickly changed back to the laser, cut a huge hole in his arm and blood started spraying everywhere. Just as Marctus was about to react to what was happening, the captain switched the Adapt to the healing square, which hovered over the wound, released some sort of mist which healed the cut, and his skin looked as if nothing had ever happened.

"You cannot heal a missing limb with this though. So keep that in mind. Any reason you may need to use any of these tools will come to you in the future, I'm sure, during your mission. I don't really need to tell you how or when to use them. Once the mission is explained tomorrow morning, I'm sure you will find uses for it should the need arise."

"The final object is the camera you saw earlier. It's useful to spy with or anything you need to have a look at. I will admit that it is not the most popular of the options but it comes in handy"

Captain Reath put his Adapt inside his pocket and motioned for them all to do the same. He then spoke very clearly, "For the rest of the day, you will be studying the diagram you saw earlier of the humans. Doctor Symborg has given each of you his file to look at. You are to return to your bunks and, as a group, will study everything available on the humans. I will escort you back. Follow me please."

When Marctus and the other male candidates returned to their room, the holoscreen was on and the human bodies were standing there nude. Marctus jumped upon walking in because he thought they were actually in the room. It was weird seeing something so different in a similar form as oneself but was sure he would get used to it sooner or later.

"So what are we supposed to study on these things?" Birgue asked Marctus.

"No idea. I guess what they are made of?" Marctus put his hand up to the view screen and moved it so that the humans rotated. He then pulled his arms back and the bodies split open revealing all their internal organs, bones, and muscles.

"So weird... I mean we are looking at ourselves basically but it's still weird." Birgue then took control and they were watching how the humans walked, ran, crawled, jumped and everything was eerily similar.

Marctus watched as the other candidates made the humans do everything you could imagine, including mating with one another which again was exactly the same. "Well, I'm off to bed, don't want to be too tired for tomorrow morning, especially when we are going to learn the sole purpose of why we are here....I hope."

Marctus walked toward the other end of the room with Birgue right behind him. As they both lay down Birgue said, "I wonder if we are going to have to go down to Earth and, like, kill these humans or something."

"Yeah, I don't know. I really don't know what we are supposed to do. I mean they showed us the modified Silpo, so I think we may be doing that with their clones... and then Dr.

Symborg mentioned abducting before the captain cut him off, so I wonder if we are also abducting them."

"Well, either way Marctus, promise me that whatever happens down on Earth we keep in touch"

"Promise," Marctus said as he rolled over and fell asleep.

Chapter 10

"Marctus! You need to run! They're coming for you! RUN!" Marctus turned to run and looked up into a giant glass eye. Birgue was behind him also looking at the eye that sat in the sky. Then, sirens. Loud sirens....

"Everybody up! It's time to go," Captain Reath yelled over the sirens and horns blaring throughout the room.

Marctus got up, pulled on his same gray pants, shoes and shirt and met all the other male candidates over by the exit door. Once there, Captain Reath opened the door and motioned everyone to follow. As soon as Marctus and the others exited the room, the sirens that were previously blasting could no longer be heard, almost as if an invisible sound proof wall had been put between that room and the rest of the ship.

The captain was leading them toward the hangar to where all the Gliders were stationed and also, as Marctus thought, the Stalker they would soon be taking to Earth. They hopped in a floater and moved toward the end of the hangar. After that, they entered an elevator that took them down. The expression on the other glowans faces made Marctus feel like they were thinking the same thing he was. Why are they going down to the ship? Is there another hangar?

The elevator came to a stop a few moments later and the doors opened to a very big, wide open hangar. The only thing there was a group of three or four sitting in the corner laughing about something. The captain entered the hangar and the people sitting in the corner rushed over coming to attention.

"Captain Reath, the Stalker is ready and awaiting your crew," said one of the men in front. They all wore yellow vests which meant they were hangar workers. "Follow me," he said

The captain and all the candidates walked toward the middle of the empty hangar following the guy in the yellow vest. But what Marctus didn't understand was where the ship was? It's not in this hangar. But just as he was about to ask the captain where they were being led, they made a turn to go around the middle of the hangar and the Stalker came into view.

"Wow, it really is invisible if you're right in front of it," one of the candidates named Jort said.

"Yep. Just yesterday Hanke here drove right into it head on and hit the front landing leg. It was pretty funny," the glowan leading the way said. They arrived directly underneath the ship. Then, just as Marctus began to look around for the entry ramp, they were all lifted off the ground arriving inside the ship a second later a bit shaken from the experience.

"First ship of its kind with an invisible transport lift directly into the ship. It keeps out unwanted people." The worker wearing the yellow vest then guided them to the front of the ship where a small crew was already sitting behind the ship's controls. A vacant captain's chair was raised above the rest. Captain Reath made his way up to the chair and sat down. Instantly a picture of Earth appeared in the front of him. Marctus looked up at the captain and the image of Earth. He watched as the captain tapped the image and the Earth vanished.

"Are we ready to go?" the captain asked.

"Yes sir!" The control crew replied.

"Launch in 10 minutes," the captain said, then walked back down to join the candidates.

"Gaik, will you lead us to the transport seats please, "The captain said or, from the tone of his voice, it was more of a command.

"Yes, sir," the glowan in the yellow vest replied. Marctus then realized the worker's name was Gaik and they all followed him out of the control room, into a room no bigger than the room they had stayed in before, but this time it was filled with seats.

"Everyone sit down and initiate your shield. We will be leaving in a matter of minutes," the captain said and left the room. Marctus and the other candidates sat down and touched a circle that was on the right arm rest. Instantly a blue light seemed to drop down from above their heads, touched the floor, and then vanished. As soon as it vanished, Marctus found he could not extend his arm or legs. It felt as if he were in a giant cocoon. The captain's voice then filed the room.

"I'm aware that none of you have ever traveled at light speed before, let alone light speed through a wormhole. You'll feel a sudden drop in your stomach then a lurch forward. By the time you try to relax in your seat, we will have arrived."

Just as Marctus registered what he said, he felt the drop in his stomach and thought he was going to be sick. Just as that thought registered in his mind, he lurched forward as if someone was pushing him forward but couldn't push him too far forward due to the invisible restraints. He was then pushed back in his seat with the same force he had felt when he was thrown forward. Then within a few seconds everything was normal again. It was frightening, but also very thrilling to him.

"We have arrived," the captain's voice echoed through the room. Marctus saw the blue light again below his feet and go from the floor upward, presumably to deactivate the shield. He was able to stand up, but instantly vomited.

"Oh," said the captain as Marctus wiped his mouth, "some of you may vomit after your first time traveling like this."

Chapter 11

Marctus stood up and, as instructed, made his way out the door with the others, some of whom looked as ill as he still felt, Birgue among them. As they made their way down the hallways of the ship, presumably toward to meet with Captain Reath, one of the candidates started freaking out and saying he should not have come.

"Be quiet or you're going to get all of us in trouble," Marctus told him.

"No way! This is crazy! We are millions of miles from home and may never even see home again. You're all crazy. I'm leaving." The male glowan then turned and ran down the hall. Seconds later a guard with an energy rifle tackled him. The guard seemed to come out of nowhere. The guard pulled the male candidate to his knees, and promptly shot him in the head. As the stunned candidates watched, his head caved in on itself and exploded blood all over the walls. Before Marctus and the other candidates could comprehend what had happened, a voice behind them made them jump and they quickly turned in that direction.

"Now you know how important this mission is and failure to cooperate will result in your death," the captain said. "We simply can't let you leave without risk of you telling someone about our mission. Please follow me." The captain walked back toward the control room of the ship. When he arrived, he took his place in the control chair. He then opened a holoscreen in front of him but just as quickly waived his hand and it disappeared. As it vanished, what Marctus had once thought was just the black of the ship, appeared to be a huge window that was covered by some sort of shutter. When it opened all the way, Earth was visible.

"Wow," one of the male candidates said.

"Beautiful," Reol said.

Captain Reath walked down to the front of the room where all the glowans stood observing Earth. He spoke to one of the crew members who seemed to be the one that flew the ship when it was not on auto pilot. After he got done speaking, the ship turned slightly and another object appeared in their view. A huge metal object orbiting the Earth. It passed right in front of the window. Marctus could see that there was a structure attached to it. It looked as if it could be a ship.

"The object that just passed in front of us is called the International Space Station, or so the humans call it," Captain Reath said to the candidates.

"There are humans on board this object. They use this vessel to study Earth from above. That ship you see attached to it is called the Space Shuttle. It's how they leave Earth and also how they return."

Captain Reath then had the pilot turn the ship a little more and a large grey object came into view. It was a little smaller than Earth, but much bigger than the Space Station.

"This is Earth's moon. They have not colonized it yet so it is of no importance to us. However, we do have plans to turn this into one of our bases for re-energizing and such in the future."

"Are we going to be going down to Earth today captain?" Birgue asked. "What exactly are we doing here?"

"You will find out soon enough, Birgue, because your first mission is going to be with Marctus here and involves the Space

Station. You two will follow me and the rest of you will return to the living quarters to await further instruction."

Captain Reath then led Marctus and Birgue through a door that stood open at the far side of the control room. Once inside, Marctus and Birgue sat down in the two chairs that were placed on one side of a long table and the captain sat down on the other side.

"I have picked you two specifically for this mission because I believe you two are the most fit for this job. It will be a chance to prove yourselves." Captain Reath then opened a screen that hovered in the middle of the table and Marctus saw the Space Station. He watched as the space station moved closer to the camera. This is footage from the camera drone Marctus thought and watched as the drone moved right up to a window of the space station. He saw two humans inside. Two Male humans. One was looking through a scope down at Earth and entering information into some sort of computer system. The other one was attaching a hose to his groin area but Marctus had no idea what he was doing.

"Your mission is simple. You will take one of the small stalker ships and fly to the entryway of the space station. Once there, you will enter and abduct the humans inside and bring them here. Is that understood?" captain Reath said without blinking at either of them.

"Failure on this mission is not possible. If you fail, this mission fails and we will be exposed," he continued.

"How are we supposed to abduct them sir? Birgue asked. "What if they put up a fight? Won't they realize that someone is coming through their entrance?"

"That's what these are for," Captain Reath said as he retrieved two weapons from under the table. "These will deliver an energy blast that simply puts them to sleep until we decide to wake them up. Unfortunately for them, they won't be waking up, but we do need them alive. As for their entrance hatch….it will be sealed and opening it will alert them, but you'll enter so quickly they'll think it is a malfunction."

"But won't they see us?" Marctus asked.

The captain then brought out another item. This one Marctus had seen before. It's how the glowans survived in the vacuum of space. It was a space suit, although this one looked a bit different from those Marctus had seen before. Instead of the bulkiness that Marctus remembered of them, this one was rather tight looking. It was black and had different insignias on it. The helmet was very different as well. The usual helmet Marctus knew was like a big bowl on your head. This helmet was the same material as the rest of the suit, but with two eye slits.

"Try them on now," the captain said.

Marctus and Birgue threw them over their clothes. As Marctus got into the suit he thought it was the most comfortable thing he had been in. It looked tight but it wasn't tight at all. He could maneuver just as easily as if he wasn't wearing it at all. As for the helmet, he didn't really feel like he was wearing anything on his head. The only thing he saw was a HUD telling him his oxygen level and other information like his suit status. An unexpected gauge was identified as his current invisibility.

"On your right arm you will see a triangle with a closed eye in the middle of it. Place two fingers on it and then remove them," the captain said.

Marctus and Birgue did as instructed and nothing happened.

"You of course cannot see, but you are now completely invisible. On your HUD you will see the invisibility gauge. This will tell you that it is on and working when you activate it. Anything you are holding or that is attached to you will also become invisible. To deactivate, do the same thing you did to activate it."

The captain then paused for a moment before speaking again, "These suits were designed specifically for you and the rest of the candidates. Not all glowans are able to put on a suit and use the invisibility feature which is why only certain glowans can."

Captain Reath then handed each of them their weapons. Marctus noticed that the HUD registered the gun as well as the amount of energy it had.

"Again, your mission is to board the space station and abduct the two humans on board, bringing them here. Alive." Captain Reath then walked them toward a door. Not the door they entered through, but a larger door behind where the captain had been sitting. Marctus and Birgue walked through and noticed a small ship that looked like it carried four occupants. It looked exactly like the Stalker, only smaller.

"Do either of you have any questions?" the captain asked as Marctus and Birgue were guided into the two pilot seats of the ship by crew members in the hangar.

"How do we fly this thing?" Birgue asked. "I don't know how to fly manually."

"It will be on auto pilot the entire time. We will be flying it remotely," Captain Reath answered.

"What is to happen to these humans once we bring them here? I mean, you did say they won't be waking up," Birgue said.

"You will be the first to see once you return with them. On the side of the ship there is a storage compartment with a suit for each of them. After they have been stunned, put them in the suits and bring them back." The Captain then said, "Remember. You must not be seen. You must not fail."

Chapter 12

"How long does it take to take a piss?" said Captain Howard as he looked back toward his companion who was attaching the urine hose to himself.

"As long as it takes you to take a shit," said his companion who went by the name of John Simmons. After a few minutes John detached the hose, floated over to Captain Howard and looked down at Earth.

"No matter how long or how many times I've been up here, this view never gets old," Captain Howard said as he continued taking pictures of Earth. John pushed himself back and floated up to another window to get a better look at the moon.

"You know, I think the moon is more amazing than the Earth in some ways. More mysterious," John said gazing out of the window.

"There are still things about our planet that we don't even know John," Captain Howard said. "I'd like to find out everything about her first before we explore other territory."

John then floated back down toward the captain and, just as Captain Howard snapped another picture, the airlock warning system went off and the voice that echoed throughout the space station was one that no astronaut wanted to hear.

"WARNING. AIR LOCK OPEN. SECURE AIRLOCK B. WARNING. AIRLOCK OPEN. SECURE AIRLOCK B."

Before the Captain could even press the emergency seal switch which would lock and seal all doors that led to the area of the space station they were in, the siren and warning shut off.

"What the hell was that about?" John asked.

"Captain Howard to Houston do you read me?" Captain Howard spoke into his ear piece. "Captain Howard to Houston do you read me?" he repeated.

"This is Houston. We read you Captain Howard. Everything okay?" a voice crackled through the earpiece.

"Negative Houston. We just had an airlock warning on airlock B. Do you see it on your end?"

"Negative we show everything is secure. Could've been an on board malfunction."

"Roger that. Will report if it happens again."

The earpiece went silent and Captain Howard and John floated toward airlock B just to verify it was sealed. Once in front of the airlock, everything looked normal. It didn't look like it had been opened. Nothing was docked there. The shuttle was over on Airlock A with the emergency shuttle on Airlock C.

Just as they started to relax, several things happened at once. Captain Howard turned around to face John and, just as he was about to speak, a ball of what looked like yellow light hit John in the chest and John went limp. Then two figures appeared in front of him in black suits, but they weren't floating. They were standing there as if there was gravity to hold them down. Captain Howard saw one of them raise what looked like a small handgun but with yellow lights pulsing on it. Just as he was about to call

Houston, his chest burned like it was on fire and everything went black.

Chapter 13

Marctus and Birgue exited the small Stalker and helped pull the two humans from the back two seats placing them on floating tables that hovered by the ship. The tables were accompanied by Dr. Symborg and three other doctor/scientist looking guys.

"Marctus and Birgue, well done, well done indeed! Please follow us back to the lab where Captain Reath awaits us," Dr. Symborg said. The floating tables started moving toward a door that led to the main hallway of the ship. Marctus and Birgue removed their helmets as they followed the scientists toward the lab. The lab was bigger than Marctus had expected. It looked the size of the hangar that the small stalker was in but contained tables, chairs and medical instruments on the walls. There was also Silpo pods in rows that ran the length of the room, Probably around 20 altogether Marctus calculated. Before Marctus could really take in his surroundings, the Captain walked in.

"Marctus and Birgue please brief me on every detail of the mission as it happened," Captain Reath said before saying anything else.

So Marctus went into what happened after they entered. How the airlock warning went off but immediately shut off. How the captain (Marctus pointed at the captain on the moving table) had called "Houston," which Marctus assumed was some command base on Earth, telling them of the airlock alarm and how Houston thought it was just an on board malfunction.

"So one of them saw you but only for a second before you shot him? He was not able to contact Houston or send any sort of distress signal?" Captain Reath asked very sternly, and very seriously.

"No Captain. He had no time. We came out of invisibility just as we shot him so the most he could have seen is a glimpse of us. He won't ever be able to tell anyone even if he did," Birgue answered.

Captain Reath paused for a moment then said, "Very true. Well done Marctus and Birgue. Now, before I take you away from Dr. Symborg's company, I think you deserve to know exactly what we are doing here at Earth. I will inform the other candidates while Dr. Symborg will inform you. He'll provide you with additional information as well."

Captain Reath left the room and Dr. Symborg came back to the front of the room looking joyous, as always. "Well then! Shall we begin?" he asked.

Chapter 14

Marctus and Birgue followed Dr. Symborg through the room and over to two tables where the two humans now lay. The space suits had been taken off of and they lay nude, face up on the tables. One of the doctors was prepping one of the medical instruments that Marctus had never seen before. Also odd was that the bodies had a floating orb above them. The orb was clear and just hovering above the bodies. It was a little bigger than their heads.

"Marctus and Birgue! Before we begin with what we are doing with these humans, I am going to tell you what our mission is here on Earth. Please do not ask any questions until I am done explaining because I don't want to forget anything important. I tend to lose my train of thought pretty easily." Dr. Symborg then motioned Marctus and Birgue to sit down on two chairs next to the table and he sat down across from them. Then the doctor began to speak.

"Now, before I explain what our mission is, understand that this is exactly what the captain is telling the other candidates, of course not showing them what we are using the humans for. You two will know everything because the captain trusts you the most it seems." Dr. Symborg paused, and then spoke in a obviously rehearsed voice Marctus thought.

"Our mission to Earth involves a number of things and may take years to complete. Our main mission is to study the humans and find out how they act, eat, sleep, and all other functions that they do which seem so similar to what we do. We will monitor and choose candidates to abduct for studying based on different characteristics --physical traits, strength --and other considerations now that we can do so face to face rather than watching from a distant camera."

"To do this, we are sending all candidates to the planet surface to live among the humans and interact with them. You will then inform us whom you feel that will be good specimens. Candidates will be stationed all over the planet's surface to ensure we have a large cross section of subjects.

"Marctus and Birgue, since you are here alone, you two will be specifically placed in the same country, but in two different parts. Marctus, you will be in a city called New York which is in the state of New York in the country of the United States of America. Birgue, you will be placed in Los Angeles which is in the state of California. You will have means of communication with each other but only between yourselves. The other candidates will not have this option."

Dr. Symborg then stood up, walked over to a cooler and grabbed three containers of water, handing one to Marctus and one to Birgue. He then sat back down and resumed speaking.

"You're probably wondering how two glowans are going to live with humans without being noticed. The answer is what I demonstrated that day onboard the mothership. You will be controlling a clone of a human with the modified Silpo. I will teach you two today how you enter the clone and how you leave the clone. These two humans will be our practice humans, but we will be abducting others shortly that are closer to your age and from the same area you will be living in. You will basically live their lives, but will be observing the humans as stated before."

"Doctor when do..." Birgue started.

"NO QUESTIONS UNTILL I AM DONE! DON'T MAKE ME LOSE MY THOUGHT PROCESS!" Dr. Symborg yelled at Birgue almost comically. He then continued.

"When you are in your clone, you are not to mate with the humans. You are not to fall in love with the humans. You are not to tell the humans what you really are. You are not to be caught doing anything that a human would think of as not normal. If something like this occurs, you will be brought back aboard this ship and be killed. I am now supposed to ask if both of you understand this."

"Yes, Doctor I do," Marctus and Birgue replied at the same time.

"These humans are very similar to us, so once you are on Earth, it will be fairly easy to adjust to their way of life without breaking any of the main rules I listed. The food they eat is okay for you to eat. Water is the same as it is on our planet. So there is nothing to worry about in that regard."

Now that you know what the mission is, let me show you how you use the modified Silpo." Doctor Symborg then stood up and motioned for Marctus and Birgue to do the same. He waived for a team of doctors to come over to the tables and, as the doctors arrived, they began.

The doctors cut the bodies in half lengthwise and removed all the organs. Once removed, the organs floated up into the orb that hovered above them. After a minute the orb glowed a bright blue. Dr. Symborg grabbed the orb and walked over to another table in the room. On the table was a matching area for the orb to fit into. The doctor put the orb there and held his hand on the orb for a few moments. After he removed his hand the orb glowed a bright green and the shape of the human's body began to grow from the orb. At first Marctus thought it looked like some deformed creature, but after about a minute the body lying on the table looked exactly like the human.

"Now for the modified Silpo." Dr. Symborg had another doctor bring over a bowl of the Silpo. Marctus saw that they had a huge storage area full of the substance, all placed in individual containers. However the size of the containers from where the bowl was brought was different than the amount that was actually in the bowl.

"Now the amount that is in the bowl is only supposed to last for a few minutes, or hours, but we should have enough time for us to practice with. The full contents will be poured into a Silpo pod which is kind of like the sleeping pods you've been in previously." Dr. Symborg then pulled out an Adapt and asked Marctus to hold out his arm. He then cut open an area on Marctus' arm, let the blood drip into the Silpo, and then healed his arm. The doctor then took some of the Silpo and poured a little into the clone's mouth.

"Marctus, I now need you to concentrate very hard on what I am going to tell you. I need you to think about who and where you are. Then I want you to look at the clone and tell your mind to become the clone." Dr. Symborg took a step back and waited for Marctus to try.

Marctus closed his eyes and thought, "I am Marctus and I am on board the Stalker above Earth for a top secret mission." He then thought about becoming the clone lying on the table. Instantly he felt a weird pulsing in his head and as if his heart was beating very rapidly. The sensation cleared and he opened his eyes. He was now looking at the ceiling of the room but couldn't remember falling over. He sat up and noticed he was on the table that the human was on. He sat up startled as he realized he *was* the human. He looked over and saw his own body lying on the floor.

"Well done Marctus! Well done! How does it feel?" the doctor asked.

"I feel normal. Just... now I feel taller," Marctus said as he got to his feet and realized the human was a few inches taller than he was.

"Very good! Now, to remove you from the clone there are only three ways. The first way is to do the same thing you did to get into the clone, but do it backwards. So think of being inside the clone, then think of being inside your normal body again. The second way is to be killed while you are in the clone form. The final way is in the pod where we have an option of pulling you from the clone by emptying the Silpo from the pod while you are submerged in it," Dr. Symborg explained.

Marctus concentrated on being back in his body. Instantly, he felt the pulsing feeling. When it stopped, he opened his eyes and got up off the floor back in his own body.

"So that concludes our practice session for now, Marctus and Birgue, do you have any questions?" Dr. Symborg asked.

"So what is going to happen to the humans you abduct but do not clone?" Birgue asked.

"We are going to examine those to study differences between them, as well as differences between them and us. We also want to see if anything they have can benefit our race and how we can use them in the future for different...things," Dr. Symborg then stopped speaking abruptly and walked toward the exit door.

"I'm afraid I may have said too much and it is time for you to meet up with Captain Reath so he can discuss abduction procedures. I wish you both the best of luck and to also tell you that what you are doing for our race is truly remarkable. Your names will be remembered once our race knows what we have accomplished here."

Marctus and Birgue walked past Dr. Symborg and toward the front of the ship where the Captain would be.

"This is pretty freaky stuff," Birgue said.

"Yeah, but we were chosen for this and it's for a good reason. So our race can expand and learn about other intelligent life forms. I am committed. I will do whatever they need," Marctus said.

"Agreed. At least we will get to stay in communication with each other from across the country," Birgue said as they approached the front of the ship.

"True. I'll be interested to hear everything you learn," Marctus said and they both walked into the control room to stand with the rest of the candidates.

Chapter 15

Marctus stood beside Birgue behind the other candidates who were all focused on Captain Reath. The captain was standing at the front of the meeting room they had all been brought to. It was similar to Dock E where Marctus first learned of Earth, but it wasn't as dark. At the front of the room the captain had a holoscreen up and was showing the candidates the different places on Earth they would be occupying.

"Once you are dropped in your observation zone you are not allowed to travel outside of that zone unless you have my permission. Is that understood?" Captain Reath asked.

"Yes Captain," the candidates replied.

"Failure to stay in your zone will result in your death. You will be living as a normal human and will not do anything suspicious. Also, there has been a change of plans regarding the human clones you will be occupying. Originally we were going to abduct a human around your age and you would be taking their place and living their life. We are changing this. We've already begun abducting humans on Earth to bring back here. These humans will be around your age, but we will be relocating you from where they originally existed. Your observation zone will still be the same, but the clone will not be around other humans it may have known. There is less chance of drawing attention."

"But won't the friends and family of the humans we abduct know something is wrong when someone goes missing?" Birgue asked.

"No. We are killing the humans while they are down on Earth so anyone they know will think they are dead. Or, what I should say is we are putting them in a deep sleep so we can bring them back alive. The humans won't be able to tell the difference." Captain Reath then shut off the holoscreen and asked if anyone had any questions. When no one answered, he told everyone to go back to their assigned sleeping quarters and get some rest before tomorrow's big day.

"The day after tomorrow we will be putting each of you into the human we have abducted for you. If all goes well, we will then go over where you will be living on Earth and your daily goals. These living arrangements have already been set up for you," the captain said.

"How have they been set up when we haven't been down there?" asked one of the candidates.

"Because we had crew members go down today to each of your living areas and arrange living quarters and so forth. Remember, we have been studying them for some time so we know how they operate…at least in a sense. Tomorrow you will all meet in Dock H so we can go over some of the basic human experiences that you will encounter." Captain Reath then left the room without another word.

Chapter 16

After waking, eating and washing up, Marctus walked into Dock H with Birgue to find that the dock was set up as an auditorium. There were 20 chairs raised on one side of the room and on the other was a holoscreen. On the holoscreen was an animal similar to one back on the home planet.

"This is one of a greater species the humans call 'birds.' This is called a bald eagle and is very similar to the Hairtin back home. For the next few minutes we are going to display a number of different species that co-exist both in the water and on the land of this planet. Some of them are very similar to creatures back home. Others are not so similar."

The holoscreen then changed into a picture of a huge creature swimming below the oceans on Earth. A label appeared below the creature identifying it as a 'blue whale.' The screen then changed to a creature crawling through tall grass and the word 'tiger' appeared below it. Marctus watched as a lot of different creatures were shown to them along with their names. After the image of an 'elephant' went away the captain spoke.

"That was just a taste of some of the creatures we have discovered since we've been here. We've had teams on the ground since we arrived observing all kinds of things. We thought this lesson would be useful in case a human were to ask you a question about anything 'normal' that someone should know."

The holoscreen then displayed a 'car,' a 'boat,' an 'airplane' and finally a 'train.' "The cars in particular you must all learn to drive once down on Earth. You will find them familiar to the manual floaters you used to operate on a daily basis, only a little more dangerous so I don't think you will have too many problems."

The holoscreen then changed into different cultural subjects such as 'celebrities,' and 'movies.' It even played samples of 'music' that the humans listened to. At first Marctus thought it was a bunch of screaming but then the sound changed and sounded relaxing. After hours of sitting in this room, Captain Reath shut the holoscreen off and spoke.

"We have showed you the basic human experiences. A lot of the things they speak about have different names, but are similar to objects or creatures on our own planet. I have no doubt you will all adjust accordingly and not reveal your mission." Captain Reath then dismissed the candidates and they all left the room. Once outside Dock H, Captain Reath gave instructions before departing for the front of the ship.

"In your quarters you will find that a holoscreen is active and has what we studied today and more. For the rest of the day you will each go through the entire holoscreen of information on human experiences and make yourselves comfortable with the information. Tomorrow, we will put you into your human clones."

Chapter 17

"Marctus, you will be living in New York City. You have an apartment that is close to the popular tourist attraction of Times Square. Within driving distance I should say. I should also say you'll have to learn how to drive." Dr. Symborg then walked Marctus over to the table where a human male was. The last time Marctus saw this table, there was another human on it that he had helped abduct. Marctus noticed the same floating orb above the body that, for the moment, was perfectly clear.

"This is your human, Marctus. He looks right around your age too. In Earth years he is 22 years old. His name is unimportant as you will be using your own name down on Earth." Marctus looked down at the human lying on the table. Marctus noted that the male human had the same muscle tonnage as he did and was slim. The human had short dark brown hair and gentle brown eyes with a sort of stern looking face.

"Once you are down on Earth Marctus you will have enough money to be comfortable living, so there is no need to get what the humans call a 'job.' Just tell anyone that asks that you 'work from home regarding business things.'" Dr. Symborg then performed the procedure and Marctus watched as the clear ball filled up once again with the organs and blood and glowed a bright blue. Then Dr. Symborg placed the orb on another table and waited till it glowed green.

"Okay, Marctus, this is our first and only test with the modified Silpo. This is either going to work or not work." Dr. Symborg then walked over to where the Silpo was stored, pulled out a large container of it and started pouring it into one of the Silpo pods. After it was completely full, the doctor had Marctus walk over and cut himself so the blood could mix in with the Silpo. Then the doctor took a container, scooped up some of it and poured it into the clone's mouth. It now occupied a previously empty table.

"Whenever you are ready, Marctus, step into the Silpo and inhale. Once you inhale, remember to think of where you want to be and who you want to be."

Marctus stepped into the ice cold pod and submerged himself below the Silpo. He inhaled and felt the cold spread through his body. He then thought of where and whom he wanted to be and closed his eyes. When he opened them, he was looking at the ceiling. He sat up and hopped off the table to his feet. This human was just as tall as he was he noticed. He was glad he wouldn't have to make a height adjustment.

"Amazing! It works! We were a bit worried that in the pod of Silpo we would have side effects, but we are good to go. The captain wants you to spend the rest of the day inside of your clone. Meet up with your fellow candidates and then sleep in your clone's body tonight as well. We will be departing for Earth tomorrow morning. The next time you will be in your own body will be when the mission is completed, when you die, or when we pull you out. Good luck Marctus."

Dr. Symborg left the room and Marctus followed. Marctus had never seen so many humans walking around. Then one of them stopped in front of him.

"Marctus it's me, Birgue," said a human with blonde hair, blue eyes, and soft looking face. He was shorter than Marctus and very thin looking.

"We leave tomorrow can you believe it!" Marctus said.

"I know. Crazy! Oh, hey, Captain Reath gave me these. It's how we will communicate with each other and also with Captain Reath." He handed Marctus an ear piece that slid into the human's ear, completely hidden from sight.

"Just talk and I will be able to hear you when you want me to. It's kind of like the ones back home but with these all you have to do is think who you want to talk to and it will do the rest. I think it's made from the modified Silpo in some way but who knows." Then Birgue and Marctus headed toward the kitchen.

When they entered the kitchen to get food, Marctus noticed the rest of the candidates were in their human clones and eating as well. But they weren't eating the usual fare, they were eating human food. Marctus and Birgue walked up to a table with different types of food with labels showing what the food was called. There were things like hamburgers, pizza, steak, apples, pears, bananas, salad, rice, chicken and pork. Then there were drinks like lemonade, water (which Marctus already knew), Coca Cola, hot chocolate and milk.

Marctus grabbed a piece of pizza, a salad, and lemonade and went and sat down with Birgue, who had grabbed the same things. Marctus took a bite of the pizza and thought it tasted okay considering he never tried human food before. The lemonade was fantastic though and he went and got more after drinking the entire glass in one gulp. He particularly enjoyed the salad.

"I hope you all get used to the food and everything else down on Earth. There will be lots of things for you to try and to adapt to. So get a feel for everything the first month you are there. After that we will begin your assignments," Captain Reath said. He was sitting at a table a row down from Marctus.

"What kind of assignments, sir?" asked a human. Marctus couldn't tell who it was that had asked the question.

"Assignments will include where you are to go and who you are to observe for a period of time; if we are going to have you leave your zone to observe somewhere a little farther away; and duties similar to that." Captain Reath then got up and left the kitchen.

"Well, tomorrow should be fun. I'll check in with you when I am on Earth," Birgue said. He left the kitchen and headed to the sleeping quarters. Marctus got up as well and followed him out.

Chapter 18

"The candidates have been placed into their human clones, have been introduced to human environments, have been briefed on what this mission is, and the risks of failing Admiral," Captain Reath said to the holoscreen that showed Admiral Schur. The admiral was pacing left and right in his quarters back on the home planet.

"Very well. Do not initiate Phase 2 of the operation until all preselected humans have been captured and executed. I don't care if it takes days, months, or years. I want everything Dr. Symborg can get out of these humans first so we know exactly what we need. I also want to know what resources the Earth contains for us besides water. Keep in mind that these candidates cannot know about the next phases until we are ready."

"Understood, Admiral. Once I know more you will know. I will contact you soon." Captain Reath shut off the holoscreen and left his private quarters. On his way back to the control room he hoped that this mission wouldn't turn into a damn war.

Chapter 19

Marctus and Birgue sat in the two back seats of a smaller Stalker while two crew members sat up front piloting the ship. They were flying from the Stalker toward Earth and paused before entering the atmosphere.

"Need to wait for the all clear," the pilot said. When a green light appeared on the holoscreen in front of him, he sent the Stalker into a dive through the atmosphere. Within a few seconds they were in and soaring right over Central Park (as Marctus learned it was called). He could also see the Empire State Building. The pilot maneuvered the craft so they could be close enough to see the hundreds of cars driving around and people walking.

The pilot then flew over trees and numerous buildings before stopping above a tall structure with many windows. "This is your stop Marctus. We will send you down to the street below. Your apartment number is 7B. It's on the 7th floor. You have a nice view of New York City and such. They have decorated the apartment to feel a little like home." Marctus wondered who 'they' could be but didn't ask. Marctus got up and the door opened.

"Let me know when you're in your apartment, Birgue," Marctus said.

"Will do, Marctus," Birgue replied. Then Marctus made sure no one was around below them. It was dark outside and he remembered that no one could possibly see anything. It was still early morning where he was. Inside the small Stalker everything looked like the sun was shining. As Marctus stepped out onto the side of the craft, he felt something grab him and lower him to the ground. Looking around he couldn't see what grabbed hold of him though. Probably another one of those secret things no one knows about. Dressed in what humans call jeans, a t-shirt, and some shoes, he made his way into the apartment building.

Once inside he knew he had to go to the elevators to get to the 7th floor. Looking around he saw they were down the hall to the left. He reached in his pocket and pulled out the apartment key that was given to him on the ship before he left. He reached the elevators, got in, pressed the 7th floor button and went up. When he reached the 7th floor he stepped out and saw that there were different doors down the hallway. He didn't have to walk far because his was right next to 7A. He put the key in the door and turned the handle.

His first thought as he entered his apartment was that he was back home and all his furniture was simply moved here. There were the same chairs, couches, and tables in the room. Marctus instantly thought that this was going to raise suspicion should anyone see this room. But then he thought to himself, who would see this room other than him? He was then startled by the sound of Birgue's voice in his ear.

"Marctus, how is your room? Mine is awesome. Just like I'm back home," Birgue said.

"Yeah. Same here. Was nervous at first that someone would see it like this but then I remembered…who would ever come in here?" Marctus responded.

Marctus then opened the fridge and got a bottle of water. He also noticed his fridge and the cabinets where the food was stored were completely stocked with human food.

"Are your fridge and food closet stocked as well, Birgue?" Marctus asked.

"Yeah, wish we could have some of our food but I guess they feel we can explain the furniture but not the food if we had it," Birgue replied.

Marctus sat down and noticed that there was a TV on the wall. When he turned it on it seemed to be connected to all the human networks and such. He selected a local news station where they were discussing the weather, and whether or not the local football team would win. Marctus also noticed that there was a holoscreen that was not activated. He activated it and saw all the previous data on humans – the different species he learned about, things like cars, trains, and information like that – were available should he need it.

"Marctus, this is Captain Reath. Please report in," Captain Reath said into his ear.

"I'm good to go sir," Marctus replied.

"Good. Now, should you have any emergency questions or concerns, simply contact me directly. Should you need a question answered, contact Specialist Naivu. She can listen in to what someone is asking you and find the answer, or you can ask her directly. That is all for now," the captain said and disengaged the connection.

Marctus could hear the sound of cars driving by outside on the street. The sun was starting to rise and he was getting hungry. He walked over to the cupboard of human food and looked for something. He had tried cereal early this morning before they left but didn't feel like having it again.

"Naivu?" Marctus spoke out, remembering to think of her so the connection would establish.

"Yes Marctus?" replied a cool female voice.

"What's a good breakfast restaurant around here? I want to go eat there and get hands-on experience early," Marctus said. Then he realized he had no idea what he meant by hands-on experience.

"Well, there is a popular breakfast restaurant just down the street," Naivu answered.

"Sounds good to me. I can even drive for the first time and see how that is."

Marctus then walked to the compartment in the wall that he had been instructed held mounds of cash and a credit card. Marctus had learned the other day that the credit card was tied to an "account" that all the candidates shared and money was already available in that account. Marctus had no idea how. The compartment also held a small energy gun for security reasons.

He walked toward the door and remembered he would need the key for the car downstairs waiting for him. He grabbed it off the kitchen counter where it was placed and headed for the elevator.

"Birgue, I'm going to breakfast," Marctus said in the elevator.

"Sweet. I'm getting pizza. Can't get enough of this stuff," Birgue replied.

Marctus was now walking out of the apartment building's front door and looked around for the car that one of Captain Reath's specialists told him about on board the ship. Marctus pressed one of the buttons on the key and heard a honk come from his right. He walked down the sidewalk a few feet and pressed it again. The car he had stopped next to honked at him. He got in the driver's seat and started up the car.

The First thing he noticed was there were some added features in the car that Marctus didn't see when he was shown a detailed image. There was an added holoscreen just below the windshield. When activated, it showed a virtual map of where he was, along with an indicator of where his apartment was. He tapped on the screen and saw that the breakfast restaurant he was going to popped up on the screen. Marctus then tapped it again and a path appeared in the middle of the road telling him where to go. He put the car in drive and followed it.

Chapter 20

"I'm telling you, Birgue, you *have* to try pancakes. They are so good!" Marctus said sitting at the table in his apartment. It had been three weeks since Marctus first went to the breakfast restaurant and tried something called a pancake. Since then, he hadn't stopped eating them. It's also been three weeks since Marctus had his first encounter with humans.

"Yeah, well, I haven't gotten around to it yet. I've been trying other things and trying to make jokes with humans. Unfortunately, this is not going too well. I'm afraid I'm not much of a comedian here on Earth," Birgue replied as Marctus finished his pancake and opened the cooler to get a bottle of orange juice.

Marctus then remembered the experience he had getting this bottle of orange juice. He had walked to the local grocery store (or so it was called) after having a glass of it at the pancake restaurant. The place was full of humans and each human looked different. Which Marctus thought these humans had an easy time of it when trying to tell who was who when in public. When Marctus had been in public with other glowans, he could only tell friends and family apart by their voices, personality, facial scarring, and of course the clothing they wore. Over time you got used to who was who. But here on Earth, each human was significantly different: height, weight, hair color, hair style, eye color, skin color, voice, personality and so many other things.

The past three weeks Marctus had learned that all humans are not nice. Some are rather rude. The other day while driving some car behind him honked at him and told him to "step on the gas idiot." Then, on another day while walking around his block, he said hi to some guys walking toward him. They replied back with "go fuck yourself." This Marctus didn't fully understand until Naivu had told him the meaning of the phrase. He had laughed when she told him.

However, there were nice humans too. Like the lady who charged him for the orange juice he bought. She was rather nice. Asked him how his day was going and if he had any coupons (whatever those were). Also, the guy that worked at the front desk of his apartment building always greeted Marctus when leaving or entering. So, all in all, not much different than what Marctus expected.

Just as Marctus was about to turn on the TV, the holoscreen started flashing which meant an incoming message or transmission from the Stalker. Marctus tapped on the holoscreen to open it and was looking at Captain Reath.

"This should be good," Marctus heard Birgue say in his ear right before the message played and thought that it was weird they were both viewing the message at the same time.

"I hope that each and every one of you so far has learned a little about these humans and have interacted with them at some point. From what we have seen, the admiral, Dr. Symborg, and I would like to inform you of what your mission next week will be."

Just then the captain disappeared from the holoscreen and Dr. Symborg appeared.

"Candidates! I sure hope you are all enjoying your time on Earth as much as we have enjoyed watching everything, but now it's time to get serious. Next week we would like you to mark the certain type of humans for abduction."

Dr. Symborg disappeared and a human now filled the holoscreen. This human was male and about as tall as Marctus.

"As you can see, these particular humans have a lot of muscle tonnage and growth and we want to know how this happens. Some of you are seeing male humans with significant muscle growth and some of you are seeing female humans. These images were taken from our drones around the world to give you an idea of what we are looking for" said the doctor, who then appeared on the screen again.

"The best place to look would be a local exercise facility or 'gym' as the humans call it. You will need to go and enroll in a 'membership' and watch for a human that fits the description. Remember, you must not draw attention to yourself."

Captain Reath then appeared on the holoscreen and started speaking. "You're probably all wondering how you 'mark' someone for abduction. Well, here's the procedure"

Captain Reath disappeared and, on screen, the space suit Marctus wore on his first abduction mission appeared as well as a small square piece of what looked like metal.

"The suit I know you are all familiar with as you watched Marctus and Birgue abduct the humans on the space station. This small device is a tracker that you will insert into the human under the skin. To do this, simply go invisible, use Adapt to make an incision in the human and then insert the chip, healing the wound once the chip is inserted. You all have the stun guns so it shouldn't be a problem, just make sure you are not seen. You will have one week to complete this mission. Failure to do so will be a signal of your termination. If you have any questions, contact me directly"

The holoscreen went blank and Marctus immediately got up and left the apartment headed for the closest gym.

"Naivu, where's the closest gym at?" he inquired.

"About three miles south, Marctus. I will send information to the holoscreen in your car," Naivu responded.

Chapter 21

Lilan woke up to sunshine coming through her bedroom window. Outside, she heard the familiar sounds of people talking, shopping and enjoying themselves. She got up and walked to the window to look at the view. The Coliseum was visible in the distance and, since arriving in Rome for her mission, she had learned pretty quickly how historically famous it was. She walked to the bathroom and started cleaning herself up for the day. She learned that females wore paint called "make up" in the belief that it would make them appear "beautiful." She had made a human friend who showed her how to do it properly.

After cleaning up in the bathroom she saw that her hologram was flashing meaning a message must be waiting for her. She had ignored the previous message and now knew there must be two messages waiting. Anxiously, she opened the message and saw both messages were from Captain Reath and had been sent in the past two weeks. She watched the first message which was two weeks old describing what the first mission would be and how to mark the selected human for abduction. The second message came a week ago where the captain said good luck on the mission and to report back when the selected human had been marked.

Ever since arriving on Earth she never thought she would fit in like she had. Not only did she learn two new languages, but she made really close human friends. She had been having second thoughts on the whole mission. Unlike back on her home planet, she felt needed and liked here, but she knew that not following orders meant her death. Or would it? She could run she thought. She could run so that they wouldn't be able to find her. They had told her that, once she was in the Silpo pod, she couldn't be awakened unless she was killed in human form, or she chose to wake up. Why would she choose to wake up? She loved being here.

She made up her mind. She wasn't going to have any part of this mission anymore. She was going to pack her things and run away. So far away from where she currently was that way they would have no way of tracking her down. She hurried to pack plenty of food, money, her stun gun and the space suit that made her invisible. She then pulled out her communication device that humans called a "cell phone" and dialed her two closest friends she met since she's been on Earth.

"Hey Aurelia, its Lilan. Can you meet me out front of the Coliseum in an hour? Something important has come up," Lilan said after her friend had answered.

"Of course Lilan is everything ok?" Aurelia asked.

"Yeah, you just need to know something. Oh, and can you bring Cassia with you?

"Yeah, I'll call, pick her up and head over there. See you soon," Aurelia said.

"See you soon," Lilan said a bit nervously.

Lilan hung up the phone and left her house. She didn't bother locking the door because she knew she wouldn't be coming back. She walked down the stone walkway between the rows of houses and headed toward the Coliseum. As she walked she was thinking of how she was going to explain this to her friends. They may not believe her. They may think she's crazy and walk away from her. Maybe she should've told them to meet at her apartment so they would see the holoscreen and everything else.

In no time she reached the front of the Coliseum and saw Aurelia and Cassia sitting at one of the dining tables across from it. Lilan waved as she ran over to them.

"So what's up Lilan? You sounded scared on the phone," Aurelia said.

"Yeah. I get a call from Aurelia and she sounded worried which then made me worried," Cassia said.

"Can we go for a walk where we won't be overheard? Lilan asked.

"Yeah I know a place we can go where no one will overhear us," Cassia replied.

The three girls walked past the Coliseum and headed south toward the beach. There was a path that led across the beach that no one seemed to ever walk on. Lilan walked between Aurelia and Cassia and, as they were walking, decided how she was going to tell them.

"I don't know how to say this without making you think I'm crazy, but here it goes. I'm not human. I'm from another planet and I've been sent here on a mission to abduct humans. I don't look like this. This is a clone of a human that we killed. Once we clone them, we place ourselves inside. I'm telling you this because I don't want to do this anymore. I want to be human."

Aurelia and Cassia stopped as soon as she ended her speech. At first Lilan thought they were going to run away and never speak to her again. But then Aurelia said something that Lilan had not been expecting.

"Prove it," she said simply and sharply. Cassia nodded her head in agreement.

"How am I supposed to prove it?" Lilan thought to herself. Then she remembered. She had an Adapt and the stun gun. She pulled them out and watched to see their expressions. Nothing on their faces changed.

"What are those supposed to be? Looks like a fancy pen and a Taser," Cassia said.

"They're not! This is called an Adapt. It can change into different things and this is our stun gun, which puts you to sleep basically, although humans would think you were dead," Lilan quickly replied.

"What does an Adapt do?" Aurelia asked.

"Watch." Lilan then made the Adapt turn into the flying drone and had it hover around them. Then she changed it back and cut a huge hole in her arm, using the Adapt to heal it. Finally, she turned it into the deadly energy gun. After Aurelia and Cassia saw everything, Aurelia spoke.

"I'm not entirely convinced …I mean that can just be technology no one else has."

"Wait! I have something else!" Lilan begged. She then pulled out the black space suit and put it on. Once she had it on she tapped the triangle with the closed eye and went invisible. She saw the shocked reactions on Aurelia's and Cassia's faces and knew they were convinced. She came out of invisibility and waited for them to speak as she put away the suit.

"Ok, I believe you Lilan. But where will we go? Surely they will find you," Cassia said and Aurelia nodded in agreement.

"I'm not sure, but we need to leave here. Go somewhere far away. Get on a boat or something and just go," Lilan answered.

"I agree. But I think we should move at night. Harder to be seen and I think we should fly out of the country. Go to Canada or the United States. A whole different country. You may be harder to find then," Aurelia said.

"Ok," Lilan said. "What time should we leave tonight?"

"Let's all go back to my place and we can plan everything before we go," Cassia said.

Lilan and Aurelia nodded in agreement and they all headed toward Cassia's house. Lilan felt so happy that they believed her. She'd only known them for a month and she already felt closer to them than she ever had to anybody of her own race. Within minutes they arrived at Cassia's house and began planning the details for how they would leave and where they would go. They planned that Lilan would go invisible so as not to be seen. Aurelia and Cassia would go as if they were just going on vacation. By the time they had everything packed and ready to go it was dark out. The sun had set hours ago and the flight they were booked on left in two hours.

"Let's go. I don't think there will be a better time than now," Aurelia said. They all walked out of Cassia's house, got in her car and started driving to the airport. About halfway to the airport, Cassia had to pull over because her car died without warning. There was no one else on the road, and no cars passing by. Cassia got out and opened the hood of her car but couldn't see what the problem was. Lilan and Aurelia also got out but couldn't figure it out either.

"Lilan, use your Adapt thing to fix it," Cassia said.

"It doesn't work like that. It wouldn't be able to fix a car," Lilan answered.

Cassia then took out her phone to call someone to pick them up and noticed she had no service.

"Do either of you have phone service?" Cassia asked

"Nope I don't," Aurelia said.

"Me either," Lilan said.

Lilan then watched Cassia walk to the back of her car and open her trunk. She brought out three jackets and handed one to each Aurelia and Lilan.

"Guess we're walking then," Cassia said and started walking down the road.

Lilan and Aurelia followed her and, after a minute, Lilan walked into Cassia because she had suddenly stopped. Aurelia also turned to look at Cassia to see why she stopped. Then Cassia suddenly rose into the air. In the next second a bright orange ball of light hit her in the chest and in another second blood exploded from her eyes, mouth, nose and ears. She crashed down on the road, dead. Aurelia screamed and tried to run back to the car, but was hoisted into the air. Within seconds the same thing happened to her. Lilan froze. Then all of a sudden her vision became increasingly foggy until she was looking up at a white ceiling.

"Welcome back Lilan," Captain Reath said.

Lilan was hoisted out of the pod by two glowans with huge guns on their backs. They forced her to her knees in front of the captain. One of the glowans pulled his gun from his back and pointed it at her head.

"I don't know why you thought you could get away. Don't you know we are constantly watching you? Maybe not every second of the day, but at least once every few hours. Fortunately for us, we saw you tell those humans who you were and your plans to leave. Good thing we didn't tell you that we can manually pull you out of your clone or you may have never gone through with it," Captain Reath said.

Lilan looked up into the captains face with tears streaming down her cheeks. She started to beg for forgiveness and another chance but the captain turned and walked away as she sobbed uncontrollably.

The captain turned around at the doorway and looked at Lilan kneeling on the ground. *How stupid did she think they were?* he thought. He nodded at the glowan who had the gun to Lilan's head and watched as he pulled the trigger and contaminated the floor with the traitor's blood.

Chapter 22

Marctus parked the car on the side of the road a few feet up the street from his apartment building. He was coming back from his fifth day at the gym and he had two possible humans in mind for abduction. He walked through the front doors and said hi to Jeremy, the guy that worked the front office, and went up to his apartment.

When he entered, he saw there was a message on the holoscreen waiting for him. It was the captain telling him that they had a week to mark a human and report back once it was completed. Marctus had two days left. He pulled out his Adapt and had it turn into the camera drone and placed it on top of the holoscreen. At once a three dimensional image of two humans appeared. These were the two candidates Marctus had selected for possible abduction.

These two humans didn't even know he existed. About a week ago Marctus had signed up for a gym membership and started scouting for an acceptable subject. After going to the gym at different times of the day for a few days, he narrowed his selection down to these two. They were both physically strong and matched the description of what Dr. Symborg wanted. The problem was which one would he select? He had followed them home a couple nights to see where they lived and knew that getting in to their homes wouldn't be a problem.

Marctus pulled out a quarter (which is human money) and assigned a side to each of the humans. He had decided that whichever side it landed on, would be the subject he selected. Tails for the human on the left. Heads for the human on the right. The quarter landed on heads and Marctus stared at the human on the right. This human lived just down the street from the gym with his female companion. He would have to stun her as well in order to make sure she didn't see anything when Marctus went there tonight.

Marctus shut off the holoscreen and turned on the regular human TV. He listened to the news about how the weather is going to be extremely rainy for the next few days. Marctus then made something to eat and continued watching the news until it was time to go. Something about watching human news interested him and he didn't know what or why.

Marctus continued watching TV until the sun set. When it finally did go down, he got up and put on the space suit that rendered him invisible. He holstered the stun gun on his side along with the Adapt and placed the tracker in one of the compartments on his chest. He got in his car, took his helmet off and came out of invisibility so he would not call attention to himself as a driverless car. He then headed toward the human's house.

After minutes of driving in a downpour of rain, he stopped a few blocks short of the house the human occupied. He put his helmet back on and got out of the car invisible. He walked up to the front door and tried the doorknob. It was locked. Marctus then walked around back and tried each of the windows on the first floor of the house. One was unlocked and open. He pushed it open a little further, crawled through then silently closed the window behind him. He then walked toward the stairs that led to the bedroom where the humans slept.

Marctus paused just outside the bedroom where he knew the humans slept, but they were not sleeping. He heard voices on the other side of the door and paused for a moment to listen.

"David, I think I heard something downstairs," Marctus heard a female voice say.

"It's nothing, babe, just the wind or something or a cat. Go back to sleep," the mail voice responded.

"No! I can't sleep thinking someone is in the house. Please go downstairs and check!" she continued.

"Oh my god okay fine," the human known as David said. Marctus heard him walking toward the door and, just before he opened it, Marctus sidestepped next to the wall to let him pass. He saw that the human was carrying a gun with him as he left the room.

It's now or never, Marctus thought to himself. He carefully entered the bedroom, standing at the far side facing the bed where the female sat. Marctus shot her with the stun gun and she slumped down on the bed. Marctus pulled the blanket over her to make it seem like she had gone back to sleep. Seconds later the male human returned to the bedroom.

"Oh, glad to see you're asleep again because there was absolutely nothing down there," he said annoyingly and crawled into bed. Marctus shot him as soon as he started to pull the covers up. Marctus made a small incision in the back of the human's head, placed the chip inside and then healed it with the Adapt. He didn't bother waking the couple as they would automatically re-awaken in 12 hours.

When Marctus was back in his car, he took off the helmet and came out of invisibility again. It was raining so hard he couldn't even see out his windows, so he doubted anyone had seen him.

"Naivu? Inform the Captain I have placed the tracking device in the human I've selected," Marctus said.

"Already done Marctus. Well done," Naivu replied.

"Birgue how did it go?" Marctus asked, because he knew Birgue was going out on the same night.

"Great. I was waiting for you to contact me. I wasn't sure if you were done. It's easy when you have the right tools to do it. Anyway I'm going to sleep. Will talk to you later," Birgue said.

Marctus drove back to his apartment and he too went to sleep without a second thought about the human he had marked for death.

Chapter 23

When Marctus woke up the next morning he could still hear the rain hitting the outside of his window. He got out of bed and walked into the main room of the apartment that had the TV and the holoscreen. He saw that he had a message waiting for him on the holoscreen but decided to wait to open it and instead sat down and watched the news while eating a couple pancakes.

The first thing he saw on the local news was a story of a missing person. Apparently the person was in bed last night with his wife and when the wife woke up this morning he was gone. They showed a picture of the missing human and Marctus saw that it was the human he had put the tracker in.

Marctus then got up and opened the holoscreen to see what the message was. He had a feeling it was probably something to do with the human abduction. Sure enough, Captain Reath was on the screen and told Marctus it was a job well done and to wait further orders regarding the next mission assignment.

"Did you get a job well done message too?" Birgue asked in his ear.

"Yeah. I wonder when the next part of the mission will take place. I also wonder how many parts of this mission there are going to be," Marctus said. He turned the holoscreen off and continued watching the news.

"Well, we don't really have a choice do we? It's either do what they want or die," Birgue replied.

Marctus didn't reply, mainly because he didn't know what to say. Also because he was sure they watched him throughout the day for signs of weakness or indications that the candidates didn't want to continue the mission. He then wondered if any of the other candidates around the world had tried running or done something as stupid as that.

Chapter 24

Dr. Symborg had the human Marctus abducted sitting alone in a room just outside of the main laboratory. He was bound to the chair by an invisible restraint and wouldn't be able to move much once awake. The doctor was waiting for the human to wake up impatiently. He had never killed a human for experimentation while they were fully conscious, but this time he had questions he needed answered before he could proceed.

A few minutes later the human's head moved and he started to look around the room. The human then tried to get up but couldn't. The human was screaming something. Dr. Symborg opened the door and walked over to face him.

"What the hell are you? Where am I? How did I get here?" the human screamed at Dr. Symborg.

"You are on a ship orbiting above the Earth. We abducted you last night. You were stunned by one of our agents on the planet. As for what I am,…let's just say I am god. No, no, I'm just kidding. Let's just say we are what you would call 'extra-terrestrials' or 'aliens.'" Dr. Symborg then deactivated the shield holding the human and, as he expected, the human lunged for him. Before the human came within a few feet of Dr. Symborg, a deep gash suddenly appeared on his face, blood flowing freely out of it. Dr. Symborg then healed the wound just as quickly as it had appeared with his Adapt and sat down in another chair.

"If you try that again, you will die," Dr. Symborg said. "Now sit. I have very important questions to ask you before we let you go."

The human sat down in the chair he had previously occupied and looked across the room at Dr. Symborg.

"As you can see, I am a very slender being. Not much muscle tone. We cannot build muscle. Our muscles do not absorb like yours do. Or, well, like I think yours do," Dr. Symborg said without taking his eyes off the human.

"What do I have to do with any of this?" the human said sharply. "There are plenty of other humans, go ask them and let me go."

"Unfortunately, we cannot do that for fear you would reveal our presence. But, then again, no one would believe you."

"You said you were going to let me go if I answered your questions," the human said.

"Yes, I will. You will see that I do as well," Dr. Symborg said. "Now, I want to know how is it you humans grow your muscles. I understand from birth they grow, as do ours, but how do you make them bigger, to become stronger? Is it an absorption factor? Certain Earth chemicals?"

The human looked at Dr. Symborg as if this was some kind of joke. This was obviously a prank or something one of his friends was pulling, and the costume they're using is so real that it's scary. Those black eyes, the weird almost glowing skin and how skinny this guy is. After a moment, the human decided to answer the questions just to be safe and play along. He was curious what would happen next.

"There are chemicals, yes, but the main thing is lifting weights and eating food that contains protein since our muscles build off of that nutrient in particular. I mean, that's the basics. There's a lot more science that goes into it, but I wouldn't be able to help you with that," the human added. "I really don't know myself so I'm not a good candidate to answer your questions. Maybe abduct a scientist next time."

After hearing this, Dr. Symborg had all he needed from this specimen. He was going to kill the human and create his clone. That way he could do whatever he needed to it without enduring the constant screaming for its release.

"That is all I needed to know for now. If you will follow me I will release you," Dr. Symborg left the room and walked toward the main lab. The human followed closely behind him anticipating his freedom. When they reached the lab, two glowans grabbed the human and slammed him onto a table. The empty orb floated above it. The attendants secured the human so fast, he had no time to even try to escape and run.

"I thought you said you were going to release me!" the human yelled. "Whoever you are, stop this prank! I'm not playing along anymore. Take the masks off immediately!"

Dr. Symborg walked over to the human and took out his Adapt. He took the human's hand and, in one quick motion, cut the human's hand off letting it bleed profusely. The human began screaming hysterically.

"Do you think this is a prank now? I said I would release you, but never said how. Death will be your release," Dr. Symborg said.

The human screamed, begging to be let go. Dr. Symborg listened as the human said he would do whatever he wanted. After a few moments of this, Dr. Symborg called over his two attending doctors and told them to begin.

The doctors cut the human in half while the human watched in terror. The human screamed and screamed as he watched his own organs and blood float up into the orb hovering above him. Then, the human stopped screaming and struggled no more.

Chapter 25

Captain Reath opened the holoscreen in his private quarters and saw that the admiral was already waiting for him. Captain Reath began speaking, telling the admiral that after the abductions they had gathered so much information from the limited number of specimens that there would be no need for constant abductions of humans. Thanks to Dr. Symborg's techniques they were able to experiment with the clones to gauge what happens to the body. Because of that, there is no longer the need for experiments on different sizes of humans, or differing races.

"So, what you are saying is that we can now initiate Phase 2?" Admiral Schur asked.

"Not necessarily. We are sending the candidates to stun certain leaders in their areas so Dr. Symborg can investigate other areas of concern. I'm not sure if he will request anything else after that," Captain Reath said.

"Very well. The ships are ready to send when you are ready. I will await your word," Admiral Schur said and the holoscreen image faded.

Captain Reath turned around and saw that Naivu was standing at the door to his quarters. He didn't think she had been there long enough to overhear anything.

"Yes Naivu?" Captain Reath asked.

"Are you ready to send the next mission task to the candidates?" she asked.

"Yes. Let's do it."

Chapter 26

Over the next few weeks while waiting for the further instructions, Marctus continued going to the gym. He enjoyed the exercise in the human body. It gave him more energy and was a good distraction. . He particularly enjoyed swimming and running. As Marctus was showering in the gym one afternoon, he heard Naivu's voice.

"Marctus, the next step in the mission will be on your holoscreen when you return home," she said

"Thanks, Naivu."

Marctus finished showering, dried off, left the gym and headed back toward his apartment. He had recently met one of his neighbors who lived a floor above him. Marctus knew this neighbor enjoyed the gym as well because they often ran into each other there. Other than that Marctus had not interacted with any humans, as per the instructions from the captain.

When he entered his apartment he opened the holoscreen and saw Captain Reath and Dr. Symborg. After a moment they began to speak.

"Hello candidates. So far you have performed above expectations. We have finished examining the first group of abductees and are ready to move on to the next phase of the mission. From examining these humans that had above normal muscle growth, we have learned how they build that muscle. Also, by experimentation, we have been able to bypass several parts of the mission. We now know how these humans get larger or skinnier, and how their bodies react to different stimuli. This is very good news." The captain paused for a moment before continuing.

"In this next phase, we wish to examine a human that holds some power over other humans. Your assignment will be to abduct what the humans call a 'governor.' In some locations the title will be different but will mean the same thing. Each of you should now see an image of your target. We have already tracked them for you. Their location will be transferred directly to the holoscreen in your vehicle. All we need you to do is stun them and anyone else in close proximity. When they are stunned, contact us and we will do the rest."

Captain Reath then had Dr. Symborg quickly explain why they wanted to examine these "governors." Marctus tuned out most of the lecture but caught phrases like 'leadership,' 'special,' 'power,' and 'control.' When the doctor was done speaking, the captain added one last thought and was very serious about it.

"Unlike last time, you will have a month to complete this abduction. You will have to watch their every move and look for the best opportunity to stun them without anyone else knowing. Breaking into their homes is not going to be easy. They have security and other precautions you will have to learn to get pass, but we think a month is enough time. We will wait to hear back from you then."

The holoscreen went blank and Marctus replayed what he had heard in his head to just clarify everything. They were now supposed to take a human of power, but had to stun them first? Why are they making them go stun these humans when they already know who to abduct? Why not just abduct them when they are alone?

"That's exactly what I was thinking," Birgue said and Marctus then realized he had been thinking out loud.

"It just doesn't make much sense to me," Marctus said. Marctus then heard Naivu's voice in his ear speaking very quickly but clearly.

"Marctus, Birgue, I'm glad I caught you communicating with each other. I don't have much time. I overheard the very end of a conversation between Captain Reath and Admiral Schur. They were discussing something about ships being ready. I'm not sure what they're planning, but I don't like it," Naivu said anxiously.

"Well there's nothing we can do about it. We are here to do what they ask or we die," Marctus said. He then heard Birgue agree with him. Nothing more was said.

Chapter 27

It was the morning of Marctus' last day to mark the governor for abduction. The sun was not yet up and Marctus was just finishing up his breakfast. After spending the last month watching the governor's every move, he was finally ready for what needed to be done. He would leave before sunrise and arrive at the governor's office before the governor got there. Marctus found that the governor was more vulnerable around his office rather than at his home. He would slip into the office where the governor sat alone every morning drinking his coffee and looking at his computer. Marctus would stun him, place the tracker inside him, and leave. The governor may wake up thinking he had been more tired than he thought and had fallen asleep in his office unexpectedly.

Marctus put his dishes in the dishwasher, grabbed the helmet to his suit, and left the apartment. As he drove to his destination, Marctus remembered how hard it was to try to follow the governor without the suit on. After a week of trying and getting caught by the governor's security detail, he had given up. Thereafter, he performed his pursuit with the suit on. He remembered the captain saying it was going to be harder than the first abduction and now understood why.

Marctus stopped about a mile away from downtown and hailed a taxi to take him deeper into the city. Surprisingly, the governor's office was not in the tallest building in New York, but in a smaller one just next to it. Marctus waited for the taxi to leave and then walked inside the building and into the bathroom. Making sure the bathroom was empty; he put the helmet on and became invisible. He made his way up to the 10th floor and pushed the door to the governor's office open as quietly as possible.

Upon entering, he saw that it was finely decorated. The desk was a deep brown wood that shined when the now rising sun's rays hit it. The chair behind the desk was large and cushiony, upholstered in red. Behind the chair and desk was a large bookshelf that contained hundreds of books. Next to the door that Marctus had entered stood an American flag and a flag symbolizing the state of New York. On the wall next to the door were historical images of people Marctus knew nothing of.

When the governor entered the office about 20 minutes later, he slammed the door behind him and seemed to be upset about something. He sat down at his desk and activated his computer. Marctus was sitting in a guest chair directly across from him, just watching. He heard the governor mumble to himself and then stormed from the office again. Thinking he should follow, Marctus got up and walked toward the door. Just as he was going to open it, the door flew open barely missing Marctus. The governor sat back down, coffee now on his desk and started clicking through different images on the computer.

Marctus pulled out his stun gun, shot the governor in the chest and watched as he fell, spilling his coffee all over his computer and desk. Marctus walked behind him, took out his Adapt and cut a small line behind his ear. Marctus inserted the chip, and healed the wound.

"Naivu, the tracker has been placed," Marctus said as he opened the door to leave.

"Confirmed, Marctus," Naivu replied.

Marctus exited the building still invisible. He had decided to walk the short distance to his car. When he arrived, he got in, removed the helmet and drove back home. It was now the morning rush hour, as Marctus had heard it called, so there were lots of cars out on the streets. Marctus hated driving around at this time of day.

Marctus got onto the freeway and saw that his exit was coming up in just a few miles. Then a lot of different things happened all at once. First, the car in front of Marctus started swerving badly. He slowed down not knowing what to expect. Second, a car was passing Marctus on his right side. As the car passed Marctus and pulled next to the car that was swerving, the first car slammed into it, forcing it into the emergency lane and then over the edge of the embankment. Out of control, the car rolled several times before reaching the bottom of a small hill. There, it came to rest on its hood.

Out of curiosity, Marctus pulled over and watched to see if a human was going to walk away from such a violent encounter. He looked to his left searching for the other car that had been swerving all over the road and found that it was nowhere to be found. He turned his attention back to the car on its hood and saw that the front of the car was now on fire. He heard a loud scream followed by the panicked cry, "Help me! Please! Anyone! Please help me!

Hearing that scream, Marctus felt a chill go through him. He jumped out of his car and ran down the hill to the burning car. There were a lot of people standing around, but doing nothing. Marctus ran up to the car and saw a female was trapped inside. Marctus took out his Adapt, cut the driver's side door off as well as most of the bottom of the car. He then climbed into the car, cut away the part of the dashboard that was pinning the woman down. Seeing that she was still not free, he also cut away most of the seat. He grabbed the female and pulled her out of the vehicle. Just as they got clear, perhaps ten feet away, the car exploded. Marctus covered the woman with his body as shrapnel flew around them.

Catching his breath, he checked her for injuries and saw that she had a huge gash on her cheek and was bleeding badly from her leg. He used the Adapt to quickly heal those two wounds, as they needed immediate attention. He then looked at the woman one more time. He saw she was about his age, thin, with soft brown eyes and dark hair. She looked up at him for an instant and then passed out. Marctus noticed that the crowd had grown and everyone was watching him. He immediately ran to his car and left the scene.

"Naivu, did anyone up there see what just happened?" Marctus asked when he was driving away.

"No, Marctus, no one was monitoring. You're fine," she replied.

"Thanks, Naivu," Marctus said.

For the rest of the drive, Marctus tried to understand just what had come over him and why he broke one of the most basic rules of the mission. He was lucky no one was watching or he might have already been woken up in his pod and executed. A chill ran down his spine and he shivered. He then thought about the female's eyes and how she looked at him before she passed out.

Chapter 28

When Marctus turned on the local news a few hours later, after taking a quick nap and showering, he saw that two of the stories involved him in a way. The first one was that the governor was missing and had last been seen entering the office building with his secretary that morning. So far, there was no information on where he was. The second story, was about a hit-and-run accident that almost killed a woman. The woman was supposedly recovering in a nearby hospital and was expected to make a full recovery.

"They abducted the governor that fast?" Marctus asked Naivu.

"Yes. It was minutes after you drove away that they did the grab while he walked outside alone. They took Birgue's target as well," Naivu said.

Marctus thought about whether or not he should tell Birgue what had happened with the female and the car crash.

"Naivu, is it clear?" Marctus asked plainly so if anyone was watching they wouldn't understand what he was talking about.

"Yes, we're clear Marctus."

"Birgue, you there?"

"Marctus! Did you mark your target? The news here is going crazy over the target I marked," Birgue crowed.

"Yeah, same here. Look, I need to tell you something," Marctus said, then explained to Birgue everything that had transpired with the car accident and what he had done. When he finished, he expected Birgue to be upset or scared for him but got a very different reaction.

"I think you did the right thing. I mean, it's good no one was watching, but I mean she didn't deserve to die," Birgue said.

"I don't know what came over me. I just had this feeling and I HAD to do something," Marctus said. He was still thinking about the female and the way she had looked at him.

"Well, it's not like she's going to tell anyone what happened or try to track you down to thank you. She has no idea who you are," Birgue said.

"Marctus, they're about to tune into your apartment!" Naivu warned.

"Anyway, Birgue, hopefully we will get to meet up and work part of this mission together. We are a solid team," Marctus said to make whoever was watching assume he was up to nothing important.

"Yeah, I agree. Guess we will see when our next mission assignment comes in. When is that supposed to be Naivu?" Birgue asked.

"Tomorrow afternoon," Naivu replied.

"Well I guess we get the rest of the day off as well as a few hours tomorrow morning to do whatever we want," Marctus said and headed out of his apartment to go to the gym.

Chapter 29

"Dr. Symborg are you done with your experiments and abductions?" Captain Reath asked. The doctor was standing over a human laying on one of the floating tables.

"I don't know yet. When I questioned him he said that all humans of power are appointed or voted into such positions. Kind of like how we do it. There is nothing significant in his body to make him seem any different than any of the other humans we've examined," Dr. Symborg said and then motioned for his crew to dispose of the body.

"What more do you need to learn before we can start with Phase 2? Admiral Schur is waiting," Captain Reath said as he and Dr. Symborg made their way down the ship's hallway toward the captain's quarters.

"Time. I still have tests I want to run to confirm certain things and I will need more humans for that. We've discussed this, Captain. Tell Admiral Schur, once I have my information we can begin Phase 2. I'm almost done," Dr. Symborg said and left the captain alone in front of the door to his quarters. Captain Reath turned on the holoscreen and saw Admiral Schur once again was waiting for his report.

"Dr. Symborg wants more humans and more time to study before beginning Phase 2," Captain Reath said to him.

"Understood. Give him what he needs. He is our best scientist. Remind him, though, that he only has two months before we begin. That will be all," Admiral Schur disconnected the holoscreen and Captain Reath exited his room to relay the message to Dr. Symborg.

Chapter 30

"Two governors seem to have disappeared in the early morning hours of yesterday. The governors of New York and California. Authorities are saying right now that the two may be together but have no leads. We will bring you more information on this story as it develops," said a news reporter on the program Marctus was watching.

"Feels weird knowing that we did this, don't you think?" Marctus asked Birgue.

"Yeah it does. But hey we're kind of famous right now if you think about it…in a way…ok, maybe not. Ignore me," Birgue said and then faded out.

"New message on your holoscreens, Marctus and Birgue," Naivu's voice said.

Marctus walked over to the holoscreen and opened it up. He sat back down in front of the screen and watched the message play. Of course, the message was relayed by Captain Reath and Dr. Symborg.

"Well done Candidates. The targets were all abducted and your participation was not noticed. Well, no more than what we had expected at least," Captain Reath said with a grin.

"Dr. Symborg will now issue your instructions for what will be happening for the next two months."

"Hello Candidates! Great job getting the trackers into these recently abducted humans. We learned so much from them. Unfortunately, there are still things I need to know. For the next two months you will be placing trackers in anyone you think is worthy of studying. We are going to leave this decision completely up to you and I will be excited to see who you mark for us," Dr. Symborg said. The captain's face appeared once again.

"You will find that more trackers have been delivered to you and we expect no fewer than five potential humans by the end of the two-month period. After this, you will be informed of the next phase of the mission. Hopefully, you will appreciate the upcoming phase. It is important to our race. We will contact you at that time. That will be all," Captain Reath finished speaking and the holoscreen shut off.

"Nice and easy. I like it," Birgue said.

"Agreed. This time we don't have to plan every step. We can just stun someone, place the tracker and be done. Much easier," Marctus said.

Later that afternoon Marctus went to a popular food place and marked one man who was very large. He thought he would be an interesting subject for the doctor. He also marked a person who was in what the humans call a wheelchair. Apparently, the humans can lose feeling in their legs and thus are forced to sit in these devices. He thought Dr. Symborg might want to look at him as well.

"Already got two people marked in one day," Marctus said to Birgue as Marctus pulled into the gym's parking lot and got out of the car.

Birgue then replied, "Yeah, well, I'm on number four."

Marctus smiled to himself and walked into the gym and headed for the locker room. As usual he put his gym bag in a locker, locked everything up (because he didn't want anyone finding his Adapt) and headed for the treadmills. After doing a short warmup he went over to the bench presses and started his routine. After his last set, he lowered the bar back onto the rack and sat up on the bench. In front of him stood a female.

"I thought I recognized you," the female said.

Marctus looked around to see who she was talking to, then realized she was talking to him. He looked at her and the first thing he noticed was her eyes. He'd seen those eyes before. He saw them on the female human he pulled from the car accident! Marctus felt something weird in his stomach. It was a pleasant good feeling, but he didn't know what it was. He thought he'd better play stupid and pretend not to know what she was talking about. Then a voice in his ear spoke.

"Don't worry Marctus no one is watching," Naiva said.

When Marctus didn't respond, the female spoke again saying, "I know it was you that pulled me from that crash. I've seen you here before and knew it was you."

"I think you are mistaking me for someone else," Marctus said as he got up and walked toward the dumbbells. He picked two up and started curling them and noticed that the female was again standing beside him.

"Look, I can understand if you don't want anyone to know what you did. I wouldn't want that kind of attention. I don't like the attention I've been getting either. I just got out of the hospital and I immediately came here to look for you. I'm Jayla by the way," the female said.

"Marctus," Marctus said as he dropped the dumbbells onto the rack. He turned to talk to her, "My name is Marctus."

"Hi, Marctus," she said. She was blushing and asked, "Can we sit down and talk?"

"Sure," Marctus said and followed her over to a part of the gym where you can get protein shakes, protein bars, and other healthy food and then sit down at tables that were spaced out in the area. They sat down and, before she could speak, Marctus asked, "So you were already released from the hospital?

"Yeah. I hate hospitals. But where would I be without it?" Jayla said.

"True. They are good places," Marctus said all though all he knew about a hospital was that sick or injured humans go there.

"Thanks for saving me by the way," Jayla said after a short pause.

At first, Marctus was going to deny knowing what she was talking about but decided not to. He wasn't being watched so why pretend.

"I wasn't going to just let you die, but you're welcome. Did you find the guy who forced you off the road?" Marctus asked.

"Yes. He is in jail. Apparently he was drunk," Jayla said.

Marctus had heard that word before. He remembered hearing it was a type of poison that impaired human's thinking and physical behavior. Jayla spoke again and asked him what he had hoped she wouldn't.

"How did you get me out of the car? I mean, …I remember bits and pieces, but mainly just you pulling pieces of the car away from me."

"I just got into the car and pulled you out. I didn't pull anything apart," Marctus lied.

"Hmm. Well from what witnesses say, you ripped off the door, the front dash, the seat and part of the bottom of the car to pull me free," Jayla said not taking her eyes off him.

Marctus looked right at her and wanted to tell her the truth, wanted to tell her what really happened but knew that he couldn't. It would jeopardize the whole mission and, most importantly, it would get them both killed.

"Well, I didn't do anything like that but I did pull you out of the car," Marctus said firmly.

They sat in silence for a moment looking at each other. Surprisingly, Marctus enjoyed talking to this human. He also liked that feeling he got in his stomach when talking to her. He wanted to know more about her. He wanted to spend more time with her and unlike other humans…did not want to see her get hurt.

"Would you like to talk again sometime?" Marctus asked her.

"Sure," Jayla said smiling. "Want my phone number?"

"Your what?" Marctus asked.

"My phone number. So you can call me? Or text me?" Jayla said laughing.

"Oh, yeah, sure," Marctus said and pulled out the phone that was issued to him when he had first arrived on Earth in order to 'blend in' or whatever Dr. Symborg had said. He handed it to her and told her to put her number in.

"Okay. I put my number in and I now have your number as well. Talk to you later then?" Jayla asked smiling.

"Yeah," Marctus said and watched Jayla get up and leave.

"Well, that was smooth," Naivu said in his ear. He could tell she was smiling when she said it.

The whole drive back to his apartment Marctus couldn't stop thinking about Jayla. Unlike the females on his home planet, he took a lot of interest in Jayla. Just thinking of her he got that flighty feeling in his stomach. He couldn't wait to talk to her again, even though being caught would mean their deaths.

Chapter 31

Three weeks later, Marctus was sitting at a popular coffee shop waiting for Jayla to arrive. It was a small shop with only a few tables and each one was full. Before he actually sat down though, he took the time to mark a few humans who Dr. Symborg could look at, one female with red hair and another male with no hair at all. Marctus wondered why he had no hair. He would let Dr. Symborg answer that question.

"Marctus, new message on the holoscreen and you're not being watched," Naivu said in his ear suddenly, making him jump.

"Thanks Naivu," Marctus said.

The past few weeks that Marctus had spent with Jayla included things like watching movies, eating dinner at restaurants, and spending time with her at her apartment playing video games and watching TV shows which Marctus got really into. The humans had a lot of good stories to tell.

The past two weeks also consisted of Jayla constantly asking about how he rescued her from the car. She was not convinced that he simply pulled her out. She had told Marctus she remembered him moving everything out of the way and doesn't think she was delirious. Marctus, on the other hand, continuously told her that that was all he had done.

She also wanted to see what Marctus' apartment looked like but Marctus would not take her there. He had to quickly come up with a lie such as saying it was his parents' place and no one was allowed to be there except him. She seemed to finally buy that and stopped asking.

To his surprise and delight one day, she reached out and held his hand as he walked her home from a restaurant they had went to. He asked Naivu what that meant and she said it's a sign of affection. The only affectionate things glowans did were kiss and sleep together, so this new hand holding thing felt good to Marctus.

Jayla walked into the coffee shop and sat down with Marctus. He had already ordered her favorite drink and she asked if he wanted to go to her house for dinner tonight.

"What are you making?" Marctus asked

"Well, I was planning on spaghetti. Are you okay with that?" Jayla asked.

"Yeah that works for me," Marctus said. "What time do you get off work again?"

"Five," Jayla said, "but I may try and leave earlier. I'll text you when I'm home."

Marctus also learned how to send text messages. It was very different than the messaging system his people use where they simply just speak in each other's ear whenever they want. If you wanted to get a hold of someone who wasn't available, you simply sent a message to their holoscreen.

"What time do you start work today?' Jayla asked

This was also another lie Marctus had created on their first date. She had asked him where he worked and he instantly said he was a waiter at some pizza restaurant downtown. He forgot to stick to the original plan that he worked from home, but hoped it wouldn't matter to the captain or anyone. Jayla had asked for the name of the place he worked and he said she wouldn't know the place. Jayla seemed suspicious at first but didn't bring it up again.

"In about an hour. I'll be off at four," Marctus said. What he was really going to do was go back to the apartment and check the message on the holoscreen.

After they finished their drinks and talked about Jayla's medical bills, which she wouldn't have to pay, Jayla left and headed to the movie theater where she worked. Marctus headed for his apartment.

As soon as he arrived, he activated the holoscreen and sat down. The message was from the captain of course and Marctus listened to what he wanted them to do next.

"Candidates, we need you for an assignment that you may not be entirely comfortable with. We need you to eliminate certain humans. The reason for this is to see how humans react when other humans suddenly die. You will you use an Adapt to kill the human using the energy gun configuration. We have assigned a human for each of you and the time the human must be killed so we can observe the reactions."

Dr. Symborg then came onto the screen and said, "I will watch the recordings of the reactions later. I want to see if the humans are at risk of having heart attacks by sudden loss of others they care about, or if they feel anything when another human dies. I will be monitoring their blood pressure and other..."

Captain Reath cut him off, "Thank you Doctor. Candidates, you will have until tomorrow night to get this done. Once completed, notify us at once." The holoscreen then shut off. Marctus sat there and, for the first time since he arrived, he was nervous about performing his duties.

He had technically killed those other humans by marking them for abduction, but he had never really killed them outright. Now he was going to have to shoot one and watch them die, knowing he had taken their life. What if he didn't get the shot off or something? Would he get in trouble? Would he be killed? Realizing he had thought about this long enough, he got up and headed out the door to meet Jayla at her apartment.

Chapter 32

"How many meatballs would you like?" Jayla asked Marctus.

"Uhh, two is fine," Marctus answered. Jayla brought the two plates over to the couch where Marctus was sitting watching one of their favorite TV shows.

"I can't believe you've never seen this show," Jayla said. "I think every human on earth has seen this show but you."

"Well, I guess I'm not from this planet then," Marctus said and Jayla laughed.

Then Naivu spoke very suddenly.

"Marctus they are about to monitor you! Get to the bathroom and stay there until I say it's clear!"

"I need to use the bathroom real quick!" Marctus said, and put his empty plate down and headed toward the bathroom. He sat in there for what seemed like forever but in reality it was only ten minutes before Naivu gave the all clear.

He came out of the bathroom and sat back on the couch with Jayla who cuddled up next to him.

"I won't be able to talk tomorrow. I am going out of town and won't have service. I'll call you when I get back the following morning," Marctus said. He thought it through and decided this would make the most sense so Jayla wouldn't get suspicious about where he was.

"Okay. I'll be waiting," Jayla said.

They finished watching their TV show and Marctus could feel himself getting sleepy. He got up to leave and Jayla walked him down to his car. He gave her a hug and said he'd see her soon and drove off.

Chapter 33

The following evening Marctus got all his things ready to go to the startling mission given to him the previous afternoon. He got into his suit, made sure his Adapt was on him, and went over the information in his head one more time. The target was supposedly already "marked" and, when Marctus had his helmet on, the human would appear green. Other than that, he was just supposed to walk up to the human and kill it.

He left his apartment just as the sun set and drove to the other side of town where a large mall was located containing a movie theater, restaurants, bowling alley, and all sorts of things that humans enjoy doing. He parked in the mall parking lot, put his helmet on, and started walking around the mall and surrounding areas.

According to his instructions, the human he was supposed to kill would be in this area sometime tonight. Marctus was supposed to kill the human in public, while everyone was out walking around the human. Marctus walked around for what must have been a few hours. The sun had now completely set and he could see the stars shining in the sky.

As Marctus sat on the hood of his car waiting for the green human to appear in the crowd of people walking around, he thought of Jayla, the smell of her hair, the feel of her hand in his and wanted nothing more than to be with her right now. The thing he loved most about her was her laugh. He couldn't stop thinking about her and even though it's only been a month or so….he felt strongly for her. He would do anything for her.

Then across the parking lot, Marctus saw what had to be the human he needed to kill. The whole body glowed green through his helmet and he started walking toward the target. The human had just come out of the movie theater across the parking lot so Marctus needed to run to reach the target before it was too late.

As he approached the human from behind he could tell it was a female. He grabbed the humans shoulder and spun her around so that he could hit her plainly in the chest. Just as he was about to pull the trigger he saw the female's eyes and he recognized them and the female's face. It was Jayla.

Chapter 34

A few weeks ago Jayla would never had thought she could be so interested in someone. She was constantly busy, going to school, to the gym, and then work and had no time for a relationship. But after the accident she put a hold on going to school to get her life back in order, including regaining the courage to drive again and to also start working again. She decided that she would start school the next semester and maybe convince Marctus to go with her maybe…

As Jayla continued giving people tickets to the movie they specified, she continued to think of Marctus. He was so mysterious and funny and was unlike anyone she had met before. Well, he did save her life but other than that she felt drawn to him. They've only really been seeing each other for a month now but she felt strongly about him…. She wanted to kiss him but knew it might be moving too fast, not to mention it might lead to other things which she didn't mind, but didn't want to force anything.

Something about this relationship made her feel happy and excited about what the future held. Her past relationships always ended in something close to violence. Every time she thought about them she tried to block the horrible memories from her mind. Hopefully, when she saw Marctus next he would wash them away. He was good at that.

She thought about her parents and if they would like him. Based on her past relationships, her parents were always skeptical about the men she dated. This was true even though she had never told them about how the relationships always seemed to end with lots of arguing and could have potentially turned violent. One day she would bring him home and show him off and hopefully get their approval.

Hours into her shift she finished doing the routine cleaning and asked her boss if anything else needed to be done before she took off for the night. When she got the all clear, she left the theater and walked out into the parking lot. As she crossed the lot a few things happened at once. A gust of wind or something pushed her around but she didn't feel any wind. The next thing was a man a few feet away seemed to rupture blood from his face and fall over dead.

Chapter 35

"Naivu, how was she the target? Do they know?" Marctus asked driving back to his apartment as fast as he could. It was just minutes ago when Marctus was going after his target and the target turned out to be Jayla. Never in his life had he ever felt so scared. If he didn't kill her, he was sure to die. If he did kill her then he wouldn't know how he could live with himself. She wasn't just another human. She was *his* human and he couldn't picture being without her. This is why he had turned around and shot another human in the crowd and ran for his car.

"I don't know Marctus! From everything I've heard I believe it was a totally random target marked by Dr. Symborg himself," Naivu replied. "As you know he did have his associates down on Earth before you candidates were sent."

Marctus didn't reply. He was too busy trying to decide if he was going to tell Jayla everything about what he is and why he is here. Marctus arrived at his apartment and began pacing the front room, trying to figure out what he was going to do. He felt strongly about Jayla and didn't want to hurt her or see her get hurt. He was sure she was still marked and would eventually be targeted. But how was she marked? Why was she marked?

"Naivu, how was Jayla marked?" Marctus asked.

"I think it must be a tracker, Marctus. I don't know for sure."

Marctus' mind was spinning. If it was a tracker, when was it placed in her? Maybe Dr. Symborg had sent his own crew down to Earth to mark humans. But if that's what he did, why didn't they just abduct her then? Nothing about this mission was making any sense to Marctus anymore. He needed to check Jayla and get the tracker out of her immediately. Then Marctus' phone rang.

"Thank god you answered. Are you home now?" Jayla's voice said when he answered.

"Yeah, I got home early," he said trying to sound casual as if he had in fact just gotten home, "Why?"

"Can I please come over? Something awful just happened," Jayla said crying on the phone.

"Yes of course…. I'll text you my address. I'll see you when you get here," Marctus said and hung up. Now that she was coming over, she would see his apartment and have questions….He would have to tell her,…but after he took the tracker out of her.

He decided he was going to stun her and then pull the tracker out of her. It was the only way. She would sleep here for the 12 hours until she woke up and then he would explain everything. After a few minutes he heard the knock on his apartment door and opened it to see Jayla in tears. She immediately ran into his arms and Marctus again got that nice feeling in his stomach and didn't want to let go of Jayla.

When they pulled apart, and before Jayla could even speak, he stunned her and eased her down on the floor. He pulled off her coat and shirt and began looking for where the tracker could be. He checked behind her ears but nothing was there. He then checked under the rib cage and saw the small incision where the tracker had been inserted. He opened the incision and removed the tracker, destroying it with the laser from his Adapt. He then healed the cut and carried her into his bed.

Leaving the room, he spoke to Birgue. "Birgue, I need to tell you something. Naivu, am I clear?" Marctus said.

"Clear, Marctus," Naivu said.

"What's up, Marctus? Is everything okay? Did you get your target?" Birgue asked, concern in his voice.

Marctus told Birgue about everything that had happened in the past month. How he saved the girl from the fiery car accident. How he's been spending time with the girl and has grown to care for her more than anyone of their own race. How he went to kill the target this evening and the target was her and, finally, how he had just removed the tracker from her. There was no reply from Birgue for a few minutes. Marctus thought Birgue was for sure going to turn him in to the captain and, at any minute, he would be killed; then Birgue spoke.

"I don't blame you at all, Marctus. I feel the same way. There are some good humans I've met that I wouldn't want to see die. I don't have the feelings you were describing about a human female myself, but whatever you need let me know."

"Thanks, Birgue. I want to explain everything to Jayla tomorrow morning. After that, I'll see what she says and go from there," Marctus said.

"I'm here too, Marctus. Let me know what you need," Naivu said.

Overwhelmed by the support he got from one of his good friends, and also from Naivu who he's never met but only spoken too, was more than Marctus could have hoped for. He could only hope that tomorrow morning's conversation with Jayla went as well as his conversation with Birgue had gone.

Chapter 36

Marctus was sitting at his kitchen table and had made pancakes for when Jayla woke up. It was exactly 12 hours ago that Marctus had stunned her to remove the tracker. She would be waking up any minute. A few minutes later, Jayla walked out of Marctus' bedroom looking lost and dazed…until she saw Marctus.

"What happened last night?" she asked. "I remember coming over to talk to you about this guy that got killed in front of my work, and next thing I know I'm waking up in your bed!"

"Come sit down. There is something I need to tell you," Marctus said.

Jayla walked over to the table and sat down opposite him. Marctus pushed the plate of pancakes he'd made toward her, along with a glass of orange juice. She smiled and took a bite of the pancake.

"This is amazing!" she said.

"Thanks," said Marctus.

"What is it you want to talk to me about?" Jayla asked looking at Marctus confused.

Marctus sat and stared at her for a few moments not knowing how to start the conversation. Should he just forget about telling her? No. It would be too dangerous now. He knew that, at any moment now, Dr. Symborg would notice that one of his marked targets was not eliminated and would be taking steps to find out why and who was responsible.

"I'm not from this planet," Marctus said very plainly.

"Well, I know that. You've never seen any of the best TV shows or movies," Jayla said laughing.

"I'm being serious, Jayla. I need you to listen to me and take every word I say seriously," Marctus said. He got up, walked over to the holoscreen and turned it on. The first image it displayed was the Earth.

He then began to explain to Jayla that he was part of a race called glowans. When he said that, he navigated the holoscreen so that a glowan appeared. He then told her of the overall mission, as he knew it and the reasons for him being on Earth. He also explained, as best he could, how he is actually inside of a clone, but still exists on the ship orbiting Earth. He explained to her the missions he's completed since he arrived on Earth. When he had told Jayla of this, he let one of the video messages from the captain play on the holoscreen.

Marctus then explained what really happened the night before, and why that guy was killed; why she had been turned around by some invisible force. When he was explaining the invisible part, he put on his suit and showed her. He also showed her his Adapt and how he was able to free her from her crumpled car after the crash. He explained why the furniture in his apartment looks different than normal furniture and, lastly, he voiced his suspicions that his race might be planning something bigger than just these small missions.

When he was done, the expression on Jayla's face was unreadable. She was simply staring at him. Then, after a minute or two, she got up and walked over to him.

She looked up at him and asked a question that Marctus was not expecting.

"So you don't look human then?" Jayla asked.

"No. I don't. I look exactly like that," and he pointed back to the holoscreen that had changed back to the male glowan.

"I don't know if I should believe you or continue thinking you're crazy. I think I'd believe you more if you show me your true self. But for now, I *do* believe you," Jayla said softly.

Marctus felt a wave of relief come over him. He was glad that she believed him without questioning anything he said (except of course the way he actually looks) and it now made the bond between them that much stronger he felt. He then spoke to Naivu and Birgue.

"Naivu, I want you to contact the other candidates as carefully as possible, and find out if anyone else is feeling the way we are toward humans. We shouldn't be killing them nor doing anything to them. We should be interacting with them and them with us. Birgue I think we need to stick together. Because when they find out what I did, I am sure they will come for you as well. Due to the captain thought we worked well together and he will suspect you."

"Okay Marctus," Naivu said

"I agree, Marctus. How did the female handle the information?" Birgue asked.

"Better than I thought she would," Marctus said and he then realized that Jayla was looking at him with a confused look on her face. She finally asked who he was talking to. He quickly explained how the glowans communicate with each other.

"Marctus, all of the candidates agree with you," Naivu said a few minutes later.

"Good. For us to interact with the humans here and stay safe, we are going to have to stand together and fight anyone that the captain sends after us. Once they find out that is," Marctus said.

"But Marctus, how *are* we going to all get together? You're across the country from me and the other candidates are all over the planet," Birgue said.

"Naivu, can I count on you to help us out?" Marctus asked.

"Of course I will, Marctus. What do you need me to do?" Naivu responded.

Chapter 37

Marctus first made sure Birgue was listening before he revealed to Naivu what the plan was going to be. When Birgue said he was, Marctus started speaking.

"The first thing we need to do is relocate. Not too far but not too close. I'm going to give Jayla money to buy or rent us a house that is still in New York, but miles away from here. I don't think they will expect us to stay here. It will be a big enough house for all of us to lay low until we can be sure we are safe."

Marctus then walked over to the safe in the wall where all the money was stored and pulled out a stack of cash and handed it to Jayla to put in her bag. He then told Jayla she needed to leave and to text him the address of the place once she had found one. He then removed his phone and set it on the counter so he could retrieve it once he is back in his own body. When he turned back around he noticed Jayla was still there.

"Jayla you need to go now, the faster the better. We should arrive there within the next day. You must be patient and stay there until we arrive," Marctus told her.

Jayla looked at him and seemed scared. She slowly walked to the doorway and opened the door. Then she looked back at him, ran across the room into his arms and kissed him, hard. Just like that all of Marctus' worries and fears went away as he returned her kiss. That funny feeling in his stomach was so strong that he didn't want to stop kissing her. Jayla pulled away after a minute and looked into his eyes. "Be safe," she said, then left the apartment closing the door behind her.

"Naivu, make sure you transmit the rest of these instructions to the other candidates. The plan will happen tonight after the sun goes down here in New York. At 10:00 pm my time all of us are going to pull ourselves out of our clones and wake up in the pods. Naivu, your job is going to be to keep the captain and anyone else away from the pod room.

Once we are all out of our pods, we will run to the hangar where the smaller Stalkers are. We'll also try and find where they keep extra of our candidate suits that turn us invisible."

Naivu then cut in and said, "Marctus they are in a room just inside the hangar. There should be enough for all of you."

"Thanks Naivu. Once we have them on and are invisible, we will all scatter and take the Stalkers back to Earth. Everyone will hover above my apartment while I go inside and grab my phone that will have the address of the house Jayla has found for us. Next, we'll find the house; park the Stalkers somewhere where they won't be easily found. That location will have to be identified once we locate the house. Does anyone have any questions?" Marctus stated.

Naivu then told Marctus she was transmitting the message and asked that he wait a moment. Birgue told him the plan was excellent and didn't see how it could fail. Marctus *did* see how it could fail. If anyone saw them wake up in their pods or saw them in the hangars they would be killed, no questions asked. They won't have any weapons to use to defend themselves unless they miraculously find some along the way. After a few minutes of waiting, Naivu finally spoke.

"All candidates understand the plan. They have set their time zones to match yours so they know exactly when to awake in the pods and will wait for you to lead them to the hangar. As for me, I will make sure no one is near the pods at that time, but Marctus, if something happens I cannot reveal myself or you may all die."

"I understand, Naivu. I hope you will eventually join us," Marctus said. It was now noon and Marctus had ten hours to prepare. He ran through the plan in his head numerous times and felt confident everything would be fine if all went according to plan. He wondered when they would find out that his target wasn't dead. Last night was the deadline and it could only be a matter of minutes before they contacted him to ask why his target was not dead.

Chapter 38

"What do you mean the target is still not eliminated?" Captain Reath said to Dr. Symborg, slamming his fist on the console. Dr. Symborg was standing on the lower landing in the control room, below where the captain sat. Dr. Symborg just moments ago ran into the control room and told the captain that the target Marctus was supposed to eliminate was still alive. To complicate matters, Dr. Symborg could not find the human he had marked anymore.

"Is it possible that Marctus forgot to tell us? Don't we have footage of the area that we can look at?" Captain Reath asked. Dr. Symborg gasped and ran from the room returning moments later with his small holoscreen. He tapped and swiped a couple times and a larger holoscreen opened in the middle of the control room. It showed an area outside of a building.

"Here is the target coming out of the building now," Dr. Symborg pointed out, and the holoscreen showed an aerial view of a human walking out of the building. "Now we won't be able to see Marctus because he is invisible and we don't have a tracker on him but he should be somewhere close."

The holoscreen then showed the girl spin around and stop suddenly and stand perfectly still. A few moments later, a different human exploded blood from his mouth and fell over dead. Dr. Symborg, the captain and the rest of the crew watched as the human glowing green ran as fast as she could away from the scene. The screen showed a crowd of humans who had gathered around the dead man's body.

"Did Marctus miss the target and hit the other human instead? Have we tried contacting him?" Captain Reath asked.

"I have, captain, and it appears he is sleeping at the moment. I have sent a message to the holoscreen in his apartment to contact us immediately," said one of the mission control agents named Naivu.

"The sun just barely set where Marctus is and he's sleeping?" the captain asked.

"Maybe the thought of killing the human upset him or something and he went to sleep," Dr. Symborg implied.

"I don't think so…. He's had plenty of time to deal with it," Captain Reath said. "Let me know when he views the message Naivu and I hope for his sake it is before the day is over."

Chapter 39

"Marctus, they know that a different human was killed and that the original target was not. The captain is expecting you to contact them before the day is over," Naivu reported.

Marctus looked at the clock after Naivu spoke and saw that it was 9:00 pm. One more hour he said to himself. He hoped that the rest of the candidates were ready because there could be no delay in the plan or everything could go horribly wrong. He just hoped Naivu was going to be able to keep everyone away from the pods.

As the time slowly progressed to 10 o'clock Marctus hoped Jayla was alright and that she will have found a place before the night was over. Just then his phone vibrated on the counter and he ran over to it. Jayla had sent him a text with the address along with a picture of the house. It was about 20 miles away with lots of trees surrounding the house. Smiling to himself Marctus put the phone back on the counter and anxiously waited for 10 o'clock to come.

With five minutes to go Marctus got up and turned the TV off. He then walked into the bedroom and sat down on the edge of the bed so that when he pulled himself out of the clone, the clone would fall onto the bed. But, then again, it's not really going to matter after this he thought to himself. Either way, it felt like the right thing to do. One minute left.

10 o'clock then arrived and Marctus closed his eyes, concentrated on where he was and where he wanted to go. He pictured himself inside his normal body again in the pod of Silpo. As these thoughts went through his mind he felt the same sensation he felt the first time he tried this. His heart felt like it was going to

beat out of his chest and then it stopped. He opened his eyes and everything was blurry. He sat up and rubbed his eyes. He had succeeded. He was back in his own body in the room with the pods. No one was in the room and, from what he could tell, no one was outside the room either. Just then all of the other candidates in the pods sat up except for one. That pod remained empty. Marctus wondered what happened to that candidate but pushed the thought from his mind.

"Is everyone good to go?" Marctus asked them as they all climbed out of the pods and stood in front of Marctus. He was standing in front of the door that led to the main hallway of the ship. It was weird to Marctus seeing his race again as they were. They looked so different from the humans that he wouldn't be surprised if Jayla screamed when she saw him. They were kind of scary looking now that Marctus thought about it.

"We're good to go Marctus. Lead the way," Birgue said and walked up right next to Marctus. Marctus nodded and they all followed him out of the pod room and down the hallway toward one of the hangars where the smaller Stalkers were. Marctus knew for sure there was one small Stalker, but he hoped that there were others; otherwise, some of them were going to be riding in the storage compartment.

Marctus thought everything was going smoothly so far, right up until one of the security glowans walked out of a door right in front of them. The glowan had one of the larger, more deadly energy guns across his back and when he first saw the group he didn't move. Then instinctively he reached for the gun on his back, sensing a threat. Before his hand reached the gun, one of the male candidates ran right into him sending him to the ground with the gun sliding across the hallway floor. Marctus ran, jumping over the downed glowan and picked up the gun. He turned to aim it at the guard before he could get up, but it was too late. The guard was already up and knocked the gun out of Marctus' hands before Marctus could take aim. The energy surge ricocheted off the wall and landed back on the hallway floor. The glowan then put Marctus in a choke hold and was squeezing so tight that Marctus started losing his vision. Then he felt the glowan release him and watched as blood exploded from the guard's face. The guard fell to the floor, dead. It seemed that one of the female candidates had retrieved the gun and shot the glowan in the back.

"Thanks," Marctus said hoarsely.

The female candidate nodded at him and handed the gun to him. Marctus took the gun and slung it over his back. They all ran down the hall toward the hangar. On their way there they had to pass the main experiment room that Dr. Symborg occupied. Marctus stopped short of the door and listened for voices inside the room. He hoped no one would be there, but then heard Dr. Symborg and the rest of his team.

"We are still waiting for one of the candidates to kill his target. Once we have that information, we will be able to make a final conclusion." The voice belonged to one of Dr. Symborg's assistants.

"It doesn't matter. We have all the information we need on the humans now. I'm not sure why Captain Reath is so focused on this one missing target. It won't change anything. Phase 2 is going to happen either way." This voice was Dr. Symborgs and he seemed extremely irritated, but Marctus couldn't understand why. He then heard footsteps heading toward the door and their voices grew louder.

"I'm going to go tell the captain right now that it's not important that the target was not killed. Please come with me," Dr.

Symborg said and seconds later he and his team exited the room. They stopped short as they saw Marctus and the rest of the candidates before them. At first no one said anything. Dr. Symborg was looking at the gun Marctus was now pointing at him and then looked at Marctus and smiled.

"We thought this would happen. You can't win Marctus. You have no idea..."

Of what, Marctus had no idea and never found out for he shot Dr. Symborg right in the head and watched his face cave inward and then explode. The shocked assistants all stood and watched as the doctor's body fell to the floor and then they began to run. Marctus shot each one of them in the back and they fell dead with pools of blood beneath them. Marctus then ran down the hall toward the hangar.

Outside the hangar door Marctus had everyone pause. He slowly peeked through one of the windows to the hangar and saw that there were no ships. But of course there were no ships because you can't see them unless you were looking right at them. It looked like there should be room for four ships. Each ship had four seats and right now there were 17 of them. He slowly explained that someone would have to ride in the storage compartment. One of the candidates nodded and volunteered to take that spot.

Marctus then noticed that there were glowans in the hangar. He would have to kill them in order to get to the ships and leave. In total he counted four. Marctus pressed the button on the hangar door to have it open and ran in. The four glowans in the hangar turned to see who was entering. Before they could even comprehend what was happening Marctus had released four shots that each hit one of the glowans in the chest. The four fell over dead. Marctus then guided everyone to a huge storage area across from the ships that he hoped contained the space suits.

Marctus shot the security lock on the door and kicked it open. Inside was more than he could've hoped for. There were guns and the suits Naivu mentioned. He told each candidate to take a suit and gun and to stow the extras in the storage compartment. The candidates all put the suits on as quickly as possible and activated the invisibility feature. As long as you had the invisibility activated, you would be able to see anyone else that also had it activated. Looking around, Marctus could see all the candidates gearing up. He grabbed a spare gun for himself and left the room.

Marctus then ran to one of the ships that they could now see since they were facing the ships. He hopped in a ship with Birgue, the female glowan who saved him, and another male. Marctus had never flown one manually but was sure it would be similar to the Glider simulators he had used. He sat in the pilot seat and opened the control screen. He tapped a few buttons that popped up and felt the ship rumble to life. He then put his hands into the two openings in front of him so he could control the ship. He felt for the handles he needed and grasped them. Instantly he felt like he was the ship and could do anything he wanted. He got the ship to hover, and then exited the hangar out into space.

Chapter 40

Jayla was sitting in the living room of a house that sat on the edge of the woods. It was quite a way outside of the city but she didn't have a problem finding it. She had seen a posting online and immediately drove out to rent the house. It was just off of a gravel road and was bigger than any house she had ever been in but, then again, money can you buy you anything you want if you have enough of it.

The house had an older look to it. It also had lots of windows and a large driveway. The trees behind the house were so tall you had to look directly up to see the top of them and a short walk into the woods there was a nice creek. Jayla, who was sitting on the same couch she had been on for over five hours now, looking out the front window, waiting for Marctus and the rest of his alien friends to show up. According to what Marctus said, they should be arriving within the hour.

When Marctus had first told her that he was not from this planet and that he was here to abduct humans and all the other incredible stuff, she didn't know what to think. At first, she thought he was crazy, that he was having hallucinations and that she should just leave. She was frightened at first, but for some reason she trusted Marctus and had feelings for him, given her past relationships, she didn't want to let a good guy go. She had decided to stick with him, even if his story was farfetched.

The more time she had to think about his explanations, the more things seemed to fit into place. He was always interested in other people especially when they were in public. He had never seen certain movies or TV shows or heard certain music that anyone on the planet should at least know about. She also thought about the furniture in his apartment. It was so futuristic looking that she couldn't dream of where he could have gotten it from. Then there was that hologram he had made appear in the middle of the room to try to explain everything to her. Yes, she decided, she would trust him and when he arrived tonight, if he arrived tonight, she would tell him so.

It was 11:45, almost midnight. Marctus had expected to arrive at the house by midnight. Jayla now had a blanket over her, drinking a cup of hot chocolate, when she heard a knock at the door. She jumped so high that she spilled her hot chocolate all over her. She cursed as she got up to answer the door. When she opened it there was no one there. She walked outside to see if someone was parked in the driveway and saw no one. After looking around for a few seconds she walked back inside and closed the door. When she entered the living room again she saw someone was standing in the middle of the room.

Jayla froze. The person standing there was wearing a black suit of some sort with some type of helmet on. Before she could run, the person spoke in an unfamiliar voice.

"Jayla, it's me," the figure said in that odd voice.

"Marctus?" Jayla asked.

The figure nodded and stepped closer to her. She noticed he was just a bit taller than the Marctus she knew, and was also skinnier.

"Before I take my helmet off, I want you to promise you won't scream or run," Marctus said.

"Of course I won't!" Jayla said impatiently.

Marctus stood there for a moment before lifting off the helmet. When he finally took it off and set it down, Jayla looked at him and began to tremble with fright. The Marctus before her had dark black eyes that were bigger than her own. He also had dark black hair that went down just above his ears. He looked extremely pale and, when the lights turned on all of a sudden, he seemed to glow.

"Wow," Jayla said out of amazement. This was actually real and not something that she was dreaming about. At first, she was kind of scared but now she could see attractiveness in him. As Marctus walked to close the blinds to the windows in the house, he said something she didn't understand at first.

"Ok, everyone, show yourselves."

When he said this, all around her appeared figures wearing the same thing Marctus was. They all removed their helmets and Jayla saw that they all looked the same with the exception of a few who had long black hair and looked more feminine. She assumed they were the females.

"Harim, Jort, Biran, and Sul I need you to go outside and scan the area. I want a one-mile map from this house in all directions," Marctus said so suddenly that Jayla again jumped in her shoes. She hated being so jumpy. After Marctus said that, four of the glowans became invisible and left the house.

"What do you want the rest of us to do Marctus?" one of the female glowans asked.

"Make yourselves as comfortable as possible. Try to get some rest. I want to see the map before I make any decisions. They should be back in a few minutes," Marctus answered. He watched as the glowans went to the kitchen to find something to eat.

"What no pizza?" Birgue asked after opening every cupboard and drawer and anything else that could possibly contain it. "I told you we should have stopped on the way."

Marctus laughed and sat down in the living room on a couch, staring at Jayla. She walked over to him, sat down next to him and took his hand in hers.

"Well, you're taking this a lot better than I thought you would," Marctus said.

"I told you I would believe you if you proved yourself to me," Jayla said and then reached up and kissed him. When her lips met his she felt a shock of cold that gradually turned into warmness. She kind of liked it and continued kissing him. They broke apart as the front door opened and the other glowans appeared.

"We've got the layout Marctus," one of them said.

"Put it on the holoscreen," Marctus said and one of the other glowans walked over and placed a small square thing on the floor and tapped it twice. It opened in front of Marctus like he was sitting at a table. They saw an aerial view of the house they were in and the surrounding areas.

"I like the trees. It provides good cover should we ever need it. Also there aren't many houses around here so there won't be a lot of suspicious humans," Marctus said.

Marctus then got up and asked all the candidates to come into the living room. Jayla didn't know what he meant by candidates but it must be in reference to the glowans and their mission here or something. She watched them all gather around Marctus and look at him as if he was some sort of leader. Jayla would follow him, which she was certain of.

"We need to provide constant watch until we know what to do next. For now our safest place is here and we need to make it as safe as we can. Naivu is keeping me informed of everything that is happening on board the Stalker," Marctus said. He paused for a second then continued.

"I want five of us on watch at all times. We will station ourselves at different areas around the house to monitor. If anything suspicious happens let us know right away. Naivu has arranged it so we can all speak to each other now. Birgue, Harim, Jort, Biran and myself will take first watch. These spots will provide us with a view of the entire property and any avenues of entry." Marctus then touched five different places around the house on the holoscreen, all evenly spaced.

"We will switch every few hours to prevent fatigue. Let's get started." Birgue, Harim, Jort, and Biran all put their helmets back on and left the house to man their designated areas. Marctus turned to Jayla and told her that she should get some sleep and that he would join her when he's done. Jayla started climbing the stairs to one of the bedrooms. At the top of the stairs she looked back over the railing into the living room and watched Marctus put his helmet on, go invisible and leave the house.

A few hours later Jayla woke up to the sound of Marctus entering the room. She watched as he removed the space suit revealing clothes that were underneath. He climbed into bed with her. She cuddled close to him and asked, "Anything out there?"

"Not yet but I'm sure there is going to be," he replied.

Jayla cuddled closer and started kissing him and felt Marctus kiss her back. Minutes passed but they didn't stop. Jayla kept thinking that they were going to die soon and didn't know how long this moment would last. She didn't want it to end. She hoped he wouldn't resist what she was about to do. She put her arm in his shirt and felt his chest and stomach. His skin felt just like hers but didn't emit any body heat which made his skin feel cool. She then slowly removed his clothing from his waist down. When Marctus didn't stop her, she felt for his groin area and found that it was identical to male humans. She climbed on top of him and made love to him until they were both exhausted. They fell asleep in each other's arms hours later.

Chapter 41

It was the following afternoon and Marctus and Jayla were sitting in bed, watching TV and eating breakfast. Jayla had left that morning and returned with a hot breakfast for everyone. It was almost time for Marctus to go back out for his watch when Jayla said, "I'm sorry about last night."

"What are you sorry for?" Marctus asked.

"For forcing myself onto you…I just felt like we might not be here much longer and I wanted to experience everything I could with you before…the end."

Marctus leaned over and grabbed her face and kissed her. "I'm glad you did. It brings us closer and gives us even more to hold onto," he said. Jayla smiled and Marctus got up, left the room and headed outside.

Last night had gone smooth on watch. The only thing Marctus saw were a few deer that walked up to the creek to drink. The other candidates had reported no unusual activity. Marctus knew it was only a matter of time before something happened. He just hoped whatever it was they would be able to get through it. Right now he had to plan to fight back. He only had 17 glowans with him and that was not nearly enough to stop anyone that would be coming after them. If anyone *was* coming after them.

He was in back of the house in the forest of trees. The lighting in the woods was very scarce. The trees were thick so the sun had trouble getting through the leaves and branches. He heard birds chirping and the trickling of the water in the creek as he walked a route around the area.

Every time he had to leave Jayla, he could do nothing but think of her. They'd only been together a little over a month but Marctus felt really close to her. Especially when she didn't care what he really looked like and particularly after what they shared together last night. She had protested when he wouldn't allow her to come out here with him. He had explained that she would be safer inside with the others than she would be with only him outside. Plus, he wasn't even sure an invisibility suit would work on her. He would have to give that a try.

Just then, he saw something ahead of him in the trees. At first he thought it was one of the candidates peeking around a tree at him. He asked the others to see if they were in the area, all he got were negative replies. He then signaled for two other glowans out on patrol with him to circle around and approach the area to confirm what he was seeing from every angle. After a few minutes they all met up with each other and had found nothing.

"Are you sure you saw something?" one of the glowans named Kilma asked.

"I'm sure. Unless my eyes are playing tricks on me, but the glowan or human was definitely outlined," Marctus said.

He then told the two glowans to go back to their positions and finish the watch. After another hour he headed back to the house and watched as Birgue took his place. Jayla came down and hugged him. As he was about to speak, he heard Naivu's voice in his ear.

"Marctus I tried to contact you sooner but we're all being watched almost constantly. We have a major problem. The captain knows where you are and is sending the Elites after you. I don't know when they will be there or the plan exactly but they've been ordered to eliminate all of you."

Marctus let go of Jayla and stood there shocked. How did he know where they were? The person he must have seen must have been an Elite and relayed their location. He had only heard about the Elites one time and thought they were just a rumor used to scare you. He remembered back in school learning about how they can run faster than any glowan, jump higher, and are stronger than any glowan. Fear came over Marctus. He had no idea how he was going to get out of this. He then came back to reality and saw Jayla was shaking him asking him what was wrong. Before he could answer her Naivu said one last thing.

"They also know about Jayla."

Chapter 42

Captain Reath was standing in front of ten glowans. These glowans though were special, part of a very secret organization. They are Elites. They are trained to perform tasks that other glowans would not be able to do. Thanks to their modified suits they were stronger, could run faster, and jump higher than normal glowans. They were also much better with the energy blasters and were very smart. The suits they wore were all white and the helmet visors were a solid red.

"Your targets this evening are the candidates that were selected for the Earth mission," Captain Reath said. Between him and the Elites appeared an image of a house that showed glowans inside along with one human female.

"They have grown to care for humans and want no further part in this mission. Not only is that against our laws but they have also killed some of our own race while escaping, including Dr. Symborg." After the captain said this a few of the Elites moved uneasily and seemed to be on edge.

"Admiral Schur has asked me to dispatch you to eliminate these traitors so that the next phase of this mission can go on uninterrupted. It is crucial that they are eliminated or this whole mission could be compromised," the captain continued.

Captain Reath then pulled up an image of the human female that occupied the house with the candidates.

"This human female has somehow turned the mind of one of the best candidates I have ever seen. He was set to become a leader of the Elites and I'm sad to see such a turn of events. But what needs to be done must be done. I want Marctus brought here, alive if possible. Kill the others."

The Elites all nodded and Captain Reath left the room heading back to the front of the ship. He gazed out at Earth and, moments later, saw five ships leave the Stalker. The candidates had taken all the smaller Stalkers and they now had to use the escape ships to get to Earth which were a little bigger but did not have the same maneuverability as the other ships. He had explained to the candidates what failing the mission meant and hoped they were ready to accept what they had coming to them.

Chapter 43

The sun was setting in the distant. It was nearly dark out and Marctus knew that whatever was going to happen was going to happen tonight, in the dark. He gathered all the glowans together in the front room and explained to them all what Naivu had told him just hours ago. He was telling them now because he had to use the time to think of a plan on how to possibly survive this.

The candidates all looked at him but showed no sign of fear or wanting to run and hide like he thought they might. Instead, they all stood up and listened to Marctus intently. After he was done, Birgue asked,

"So what's the plan Marctus?"

"You guys want to fight?" Marctus asked.

"Of course we do. It was going to come to this eventually. Plus, I have a feeling that this will only be the first battle," Jort said and the other candidates nodded in unison.

Marctus looked at each of them and went over the plan in his head one more time. He then opened a holoscreen in the center of the room, displaying not just the usual one mile surrounding the house, but several miles of terrain.

"As you can see, we are here," Marctus pointed to the house they were in. "There are two other houses in this area, one here and one here," he pointed out the other houses. One was about a mile away and the other less than half a mile. From what Jayla had told him, they were both vacant.

"We will split up into two groups of six and one group of five. Five of you will stay at this house with Jayla and myself. Six of you will go to this house, and five to the other. That way they won't know which house I'm in, as I'm sure their primary mission is going to be to capture me and kill the rest of you. I think if we split up and they realize we're separated it might confuse them for a time."

"Is Jayla going to be fighting Marctus or are we hiding her?" Sul asked.

"There's an underground shelter in this house where I'll have Jayla hide until this is all over. We found it earlier while exploring for a room to keep Jayla in. It should be safe. I don't think they will find her. The door to get into it is behind a bookshelf in the basement, so it's pretty hidden. She will be much safer there."

Marctus then pulled up a detailed view of each room in the house. He navigated to the top floor where there were windows looking out back toward the woods and out front. "I want one person up here watching the back and one watching the front. We are going to remove the windows so we have easy shots if we need to take them." Marctus then navigated to the main floor and explained he wanted one person watching through the front window and another through the back window on this floor as well and, lastly, said he wanted the last person to guard the bookshelf downstairs. He said that he would be monitoring each post to see what help might be needed should anything happen. He then told the other candidates he wanted the same formation in the other houses.

He then split up the candidates into the groups. He told Harim, Jort, Biran, Sul and Birgue that they would be in this house with him, and assigned Biran to guard the basement. Birgue and Sul were to be upstairs, with Harim and Jort on the main floor. He told the rest of the candidates where they were assigned in the other houses and they all nodded.

"I want to know as soon as you see them and how many you see. I'm not sure how many they will send but I don't expect less than five," Marctus said and wished them all good luck and voiced his hope that this would all be over soon.

Marctus then grabbed Jayla by the hand and led her to the basement. He slid the bookshelf aside and walked her down to the shelter. It was full of food and water. Marctus assumed it was an emergency bunker of some sort. He was glad it was here.

"You'll be safe here. No matter what, do not make any noise or come out of this room until I come and get you. Do you understand?" Marctus asked Jayla looking at her intently.

"I understand. Please come back," Jayla said looking up at him.

"I promise," Marctus said and then Jayla kissed him. He kissed her back as if he were putting all his feelings for her into the kiss. They broke apart and Marctus shut the bookshelf behind him. He saw Biran was already standing there on guard.

"Make sure nothing happens to her Biran," Marctus said and put a hand on his shoulder.

"I'll protect her with my life Marctus."

Marctus then walked back upstairs and saw that all the candidates were in position. Birgue and Sul were upstairs, windows already shot out and had their rifles perched on the window sill. Harim and Jort were in their positions as well with the windows removed and were looking out intently.

After a few hours there was no reported activity. Marctus looked at the time and saw it was almost 10 pm. Maybe they weren't coming tonight? Maybe he should just call everyone back and have everyone get some rest, and keep a lookout using the drone and a holoscreen. Just as this thought crossed his mind, he saw ten figures approaching through the window where Harim was stationed. They were outlined in white and Marctus saw they were in fact Elites. He then saw them stop suddenly, and told everyone to hold their fire. Three of them split away from the main group and headed toward one of the other houses. Seconds later another group of three headed toward the last house. The remaining four started sprinting toward Marctus and the base house.

Chapter 44

Marctus ordered everyone to open fire and called out to have everyone help cover the back of the house. Birgue and Jort took up positions and started firing at the Elites. The Elites were so fast that they seemed to dodge every blast while firing back toward the house as they ran between trees. When they got into the backyard, they took cover behind the slope that led down into the woods. For the time being they were pinned down behind the hill.

Marctus hurried to warn the glowans in the other houses what had happened and to expect three of the Elites to approach each house. They all said ok and moments later Marctus got reports that they were engaging as well. Marctus then focused his attention on the hill that the current Elites were hiding behind. They weren't moving at all. Just sitting behind the hill. All of a sudden the front door of the house blew open and one of the Elites moved in. Expecting it, Marctus dropped to the floor as a ball of energy flew over his head. At the same instant he fired his blaster at the Elite and hit him right in the chest. The Elite froze and then blood exploded from his helmet.

While that happened though, the four Elites behind the hill stormed the house and one of them was able to hit Harim in the face. Marctus watched the glowan scream in pain as his head caved in on itself and Harim fell dead across the window sill. Marctus watched then as the four Elites jumped and landed on top of the house. They then started shooting down through the roof. Marctus watched as balls of energy fell everywhere. He told the glowans to hurry outside and start shooting them off the roof. Marctus followed Birgue, Sul, and Jort outside and opened fire at the four Elites. Birgue was able to hit one who collapsed and fell off the roof. The other three then ran to the backside of the house again.

Marctus called for an update from the other candidates at the other houses as his group ran back inside to see where the Elites had gotten to. He got confirmation that, at house Number 2, they were fighting two Elites who had already taken out three of the candidates. Marctus cursed to himself as he also learned that house Number 3 was engaging three Elites. They had managed to take out two of the Elites, but had lost three candidates in the process. They were unsure where the last Elite was hiding.

Marctus was inside now and the three Elites they had been fighting were nowhere to be seen. Birgue, Sul, and Jort were looking all over the backyard of the house but couldn't see anyone. They were obviously waiting for the candidates to make some sort of mistake and show themselves. Marctus had a better idea.

"Jort, I need you to run out the front door and head to house Number 2. I need you to draw their fire so we can see where they are and take them out. Also, house Number 2 needs help. See if you can flank the last Elite there," Marctus said to Jort.

"Okay. Ready?" Jort said.

"Ready," Marctus, Birgue, and Sul said in unison.

Jort then bolted out the front door and ran down the road. Almost immediately there was fire coming from the roof again. Marctus and Birgue went outside and started shooting at the Elites on the roof while Sul stayed inside and fired up through the ceiling at them. Marctus saw that Sul was able to hit one and Marctus hit one as well. They both fell off the roof with blood pooling beneath them. The final Elite ran into the woods and then out of sight.

"We have an Elite who ran from our house. Be aware he may be headed to either of your locations," Marctus said. After a moment one of the candidates in the other house spoke to Marctus.

"Marctus we eliminated the three Elites here, but everyone else here died before I could finish the last one off." These remarks were made with anguish in the glowan's voice, and he seemed to be upset.

Marctus cursed to himself. He didn't want to even think how many candidates were dead right now. He then asked for someone from house Number 2 to respond. He got no answer.

"Biran, we are going to head to house number 2. Stay downstairs," Marctus said.

"Okay Marctus. All is good here," Biran responded

Marctus, Birgue, and Sul all ran to house Number 2 and Marctus told Reol, the last survivor of house Number 3, to meet them there. If Marctus was correct, there were only three Elites left. Two were last reported attacking house Number 2 and the last one Marctus saw run away.

Marctus, Birgue, Sul, and Reol arrived at house Number 2 and saw Jort's dead body lying on the front porch. They stepped over him and moved into the front room where they saw six more glowan bodies all piled on top of each other. On the wall, written in blood, there was a message: Surrender.

Marctus then realized this was a trap and as he turned around an energy ball narrowly missed hitting his head. He fired back and hit one of the Elites in the face who fell over in the front yard of the house. The other Elite hopped on the roof after seeing his comrade fall and Birgue, Sul, and Reol fired up through the ceiling. They ran out the back of the house ready to continue the fight and saw that the Elite was dead and hanging by his suit from the roof.

Marctus walked back into the house and made sure Biran was still okay. Biran responded with an "all clear." Marctus sat down and cursed the captain, Admiral Schur, and anyone else involved in the killing of his fellow candidates. He had gone from 17 candidates to just a few. Biran, Birgue, Sul, Reol, and himself were the only ones left. Reol was the only female. She was in the room with the pile of bodies crying over the loss of one of her friends. Birgue went and comforted her.

"Well, there is only one left and he ran away after we killed three of them. I'm sure he's going back to the captain to explain what happened," Marctus said to the rest of them.

"Are we going to burn the bodies Marctus?" Reol looked up at him with tears streaming down her face.

"Of course, Reol. We will honor their sacrifice," Marctus said. He then picked up one of the dead bodies and motioned for the rest of them to do the same. He told them they were going to bring them into the woods behind the main house and burn them. They walked into the woods and made their way toward the back of the main house. After a few trips bringing all the fallen candidates to the back of the house Marctus made his way to the clearing that opened up at the bottom of the hill behind the house. As he approached the hill he looked up and saw that Biran was standing just inside the house looking out the broken window where Harim had died.

When Marctus walked inside the house and walked up to Biran, fear and shock came over him. Biran was standing up against the window with his helmet on but wasn't moving or responding when Marctus and the rest of the candidates tried to talk to him. Marctus removed Biran's helmet and, as he did, blood spilled out all over Biran's body. Marctus then saw Biran was not standing by the window; he was hanging from an invisible rope of some sort attached to the upstairs balcony that overlooked the front room and the back room where he stood.

Then Marctus heard a scream that sounded like it came from the back of the house. He looked out toward the woods and at the bottom of the hill he saw the Elite that had run away. The Elite was just standing there holding something large in his arms and the object was moving around a lot. The Elite just stood there staring at the glowans in the house. Then Marctus saw what was trying to escape the Elite's grasp. The figure in the Elites arms screamed out Marctus' name and Marctus watched as the Elite ran off into the woods with Jayla.

Chapter 45

Marctus was sprinting as fast as he could toward where the Elite disappeared. He checked behind every tree, every rock, and anywhere else the Elite could be hiding with Jayla. He couldn't hear her screams anymore and he thought the worst. After running through the woods for what seemed like an hour, he entered the clearing where they had originally landed the smaller Stalker ships. Immediately he noticed one was missing.

Marctus cursed himself and walked back toward the house where his surviving friends had already started burning the bodies of the friends they had lost. He stood with them for a while until the fire started to die down and all that remained was ash and burnt wood. Marctus, Birgue, Reol, and Sul walked back in the house and all sat in the front room where Jayla once sat waiting for them to arrive.

For a while no one said anything. The early morning sun had begun to illuminate the house. "What do we do now Marctus?" Sul asked. For the first time in a long time, Marctus didn't know what to do. Almost every second of these missions he had something to look forward to and something to do while he waited. But now it was different. Jayla was gone and he had no idea how to find out if she was even alive.

Marctus stood up so suddenly that the other glowans all jumped at the sudden movement. "Naivu, are you there?" Marctus said with hope in his voice. No answer. He decided to wait a few minutes before trying again but still got no answer. He hoped Naivu didn't get caught for helping them. After about ten minutes of sitting there waiting for a response, Naivu finally spoke in his earpiece and it seemed she spoke to the other glowans as well.

"Jayla is fine, Marctus, for now at least. She was brought in a few moments ago and the captain had her taken to a room. I'm sure he will be questioning her and keeping her hostage to get to you," Naivu said speaking quickly. "I will contact you when I know more."

After hearing Jayla was alive Marctus finally felt a little better, but this was quickly erased by worry once again when he thought about what they might do to her. There was also the fact that he couldn't think of a way to fight back or to even try to get her back with only three glowans by his side. The only option that came to his mind was to surrender himself to the captain in hopes that Jayla would be released and live…even if they could not be together.

"I know you're not thinking about giving up, Marctus," Birgue said. "You know we are all with you on whatever you decide. Personally, we should fight and get her back." Reol and Sul nodded in agreement.

"I appreciate you all standing with me and wanting to fight but one big problem exists. There are four of us now. Even if we went back up to the ship, we are facing who knows how many glowans on board. If there were Elites secretly on board that ship with us who's to say there aren't more?" Marctus said. He put his head in his hands and tried to think of how to get an army of some sort to ally with him. Could he send a message to glowans back on his home planet? Even if he did, who would join him and how would they get here? He could have Naivu send it and have it open across the planet and on every holoscreen everywhere. He decided to give it a shot because he had nothing else he could do at the moment.

After explaining what he was going to do to the group, Birgue had his Adapt turn into the drone and had it hover in front of Marctus. "Speak whenever you're ready Marctus." Marctus stood there for a moment looking at the small floating drone looking at him. With Jayla on his mind, he started to speak.

"Fellow glowans, my name is Marctus and I was selected along with twenty other candidates for a top secret mission to a planet with intelligent life called Earth. Earth is inhabited by beings very similar to us called humans. Our mission was to abduct, kill, and find out about them to better our own lives. Once we arrived on Earth we learned a lot about them, grew close to them, and no longer want to harm these humans. We realized, too late it seems, that what was expected of us is wrong. We ask you to join us on Earth and help us fight to save the innocent humans they have captured and to prevent any more abductions."

When he had finished, Marctus sat back down and the glowans around him nodded and told him it was well said. Marctus then spoke to Naivu, "Naivu, if you can hear me, I am sending a message to you and I would like you to send it to every holoscreen back on our home planet and anywhere else it can be heard by fellow glowans." He didn't receive a response, nor did he expect one right away.

"Marctus, should we try and get the humans on our side?" Reol asked unexpectedly. At first Marctus thought it was an excellent idea. But the main concern was what would the leaders of the humans do once they saw them? Would they think it was a joke or would they take hostile action trying to hold them hostage or kill them to experiment on? Marctus decided he was going to wait to involve humans until they had some proof to show them that their world was in danger.

"Marctus your message has played on every holoscreen. As you might have expected, the captain and admiral know what you did and are now sending out messages of their own basically calling all the candidates traitors and that you and the humans must be eliminated. Also, the captain and admiral have threatened that if anyone attempts to contact or join you, they will be killed." Naivu said this so suddenly that the glowans all jumped when her voice crackled in their ears.

Marctus was not surprised by what he heard and knew that, at any moment, he would see the mothership above Earth. This would be all the proof he would need to try and ally with the humans.

Chapter 46

Captain Reath was sitting in his quarters with the last of the ten Elites behind him. They were both looking at Admiral Schur on the holoscreen before them. Admiral Schur was extremely upset and when he finally spoke the captain knew he was livid.

"YOU MEAN TO TELL ME THAT NINE ELITE SOLDIERS COULD NOT KILL 18 CANDIDATES WHO HAVE HAD NO SPECIAL TRAINING?" Admiral Schur yelled.

The Elite and the captain didn't speak for a moment and then the Elite finally said, "With all due respect, sir, they outnumbered and surprised us. By the time we realized what we were dealing with, it was too late." Admiral Schur didn't speak for a few moments but when he did he seemed to have calmed down a little.

"Werz, I understand you were outnumbered, but Elite soldiers have a five to one kill death ratio! We should have lost at MOST four of you." Captain Reath didn't speak, instead deciding it was best to speak only when spoken to by the admiral. "What's done is done. They will still die in the coming weeks. Captain Reath I am initiating the next phase of the mission. Once we arrive, please join me on board in my quarters." Captain Reath looked up now and acknowledged the admiral.

"Once we arrive we will simply sit in orbit of Earth until we are ready to invade. We will give the humans something to be scared of when they look up and see that our ship takes up most of their sky. The purpose of meeting me in my quarters is to go over the plan with the other captains who will be on the planet exterminating the humans. I expect to invade no later than one week after our arrival," Admiral Schur said. Captain Reath nodded and said he understood, and would await orders when he arrived on the mother ship.

"Now, I also understand we have a human on board your ship?" Admiral Schur asked.

"We do, Admiral. It is the human female that was associating with Marctus and who we believe drove him to turn against us," Captain Reath said.

"Send a message to Marctus that if he wants to see her alive again, to surrender before we invade. Send the message after we arrive in orbit so he understands he has just one week. In the meantime, interrogate her. Torture her if necessary to reveal any plans Marctus may have confided in her." Admiral Schur then paused and said one last thing before he signed off, "The ship will arrive early tomorrow so that the first thing Marctus sees when he wakes up is our craft blocking out most of the sky."

The holoscreen shut off and Captain Reath told the Elite he was dismissed. Captain Reath then made his way to where the human was being held. When he opened the door he saw she was awake and struggling to move in the chair that she was in. He walked over and looked down at her. She looked up at him with fear in her eyes.

"I'm going to ask you some questions. If you answer them truthfully, you will live. If you don't, you will die a slow painful death. Is that understood?" Captain Reath asked the human female and he saw her nod.

"Good. Now, what is Marctus planning to do down on Earth to fight us?" Captain Reath asked. She looked up at him and shook her head and cried out that she didn't know. Captain Reath starred at her for a moment before asking the question one more time. She cried out even more desperately when she said she didn't know. Captain Reath took out his Adapt and made a slash down the length of her forearm. Blood ran down her arm and dripped off her fingers onto the floor. She screamed loudly and continued saying she didn't know. After a moment the captain healed her arm before she bled out. Next, he grabbed her face and lowered his so their eyes were only an inch apart.

"I will ask you one more time. What are his plans to fight us?" he asked. The female human tried to speak and the captain let go of her face so she could. She then told him that Marctus had mentioned allying with humans in some way but didn't know how. She swore that this was all she knew. Captain Reath stared at her for a moment before asking another question.

"How did you come in contact with Marctus?" he asked. The human explained how Marctus had rescued her from a car crash. Her words were interrupted by sobs and sniffles. The captain then paused for a moment and stared at her. The human female looked at him terrified. She was shaking almost uncontrollably. The captain then asked one last question to her.

"Why did he not kill you when he was ordered to do so?" he asked. The human's eyes widened and she shook her head and cried and said she didn't know why he didn't. He only said that he cared for her and didn't want her to get hurt.

"Well, he's not doing a very good job making sure you don't get hurt is he?" the captain said. Immediately, he grabbed her left wrist, extended her arm sideways and used his Adapt to sever her arm in one fluid motion. She screamed with pain as she watched blood pour out of what remained of her arm as the captain threw her arm in her own lap. She took one look at it and then passed out. Captain Reath then healed the stump of her arm to stop the bleeding and left the room.

When he shut the door behind him he saw Naivu standing there.

"What do you want?" Captain Reath asked.

"Sir, are you ready to record the message to Marctus so I can send it to him?" she asked.

"Yes, let's get it over with," he said and he followed Naivu back to the control room of the ship.

Chapter 47

Captain Reath was up early and staring out at Earth the following day. At any moment now the mother ship would appear somewhere near them. As he watched Earth he wondered if this planet would surrender itself and the glowans would have a new planet to harvest resources and other materials they needed, but first the humans needed to be exterminated. They had no need for them anymore.

Then, out of the blackness of space the mother ship appeared in front of the Stalker. It grew larger with every passing second until it finally stopped and sat above the Earth. "Proceed to the hangar to land," Captain Reath said to one of the glowans. "Yes sir," was the reply and the Stalker flew toward the mother ship. The hangar door was so tiny in the distance that when you finally approached it the size of the mother ship really shocked you. Even to this day it amazed the captain.

After the Stalker landed in the hangar, Captain Reath walked out accompanied by the crew of glowans. The Elite was holding the female and Captain Reath instructed him to take her to the holding chambers to wait for further questioning. In reality the only thing that would await the human is death if Marctus did not surrender in a week's time. Captain Reath then boarded a floater that would take him to one of the main elevators that led to the Admiral's quarters.

When he exited the elevator and walked down the hallway toward the Admiral's quarters, he noticed that, all along the wall, were images of previous admirals dating back hundreds of years. He arrived at the door to the admiral's quarters and knocked on the door. The door immediately slid upward into the ceiling and

Captain Reath walked in. In front of him was a large round table with chairs all around it. On the table there were what looked like landscapes, buildings, water, amongst other things. Around the table sat Admiral Schur and other captains.

"Captain Reath welcome!" Admiral Schur said getting to his feet and greeting the captain showing him to his seat at the table.

"Let's begin," Admiral Schur said and the table in front of them zoomed out to show one of the continents on Earth. "This is North America and contains the United States of America and Canada which are each called countries. Captain Reath you will be in charge of the forces in the United States and Captain Blach you will be in charge of Canada. You will not be on the ground but will command from here."

The table then zoomed in to show the United States in detail with red dots all over the country. "These red dots indicate where the drop ships will place glowans to begin the extermination. Each drop ship will contain anywhere from 500-1000 glowans depending on the area. Once on the ground, the captain will make sure that they move out in a diameter that covers enough area around the major cities. No airstrikes will be used as we want the Earth unharmed."

"Initially, we did not foresee any resistance and this part of the mission would only last a day at the most. Unfortunately, we have run into some complications." The Admiral then explained to the other captains about Marctus and the human female, and his desire to fight back. The other captains already knew about it, but not in the detail the Admiral provided.

"We are hoping Marctus will surrender and we won't have to fight any humans. This is not to say that we would lose against them, but we risk losing more glowans and it will take longer." Admiral Schur then zoomed to another country and assigned it to one of the captains around the table. He continued in this fashion until every country was assigned.

"At first you will have your glowans simply exit the drop ship and kill any humans they encounter. Once your area is secure, you are to report to me and await further orders. I do not expect this to take longer than a couple days at the *most*, is that understood? The Elites leading each group will be invisible which will be a nice surprise to the humans. Also something that should be noted, we are going to be shooting the main gun of the mother ship at Earth before the invasion begins, but not to burn the planet. The purpose is to eliminate their communications, transportation, and basically anything that runs on electricity," Admiral Schur then stood up and the other captains left the room. He asked Captain Reath to walk with him.

"What did you learn from the human?" Admiral Schur asked as they walked down the hall toward the elevator.

"Nothing we couldn't have guessed ourselves," said Captain Reath and he then described how Marctus came in contact with the human and Marctus saying he was going to ally with the humans.

"Even if he did try to ally with the humans, would they believe him? If they did they would capture him and try to experiment on him just like we did with the humans," Admiral Schur said. "Make sure the message gets to him that he has one week. The plans for this invasion are simple. I don't want to use any of our larger weapons because I want the Earth intact. Ground forces should do for this mission. If it comes to a worst case scenario, we will launch airstrikes before we use the mother ships main gun for anything other than what I specified in the briefing."

Captain Reath then entered the elevator and turned around to see that Admiral Schur had not entered with him. "I will meet with you later. Inform me immediately if Marctus surrenders," said the admiral. He then nodded as a form of goodbye and the elevator doors closed.

Chapter 48

Marctus, Birgue, Sul, and Reol were all invisible and standing outside looking up at the mother ship that had appeared in the blue sky. Even though it meant something bad was going to happen it was hard not to admire its beauty. As they were staring at it, Marctus heard Naivu speak into his earpiece, but her tone suggested she was being watched as she spoke.

"Marctus, I am relaying a message to you from Captain Reath and Admiral Schur. If you accept the terms of the message, reply at once," Naivu said. Shortly thereafter the voice of Captain Reath came through the earpiece.

"Marctus, you have one simple option. Surrender to us now and your female human will live. Don't surrender and we will kill her, your glowan friends on Earth, and kill you. You have one week to respond." Once the message ended there was a high pitched scream in his ear and he knew the scream to be Jayla's. He dropped to his knees and put his head in his hands and yelled in frustration.

"Marctus, this is your proof right here," Birgue said pointing to the sky. "This is your proof to offer the humans, to let them know what we know is going to happen to Earth and what has already happened. It's our only choice, our only chance."

"But we're not sure what they're doing here. Are they going to fire the main gun of the mother ship, wipe everyone out and burn the planet? Or something else?" Marctus replied.

"Marctus, its, Naivu, I don't have much time," Naivu addressed the group suddenly. "Jayla is alive but the captain tortured her for information about you and your plans and…well…he cut one of her arms off in the process. He doesn't mean to do anything else to her unless you don't surrender. In that case he plans to kill her."

Still on his knees, Marctus sank even lower and felt anger and hate course through him. He would give anything right now to fly up there and kill Captain Reath and anyone else associated with him. He wanted to blow that mother ship right out of the sky and watch them die in the vacuum of space. Naivu's voice brought him back to reality.

"As for what you think they are going to do down on Earth, I have the information for you. They plan to drop glowans in all major cities all over the world in groups of 500-1000 glowans depending on the cities. The main army won't be invisible of course, but each group will have an Elite that will be. As for the number of them per drop ship I do not know. They plan to start in a week's time….I've got to go," Naivu then cut off.

"Marctus this is perfect! We now know the plans and can go to the humans and tell them what's going to happen. They'll have to believe us," Birgue insisted and the rest of the glowans nodded with him.

Marctus stood up and looked at them for a moment before speaking, "How are we going to talk to them though? In this country we would have to talk to the President of the United States and I can only image he is well guarded, even more so than the governors we had to eliminate."

"Did you forget we can go invisible?" asked Sul smiling.

"I know that but we can't just sneak in invisible and then randomly appear in front of him. For one thing, it would frighten the human and, second, I feel like we need to walk in as we are. Or at least in a disguise of some sort at first," Marctus said. "I feel like it would be more…proper."

They all agreed and started discussing what the best disguise would be and how to approach the president. "Well, I know he lives in the White House which is in another state. We will have to travel there right away. It shouldn't take more than four hours," Birgue said.

"As for disguises, let's worry about that after we get there and scout out the White House and how we should approach it," Reol said as she walked back inside to get the keys to Jayla's car. She threw the keys to Marctus. Marctus caught them and they all got into the car. The first thing Marctus noticed was Jayla's perfume. He didn't think it was possible to miss someone as much as he missed her right now. He made a promise to himself that, if he ever came in contact with the captain again, he would cut off all of his limbs before beheading him.

Chapter 49

Driving to Washington DC while invisible was one of the weirdest things Marctus had ever done. For one thing, people in every car that passed them turned to look and did at least a double take when they noticed nobody was driving the car. The look on their faces was pretty funny, especially because Birgue couldn't stop laughing. One thing they had not considered when they left was where they were going to live.

"I think our main priority right now is to get in to speak with the President. It needs to be done today," Marctus said after Sul brought up the question of where they were going to live. "What's the address to the White House, Birgue?"

"1600 Pennsylvania Avenue. Five minutes away," Birgue replied looking at his holoscreen that was giving him directions.

Marctus turned down a street following Birgue's instructions and they drove right in front of the house. It was a very large house with tall fences and gates all around it. There was only one way in and out which was very heavily guarded. There were additional humans on the roof of the building as well and guards patrolling all around the fences. The mother ship appearing must have something to do with all the heightened security. Marctus parked a few blocks down the road and they all got out of the vehicle to walk around the building.

"Our best bet is going to be to walk up to this gate with our disguise on and ask to see the president; or we go to Plan B and stay invisible and just walk in," Birgue said.

"There is no Plan B. This is the only plan," Marctus insisted, seeming kind of irritated as he stared at the front gate and at the guards that were heavily armored and carried large rifles. "Let's go figure out a disguise that will cover us completely including our faces." They all followed Marctus back to the car and got in. Marctus had Birgue track down the nearest shopping mall where they may be able to find these items.

"About 10 minutes away," Birgue said as Marctus pulled onto the highway and in the sky ahead of them, the mother ship still took up most of the sky. Surprisingly to Marctus, he didn't see that the humans were acting any differently so far. People were still driving faster than the posted speed limits and out front of the White House there were no riots or demonstrations. Were the humans really that calm about this, or had they just not noticed the ship?

When they arrived at the mall Marctus' thoughts about the humans being calm changed. There were humans with guns standing in front of the shops and one of the shops seemed to have already been broken into. Marctus and the glowans walked through the mall and into and out of stores looking for what they should wear. They decided on black jackets with hoods and black pants. "We need to find something to cover our faces," Reol said.

As Marctus and the glowans made their way through numerous other stores with no luck finding any type of mask, he noticed that one of the TV's that hung in the mall all of a sudden started blaring an emergency message with the words appearing on the screen which said: "Emergency Presidential News Conference." A second later the president walked out of a side door, up to a podium and began speaking.

"Earlier this morning a ship of extra-terrestrial origin entered our planet's orbit. Since then we have tried to contact the ship but with no success. We are continuing to try to contact the craft and ask that everyone continue their daily activities as normal. All laws of this land still stand and any looting, killing, or impediments of movement will still be punishable to the full extent of the law. When we have more to share on this subject, we will inform you. Thank you." The president then entered the same door he had originally exited, and the TV went back to the normal mall programming.

"I wonder how they are trying to contact the ship." Sul said.

"No idea," Marctus said.

"Hey, Marctus, how about these? Would they work?" Reol asked Marctus who was inside a store just below the TV. She was holding up masks that looked like human faces with white hair and had a large white smile.

"Well, we're not finding anything else, so that should do," Marctus said.

"What about these?" Birgue asked and when Marctus turned around to see what Birgue was talking about he saw Birgue was wearing a horse's head.

"Are you trying to draw attention to yourself?" Marctus asked. "Take that off before someone sees you." Birgue removed the horse head mask while mumbling "we're invisible", and they all started walking toward the exit from the mall. Just as they walked outside they saw a bunch of the humans with large rifles running past them headed for a building down the road. The building was actually a gun store and they could hear shooting coming from inside it.

"Let's get out of here, quick," Sul said. They all got back in the car and headed back toward the White House.

Chapter 50

Jayla was floating in midair unable to move. Above her was a circle with a blue light illuminating out of it which seemed to be the source of her imprisonment. She looked over at her missing arm and started crying again. She couldn't help it. She was scared out of her mind and knew she was going to die soon. She thought of Marctus and all the great times she'd shared with him. She had never felt so close to another person before. The funny thing was, he wasn't a person really. He was an alien and she felt closer to an alien than she ever had to anyone on Earth.

Just as she was thinking about Marctus and what he was doing right now, a glowan walked in to the room with long black hair. Jayla watched as the glowan turned the lights out in the room and everything was put into darkness except the blue light that illuminated Jayla. "What do you want?" Jayla demanded.

"I'm a friend of Marctus'," said the glowan and Jayla knew it was a female.

"I don't know anything, I promise. Please let me go!" Jayla said convinced that this voice was indeed no friend of Marctus but just a plot to try to get more information out of her.

"My name is Naivu," the woman said and Jayla recognized that name. It was a name she heard Marctus speak to on occasions. If she remembered right, this was the one who helped Marctus escape. "I just want to let you know I am going to try and get you out of here but it's going to take time. As soon as I can, I'm going to speak with Marctus and let him know my plan, but I need you to be patient."

Jayla didn't say anything because Naivu immediately left the room leaving Jayla to her thoughts of what the plan could be and when it would take place. Most of all Jayla thought about when she could see Marctus again.

Chapter 51

Marctus, Birgue, Sul, and Reol were all standing across from the White House in their disguises watching numerous humans rally outside the fence and gates. They were holding signs that depicted blowing up the mother ship, killing the aliens and other things along that line. But there were also signs of the opposite opinion, like making peace with the aliens and 'Learn from them don't kill them' signs.

"You guys ready to do this?" Marctus asked. "I'm not sure what's going to happen but we could all be killed."

"We're ready, Marctus," said Sul. Birgue and Reol nodded in agreement. Just as Marctus was going to start walking toward the main gate to tell the guards he wanted to see the president, Naivu spoke in his earpiece.

"Marctus hold on" she said.

"Naivu? What's wrong?" Marctus asked her with worry in his voice.

"I have a plan to free Jayla but it's risky and I'll have to do it on the day you're supposed to surrender. This would mean the invasion may start anyways." Marctus was glad to hear she had a plan but didn't want her putting herself at risk to help him any more than she already had.

"Naivu, I don't want you risking your life to help me anymore. I feel that's a big risk and so many things can go wrong," Marctus said but holding out hope that she would ignore him and proceed with her plan anyway.

"I'm on your side, Marctus. If I could, I would leave here and join you today but I feel like I'm more useful to you up here and I will do what I can when I can," Naivu spoke with certainty and a sense of pride in her voice.

"I am very thankful, Naivu. What is your plan?" Marctus asked.

"In a week I will escort her to one of the small escape pods and will program it to go to you. If any questions are asked I will simply say I was ordered to release the prisoner. I think it should go fine. I think, with all the chaos of starting the invasion, they won't be focused on it very much. It's worth a try if you're okay with it." Marctus went over the plan in his head a couple times and found numerous things that could go wrong. But if he didn't surrender she was dead anyways and surrendering wasn't an option.

"I think it will work, Naivu. Please let me know if you succeed and good luck," Marctus said. Naivu said, "of course" then ended the transmission. Marctus then pulled his focus back to the task at hand which could also not fail or Jayla would be released to nothing but an Earth that is certainly doomed.

"Okay. Let's go," Marctus said and he began walking toward the front gates of the White House with Birgue, Sul, and Reol following behind him. As he approached the gate all the guards pointed their rifles at them and the humans on the roof took aim at them as well. One of the guards next to the gate shouted at him to stop and he obeyed. The human then walked up to him and asked his purpose for approaching the gate.

"I need to speak with the president. It is of upmost importance you let me," Marctus said calmly. The guard looked at him for a moment before pointing the barrel of the rifle at Marctus' chest and saying, "I think it's of upmost importance that you turn around and leave." Marctus then turned around to look at Birgue, Sul, and Reol and saw Birgue nod his head at him. Marctus turned back around to the guard and reached up to remove his mask. As he did that he saw that all the guards were now intently watching him, rifles pointed at his head, chest, everywhere. Marctus grabbed the top of the mask and lowered it just enough so that the human would see his eyes and only his eyes and said, "It is important that I speak with him." The human's face turned from stern and threatening, to shock and confusion. At first the human didn't lower his weapon and seemed to be working something out in his mind. The guard then lowered his weapon and raised his arm to signal the other guards to do the same. "Follow me," the guard said and opened the gate.

Marctus, Birgue, Sul, and Reol all followed the soldier up the drive and toward some stairs that led into the basement of the White House. They entered a square room just big enough for them to fit into and Marctus heard a few clicks and chinks ahead of him and saw the wall open into a larger room. They followed the guard into the room which reminded Marctus of a normal family room that you would see at any human's house. It had couches, TV's, and pictures of other humans on the wall.

"Before we continue I need you to remove your masks completely," the guard said.

"Not until I am in front of the president," Marctus said.

The soldier stared at him and Marctus had a feeling the soldier was scared of what was about to happen. The soldier nodded and spoke to someone in what seemed the same manner that Marctus spoke to Naivu. "I need to see the president. I have something he's going to want to see," said the guard. After a few moments the guard nodded and motioned for Marctus to follow. They got in an elevator that took them even further down below the White House.

When they stepped out of the elevator Marctus looked out at a huge room filled with people at computers and huge TV's on the wall that showed an image of the mother ship and what seemed to be missiles on a launch pad. His time of gazing around the room was cut short when the guard motioned to him to follow once again down the middle aisle between the rows of computers and towards a door at the far end of the aisle just under the huge TV's on the wall.

When Marctus entered the room there was a red leather desk chair behind a desk and, behind that, was an American flag and the seal of the President of the United States. In the room across from the desk were chairs that the guard motioned Marctus and the glowans to sit in. Marctus refused and remained standing. After a moment of looking around the room, he realized that they were in some sort of underground bunker/ intelligence gathering type of room. The door opened and Marctus watched as more armed guards entered with their guns raised. The guards were followed by the president.

The president entered and, before he walked behind his desk, took a good long look at Marctus and the glowans in their masks then proceeded to sit down. "So, I was called down here to look at four people in masks?" The president said looking at the guard who had brought Marctus and the glowans here.

"Sir, you don't understand he…" the guard was cut off and watched as Marctus, Birgue, Sul, and Reol all lowered their hoods and removed their masks. At first no one did or said anything. The guards that had their guns aimed at Marctus and the glowans mere seconds ago now lowered them in shock; however, after a moment they raised them up and were ready to fire once again. The president also had a shocked look on his face, but held up his hand to signal the guards to lower their weapons.

"Whom do I have the pleasure of speaking to?" the president asked unexpectedly.

Marctus stepped forward and said, "I am Marctus. This is Birgue, Sul, and Reol." He pointed to each glowan as he said their name. The president nodded and introduced himself as well and motioned for Marctus and the glowans to sit down. Marctus accepted and sat in the comfy smaller leather chairs that were in front of the desk.

"I must say it is a surprise you showed up in such an interesting disguise when your ship is most certainly not hidden." the president said and looked at Marctus for a further answer. Marctus waited a moment and then said, "It's not technically our ship." The president leaned back in his chair and didn't say anything, waiting for Marctus to elaborate.

"What I mean to say is, we did not come from that ship, we were already here," Marctus said and the president leaned forward with interest marking his rough face. The president looked at him for a moment then asked, "Care to elaborate?"

"It's a long story," Marctus said plainly but the president nodded for him to continue so Marctus started out telling him that he was from a race called the glowans. He explained that they found Earth back when life was just forming on the planet and have been watching it ever since. He then explained that he and his fellow glowans were selected for a mission to Earth to learn more about the humans. He explained how they had abducted humans for experimentation and termination. "So that explains the two missing governors, I assume?" the president cut in.

Marctus nodded with his head downcast, then continued. He told the president about Jayla and that she had been taken hostage because Marctus and his fellow candidates refused to abduct or kill anymore humans.

"So this is the reason that your whole race has come here now?" the president asked.

"No," Marctus said, "there was always a bigger plan, one that we were not aware of until yesterday." Marctus continued to divulge that the main plan is to eliminate all humans on Earth so that the glowans can colonize the planet and use it for resources. He then explained that the main reason for abducting humans at first was to see if anything could be learned or gained from them. Marctus went on to explain how he had grown to care for humans like Jayla and how his fellow candidates agreed with him. He then told the president of his source onboard the mother ship and the plans of invasion involving the drop ships of glowan and Elite soldiers. He informed the president that these soldiers have the ability to become invisible by wearing specialized suits and the only way to see them is if those same type suits are used.

"Can you get these space suits freely?" the president asked, interested. "Not unless I go on board and steal some and I would never make it out alive," Marctus replied. He then explained that only the candidates and the Elites could take advantage of the invisibility feature of the special suits. If a regular glowan were to wear them, it wouldn't work. When the president asked why, Marctus told him that the suits were specially designed for them and had no other explanation.

After Marctus was done explaining everything he knew the president just stared at him. Marctus wondered if the president thought this was some joke or if he was even taking it seriously. After a few minutes the president asked what kind of weapons the glowans used. Marctus took out his Adapt and showed the president the different things it could turn into including the gun. He then explained what the balls of energy do once they hit a body. He also explained that there were more accurate versions of this gun similar to the ones the guards were holding in the room.

Then Marctus explained about the main gun on the mother ship and how it could wipe out everything on Earth. He continued to say that he didn't think they would use it unless they found Earth unattainable and would use it only in a last case scenario. He also said that any type of airstrike or similar action would not be used because they want Earth in good condition. It would be strictly ground forces....at least for the first part of the action. The president looked down at his hands for a moment then said, "This is beyond anything I imagined." The guards around the walls were also shocked at what they had just heard. A number of them actually sat on the floor to listen to Marctus.

The president then stood up and the guards stood at attention. "Marctus, I hope you don't mind but that whole scene was recorded. With your permission, I would like to show it to everyone in the country and share it with the world as well." Marctus nodded and was shocked that this whole operation went so well. "Does this mean you are going to fight?" Marctus said.

"I don't think we have a choice," the president said. "I assume you will be fighting by our side?"

"Absolutely sir," Marctus said and then told him about the message he had sent to his home world trying to recruit other glowans to join their cause. He added that he had not heard anything about any resistance forming there or any glowans wanting to join the fight. The president nodded and said, "Humanity vs. aliens. I never would have thought I would see the day this happened. You four will stay here. You will be safer here than anywhere else. I will have George show you where you can stay. I am going to be contacting other world leaders and playing your message for them and, if they are stupid enough to ignore these facts, we will all die. As for us, here, we will immediately send out national security warnings and play your message across the United States. Every soldier will be ordered to the main cities and surrounding areas. Anyone that wants to fight will not be turned down no matter their age. I'm going to gather my head generals and the Security Council. They will want to go over what you've told me about the attack plans. I hope you will cooperate."

"Absolutely," Marctus said. The president then left the room and one of the guards, who Marctus guessed to be George, told them to follow him. He led them to a large room where they sat down, but before Marctus let George leave he asked him if they could retrieve their weapons from their car. George said he would have the car brought onto the White House property and they could retrieve them from there. Marctus threw him the keys and he left.

"Well, that went better than expected," Birgue said.

"Yeah it did," Reol said.

"Do you guys feel like the humans stand a chance?" Sul asked.

"At first, yes, but I know the admiral will send more and more glowans and then I think they'll be in trouble. We'll have to wait and see," Marctus said and he hoped it wouldn't come to that. He also hoped that some glowans would join them and the humans and fight. He also thought about Jayla and what role she would play once she was back on Earth. If she did make it back to Earth.

Chapter 52

The following days were filled with Marctus talking to other world leaders via computer and also talking to generals and other important people about the glowans' plan of attack. He couldn't count the number of times he had outlined everything that he had explained to the president, and told them again and again that that no type of air weaponry would be used. The humans liked this fact and felt they could use it to their advantage. During one of the meetings with numerous people one general had asked if the mother ship was able to be destroyed.

Marctus thought for a few minutes on that question, because he had never learned how the ship operated and, therefore, if or how it could be destroyed. Then Marctus admitted that he wasn't positive how the mothership operated. It could use Silpo or it could use something he has no knowledge of. At the mention of the word Silpo, Marctus also had to tell them about the fluid on their planet that was used for so many different applications.

"Well our plans of getting to that ship are slim to none," said a general sitting at a long table with the president and Marctus, with several other leaders from around the world on a computer screen above them. "We don't have the technology to fly there fast enough to make any impact." the general added.

Marctus then remembered the smaller Stalker ships that were still sitting in the woods outside of New York and thought they could use those to fly there if they needed. The president immediately had a helicopter pick Marctus and the glowans up and take them to the location where the Stalkers where in order to fly them somewhere closer and more secure.

Marctus left the table and as he was escorted outside, the helicopter was already landing on the front lawn. He boarded the helicopter and it took off toward New York. Along the way Marctus saw that almost every street was filled with cars. He assumed it was humans trying to get to other family members to hide or to fight. In no time they were above where Marctus had landed the Stalkers. He told the pilot not to land just to hover and let them climb down. Another pilot threw down a ladder and Marctus and the glowans descended into the clearing.

Marctus walked around to the front of where the Stalkers should be, but didn't see anything. Heart pounding, he continued to pace around the clearing hoping to find the right angle to view the ships, but couldn't see them. He motioned for the pilot to land. When the pilot landed and didn't hit anything on the ground, Marctus realized that the captain or the admiral must have had the Stalkers picked up before he could.

Cursing himself he climbed back onboard the helicopter and headed back to the White House. How could he have been so stupid as to not move them when they left? Now they had no way to approach the mother ship. Feeling like he had just doomed the entire human race, Marctus sat in silence the whole ride back.

Chapter 53

Marctus woke on the day he was to surrender. It was still dark out; the sun had not risen. A guard was stationed just inside the doorway of the quarters. When he noticed Marctus was awake, he told Marctus the president was expecting him and to follow him. As Marctus ate a bagel – a type of bread breakfast food he had come to enjoy – he hoped he wasn't going to be telling more people about the plans of the attack. The past week had consisted of nothing but Marctus explaining every detail that had been relayed to him from Naivu. The one piece of information that was missing, though, was the time of the attack. Would it be morning? Afternoon? Night? He hoped Naivu would tell him when it was starting, but, either way, they had to be ready.

The guard was leading Marctus into the underground bunker where the huge TV's were located, and the many people manning the computers. As he walked in and looked at the TV's on the wall he saw footage of different areas of the country where soldiers were stationed with tanks, Humvees, and other military weaponry just waiting. When Marctus saw the tanks and Humvees he told the president that they were a waste of time since they were going to be wiping out all electronics before the invasion. The president smiled and said, "Yes we know. The tanks won't be able to start but they can still turn and fire. That part runs on hydraulics and machinery, Humvees as well."

Marctus nodded and understood what he was saying and any additional fire power was good so Marctus decided not to argue the decision. The president then went on to say that he had around 1000 troops in each major city and between 200-500 in the smaller surrounding cities. He hoped it would be enough. He also said that those numbers did not include civilians. Around the world leaders were doing the same thing. They all took Marctus' message seriously and put their defensive strategies in motion.

The president said that Russia had attempted to fire a nuclear bomb at the mother ship. Apparently, when it made contact with the mother ship, it did absolutely no damage. Marctus explained that unless you were using weapons of their own design, nothing would hurt it. The president had that information relayed to the rest of the leaders around the world. "We have precious little time before all means of communication are cut out. Hurry and get that information transmitted!" A human at one of the many computer terminals started typing very fast into her system.

"Marctus are you and your squad ready?" the president asked.

"Yes sir," Marctus said.

"Good. I'm sending you all back to New York City. It's one of the most populated cities and they will need all the help you can provide." When Marctus started to protest about staying here and keeping him safe, the president shook his head and said he would be fine underground. Marctus nodded and the president shook Marctus' hand. "God be with you," he said. "I hope we will see each other again." Marctus didn't say anything because he honestly didn't know how they were going to win this war.

A guard then motioned for Marctus to follow. Marctus followed him back to the elevator and up to the floor where Birgue, Sul and Reol were waiting. Before Marctus forgot, he spoke to Naivu and hoped she was listening. He told her they would be in New York City if she is able to free Jayla. Surprisingly, he heard her say back very quickly, "Okay. I'll be trying to release her soon. Will contact you if I succeed."

Marctus put on his suit and followed the guard out to the helicopter that was waiting on the front lawn of the White House. The sun was now rising and the helicopter lifted up and headed for New York City.

Chapter 54

Captain Reath and Admiral Schur were watching a video of Marctus telling the humans about the mother ship and what was going to happen. They were hours away from starting the invasion when Admiral Schur was informed about this message that was broadcast all across the planet.

"Do you think he has inside information on our plans?" Admiral Schur asked the captain.

"It's hard to say. It seems like he does, but where would he have gotten it?" Captain Reath responded with anger building in his voice.

"No matter. We will double glowan soldiers per drop ship. We will launch at the same time," Admiral Schur said and a glowan that was standing in the admiral's quarters with them nodded and left the room to deliver the order.

"Are we ready to eliminate their electronics?" Captain Reath asked.

"Yes. The block of their electronics will last only 24 hours, we will need to fire again at the same time tomorrow if necessary," Admiral Schur replied.

The captain nodded and left the room making his way to the mother ship's control deck. This is where the responsibility for the main weapon rested on the shoulders of a new recruit. The captain walked up behind him and told him the admiral was ready for it to fire. The glowan nodded, flipped a few switches and hit a green button.

A few moments later Captain Reath looked at the Earth below them and saw that a green beam was making its way toward the Earth. It seemed to be pulsing and sent a green wave of energy across the entire planet, then disappeared.

"Captain, electronics on Earth have been disabled," another glowan said who sat next to the new recruit.

"Good," said the Admiral walking into the room behind the captain. "Ready the drop ships. We invade in an hour."

"What of the human?" Captain Reath asked the Admiral.

"After seeing the video Marctus sent to the humans, I don't think he is surrendering. Kill her and send her in a pod back to Earth near New York City so Marctus can find her," Admiral Schur said.

"It will be done," Captain Reath said and left the control room.

Chapter 55

Marctus woke up lying on his back in the middle of a street. He looked around and saw pieces of the helicopter they had been flying in all around him. Buildings in the immediate area were on fire. He looked around him and couldn't see Birgue, Reol or Sul anywhere. He did see the pilot of the helicopter and just looking at the body he knew he was dead. Marctus got to his feet, found his energy rifle lying a few feet away from him, and started walking down the street between the burning buildings looking for his fellow glowans.

He remembered being close to the landing zone and then the sky lit up with a green light. The next second, the helicopter was spinning out of control and crashed into the building below them. Not only did the helicopter crash, but airplanes were dropping out of the sky like dead birds. As he walked down the road he saw Birgue lying face down on the road with a pool of blood under him. Marctus quickly ran over to him and turned him over. He saw that Birgue had a piece of metal or something sticking out of him which was the source of the blood. Marctus pulled the piece of metal out and healed the wound with his Adapt. After a moment Birgue woke up and asked what happened and Marctus told him everything. Birgue got to his feet making sure he was okay and he and Marctus continued looking for Sul and Reol.

They walked past a house that was completely on fire and saw Reol running out of the building. Marctus yelled for her and she turned and ran toward them. "I'm lucky I woke up in time. That fire would have killed me," she said out of breath. "Where's Sul?"

"We're still looking for him," Marctus said and they continued down the road checking the houses as they went. After passing six houses with no luck, Marctus decided to head back the other way and check the opposite direction. When they got to where Marctus previously was, he saw in the distance a body lying on top of a fence. As they got closer they saw that the fence had sharp ends at the top of each post and, on top of one of the ends, was Sul. He locked over at Marctus, Birgue and Reol as they approached and grabbed Marctus' hand.

Coughing up blood he managed to get a few words out before Marctus felt his hand go limp, "Kill them all". Marctus released his hand and a new fury came over him. He lifted Sul off of the fence and walked him over to the burning house. Wishing he had a better time and place to burn Sul, he placed him at the foot of the burning house and watched as the flames took his friend. Marctus turned around to look at Birgue and Reol and said, "Let's go." They started running toward the city with renewed energy and Marctus had a hungry desire to kill every last glowan that stood in his way.

Chapter 56

Naivu walked quickly and quietly toward where Jayla was being held. As she passed one of the many large windows on the mother ship, she saw the hundreds of drop ships heading toward Earth and hoped that the humans and Marctus were going to survive. She would leave to join them as soon as she thought she wasn't needed on board to help Marctus.

Naivu approached the door to Jayla's holding cell, opened the door and walked in. Jayla was still there floating in midair and seemed to be asleep. Naivu deactivated the device keeping Jayla afloat and caught her as she fell. The fall woke Jayla and she momentarily forgot where she was. She started to scream but Naivu covered her mouth. "Quiet. I'm getting you out of here. Follow me."

Naivu sat Jayla down and Jayla got to her feet. Naivu walked over to the door and opened it just a crack to make sure that all was clear. When she saw no one outside she motioned for Jayla to follow. They made their way through numerous hallways of the ship turning left, right, left, left and right many times to the point it made Jayla wonder how Naivu knew where she was going. Finally, they arrived in a room where guns and space suits were aligned along the walls.

Naivu quickly grabbed one of the suits that the Elites used and threw it to Jayla. She also attached one of the rifles to Jayla's back in case she needed it when she landed on Earth. She also cut off the sleeve so it wasn't hanging freely off of her missing arm. She then told Jayla to put the helmet on and to tap her forearm on her knee to activate the invisibility. Jayla did and Naivu lost sight of her. At first Naivu was unsure if the invisibility would work on a human because not all the invisibility suits worked on all the glowans. "Great! Now follow me and keep quiet," she said to Jayla and headed toward an elevator.

As they exited the elevator a few floors down Naivu quickly hid behind a door as a few glowans walked past. Even though Jayla is not visible, if Naivu was seen down here it would draw suspicion. Being on good terms with the captain, she was sure she could talk her way out of it if she did get caught. When the glowans finally passed they ran down a hallway and made another series of turns before arriving at a long room covered in windows. Below each window panel was a small square that led to an escape pod. These were for emergency use only so when it was detached someone would know about it. Naivu would have to get Jayla in and then leave this area immediately.

Naivu briefly paused just inside the room to make sure no one was in the long room. When she was convinced that no one was there, she told Jayla to follow and made her way over to one of the square doors below the windows. Naivu quickly typed in a code and the door opened up into a small area with enough room for maybe five glowans. It was one of the smaller pods but it was all Jayla needed. She saw Jayla take off her helmet and sit down as Naivu put coordinates into a holoscreen that appeared in front of the pod.

"Marctus is in New York City ready to fight. I am sending you just outside the city so your pod does not draw too much attention. It is important that you keep that helmet on when you land and exit. Make your way into the city and try to find him. I will let him know you are on your way once I am back in the control room," Naivu said to Jayla.

Jayla grabbed her hand and said thank you and that she hoped to see her again. Naivu smiled and said, "Hopefully soon." Naivu finished pressing something on the holoscreen, the pod lit up and started shaking. Jayla strapped herself in and watched as Naivu stepped outside the square door. Just as Naivu was about to close the door a ball of energy shot right past Jayla's head and hit the pod. Jayla screamed and Naivu quickly shut the door.

"So you're the one leaking information," said a voice behind Naivu. She slowly turned around and saw Captain Reath standing there, energy rifle pointed at her. "I have to admit that this is quite a shock. I never expected it of you." Naivu had her hands up and the button to launch the pod was right behind her but she didn't dare make a move to press it.

"Captain, you must know this is wrong. Please stop...," Naivu was cut off by a ball of energy exploding right next to her head. She screamed and stood frozen, hands still in the air.

"Open the doors to that pod immediately and I will forget you had any part in this," Captain Reath said. "You have my word." Naivu opened her eyes and saw the captain approaching her. Jayla was watching with tears in her eyes and didn't know what to do or say. Naivu nodded to the captain and turned around to open the door. But looking at Jayla's face and thinking of what she meant to Marctus made her think about how wrong all of this was. She would rather die than watch Jayla die. Jayla was motivation for Marctus and returning her to him meant that the humans and Marctus had a chance to win. A small chance, but a chance nonetheless.

Naivu hit the button to release the pod. Just as the pod broke away from the ship, Jayla watched as Captain Reath shot Naivu with the ball of energy from the rifle and watched as Naivu toppled over. She screamed and closed her teary eyes as the pod descended toward Earth.

Chapter 57

When Marctus arrived in the heart of New York City, Times Square, he was ordered to relocate to the Brooklyn Bridge. "If the bastards land outside the city and try to enter across the bridges, I want forces to stop them. I have a small group there already but they could use your help," said one of the army Sergeants named Carter to Marctus. Marctus immediately sprinted away from Times Square toward the bridge.

The bridge was about 30 minutes away but Marctus knew if they kept up their speed they could reach it in under 20. As he ran down the main road that led to the bridge, there were a lot of abandoned cars on the road. "I overheard one of the soldiers talking about how they had to threaten everyone to get out of their cars and get inside to shelter. That would explain all the abandoned cars," Birgue said. Marctus and Reol were now jumping from car hood to car hood as a faster way to get around all the cars.

They reached the end of the road, turned left and saw that someone had cleared a path between the cars. Looking at the way the cars were on the sidewalk and crammed into the surrounding buildings, Marctus assumed a tank must have drove through and pushed them all to the sides at some point before the electronics went out. They now sprinted down the cleared road with the bridge in sight. Another few minutes and they would be there. Then all of a sudden there was a loud bang that echoed around them and the road in front of Marctus' feet seemed to crack. He stopped and looked around and watched as five humans ran out from one of the buildings, guns raised and pointing at Marctus, Birgue and Reol.,

"Weapons on the ground aliens or we shoot to kill" said a plump male human with a round face. It was at this moment that

Marctus realized they were not invisible. He had forgotten to enable it after they left Times Square. Marctus didn't lower his gun and saw that Birgue and Reol were not lowering theirs either but kept them up and pointed at the humans.

"We're on your side," Marctus said and the human took another step closer.

"I don't care whose side you're on. Maybe if we turn you in, the rest of your race will leave." The human took another step forward; he was only about ten feet away from Marctus. Marctus also noticed that the other humans around him were slowly approaching him as well. Then Marctus realized that they weren't going to shoot to kill. If they wanted to kill him he'd be dead by now. They wanted him alive so they could turn him in and be the saviors of the human race. Foolish human.

"Even if you turn us in, they are not going to stop what they plan to do. They will capture you and make you experience pain beyond words," Marctus said trying to scare the human. The humans then all stopped in front of him. The plump one then spoke again.

"I seriously doubt that. You're obviously wanted if you are rebelling. I see a fine reward for us boys," the human said looking around at the rest of the humans. "You're going to take us to where we can turn you in right now." As the human said this, he lowered his gun to point at Marctus and in that brief second, Marctus tapped the invisibility button and saw Birgue and Reol do the same. The second they disappeared they crouched and slid behind the humans who were now firing blindly all around them. Marctus told Birgue and Reol to take their guns and within a few seconds the guns were snatched from their hands.

Marctus reappeared and said once again, "We are not your enemy. Either fight with us, or die." The plump human who was on his knees now spat at Marctus and told him to "Go to hell." Marctus was not going to kill them. That would make him no better than the commanders of the mother ship. Just as he was about to hit him over the head and knock him out, the humans head exploded and a loud bang echoed through the street. Then one by one the other humans' heads exploded and the limp bodies fell over. Looking around for who had fired, Marctus saw that down the street in the original direction they were heading were a couple soldiers with long rifles and big scopes aimed at them.

"Why did you kill them?" Marctus asked the soldier when they approached.

"We've been ordered to eliminate anyone who poses as a threat or anyone who tries to…interfere for lack of a better word," the soldier said. Marctus saw the name on his uniform was Mendoza.

Marctus nodded and understood why they were ordered to do it but didn't know if he agreed with the decision or not. "The bridge is just up here, sir. Let me show you the layout and plan," Mendoza said and led Marctus down the road where they took another left and then a right that opened up to the bridge. Marctus admired the huge bridge and the open arches to the roadways. Marctus saw that the bridge was also crammed with abandoned cars and a tank stood just a few yards onto each side of the bridge. A few yards before the entrance of the bridge were mounds of sandbags and cars that were being used by other soldiers who had large guns perched on them. Marctus also saw that there were at least a few hundred soldiers that stood behind the front lines of the sandbags. Marctus saw that walls of sandbags extended back as far as the soldiers. If anyone noticed them from the bridge, they would have a hard time hitting the soldiers from a distance.

"Now that you're here, we can activate these," Mendoza said and stepped on a sort of steel square pedal a little bigger than his foot. Each time it was stepped on, a large steel wall rose until it covered the entire entrance, effectively sealing the tank on the other side. "Is anyone in that tank?" Marctus asked.

"No. It's there now as a roadblock, should anyone try to come across the bridge," the soldier said. He then went up to the steel barrier and tapped it with his gun. The soldier walked with Marctus, Birgue, and Reol back to the other soldiers and introduced them.

"We're glad you're here. …sir," said a soldier who hesitated on the word sir because he didn't know what he should call Marctus. Marctus smiled at the human then asked where they wanted him, Birgue and Reol to be positioned.

"Up there," said Mendoza and Marctus saw he was pointing to a tall building that overlooked the squad of soldiers. The building provided a great view of anyone who attempted to cross the bridge. "I know you have some nice weaponry, but we also put some of our own up there for you to use if you want to. They have long scopes on them and are very accurate," Mendoza said with a slight smile.

Marctus gave his thanks and followed another soldier with the name Limars on his uniform to the building and then up to the roof. When Marctus walked out of the door and onto the roof, the first thing he noticed was the view of the water in the distance and how it flowed under the bridge, not to mention how big the bridge was. He then saw three of the rifles Mendoza had told him were up here. Marctus realized they would have to lay prone to fire them.

He walked over to the edge of the roof and saw the group of soldiers below on the street. Looking at them gave Marctus some hope because they were in such a position that if any glowans came across the bridge, they would be funneled into the entrance and slaughtered. However, if they came in from behind, that was going to be a very different story.

"What happens if they attack from behind and not from the bridge?" Reol asked Limars before he left the roof.

"The plan is to lower the steel walls and group up on the bridge behind the cars," Limars said. Marctus hoped it wouldn't come to that because the position here was so much better. Knowing that the plan was to land drop ships in every major city and the surrounding areas of that city, he was sure there would be one deployed near Times Square. He had a feeling that if the soldiers back there failed, they would be forced onto the bridge.

Marctus lay down at one of the human rifles and looked through the scope. He could see clear across the bridge with the scope. He moved a dial on the scope and it zoomed out so he could see a lot closer but still have some sort of magnification. Just as he was getting used to the gun, he heard a loud rumble above him. He looked away from the scope, up at the sky and saw ships all across the sky falling to Earth. Marctus had never seen this type of ship before and it looked like a large black box falling to Earth. Some were almost right on top of him and others were far away in the distance. It looked like the sky was filled with black squares for a moment and then Marctus watched as one drop ship landed behind them in the area of Times Square and saw one land somewhere across the bridge.

"Here we go," he heard Birgue say and Marctus saw the soldiers below all bunkering behind the cars and sandbags readying their guns. Marcus moved the dial on the scope and looked across the bridge.

Chapter 58

Sargent Carter was stationed inside one of the man-made bunkers placed around Times Square. It was a structure made of solid steel and stood about 10 feet off the ground with windows to shoot out of. It looked like a large steel shoe box. The past few days entailed construction of these steel bunkers in major cities all across the United States. It was something that was designed in case any foreign invaders decided to invade the country. They had never been tested but, in order to break through the steel, you would need some serious firepower.

Carter was inside with several other men that he knew well. Their names were: Ramirez, Grubber, Johnson, Cort, Wong, and Spear. Their orders were to stay inside until ordered to come out. They had a good view of two main roads that entered the middle of Times Square and any aliens that came through those roads would be killed. If they came from behind which was the middle of Times Square, then they would have to funnel through one narrow road to get to them.

None of the men were talking. They sat. They waited. Carter knew they were scared and admitted he was scared too. An alien race that were years ahead of them in technology were about to invade their planet and when it came down to it, what chance did they really have? He remembered the three aliens that came up to him about an hour ago that he redirected to the Brooklyn Bridge. If only we had an army of them on our side, then he would feel a little more comfortable about this war. But they only had three and what was three aliens compared to who knows how many on board that ship that still hovered in the sky.

Suddenly, there was a loud rumble that shook the bunker. Carter looked outside and up at the sky and saw a bunch of black objects falling toward Earth. "Get ready guys. It's starting," he said to his squad who all cocked their guns and checked their ammo. A few moments later the whole ground shook as if something hard had slammed into the Earth. He heard the sound of what he thought were buildings falling down from the impact of the ships landing. The ground continued to shake as if an earthquake was taking place. His thoughts were confirmed as a plume of dust and smoke began to fill the streets.

The soldiers inside the bunker put their masks on to breathe and after a few moments they heard gunfire and another unfamiliar sound which Carter guessed as the aliens' guns. As he turned away from the window facing south, he saw Johnson throw up all over the wall. Not long after that, Ramirez did as well and then Wong. He asked them if they were okay and they nodded. Minutes later the smoke and dust started to clear a little and, in front of them from one of the main roads, a group of the aliens were running right at them firing their guns.

"Fire at will!" Carter said and he heard every gun in the bunker start shooting at the approaching aliens. There were bullets and little balls of orange light flying back and forth. Carter watched as the aliens tried to dodge the bullets and, to his surprise, they were actually able to dodge a few before being hit. They were fast and gaining ground quickly. He had no idea how many there were. They were lined up in a row of at least ten and just continued to run at the bunker even after comrades next to them were killed and torn apart.

After what seemed like hours, the aliens ran back toward the street they had come from and seemed to be retreating. There was still gunfire in the distance and Carter and the rest of his soldiers cheered at the thought that they had been able to fight them off. But just as the cheering started, Carter saw down the road a large floating orange ball. It looked almost like the sun, but in a smaller form and not as bright and it was approaching their bunker. As it got closer, the air around him seemed to get hotter. Carter ordered his men to shoot at it. The object took a lot of rounds, but nothing happened. It was about a yard away from the bunker and Carter, now sweating profusely, ordered his men to leave the bunker. Before his men were able to evacuate, the orange ball engulfed the bunker and Carter watched as the steel melted like it was an ice cube. He watched as melted steel fell on his friends and burn right through their bodies, killing them instantly.

He had just made it out of the bunker when he looked back to see that the entire bunker was now a pool of melted black steel. The orange ball then disappeared and Carter watched as the aliens once again charged the location. He fired what ammo he had left but only managed to take down a couple before being hit in the chest with what looked like a smaller orange ball the size of a baseball. At first he thought he was okay, then he felt pain beyond measure, tasted blood and then everything went black.

Chapter 59

For a moment, all was quiet. The sun was getting low in the sky and darkness would be settling in within the next few hours. Marctus, Birgue and Reol were all lying down looking through the scopes of the three sniper rifles aimed toward the bridge. A few moments after the drop ships had vanished from the sky, Marctus felt the ground shake. He knew it was from the dropships hitting the Earth and he watched as tall buildings fell to the ground from the shaking and impact of the drop ships. Then he heard gunshots coming from every direction. The sound seemed to echo all around. The mixture of the sounds from the human guns and the glowans' energy guns carried for miles. To the north, Marctus was positive there was a fight in Times Square, like he predicted, and he also heard gunfire from across the bridge.

He looked down at the human soldiers and a lot of them were throwing up from what he assumed was being scared or nervous. As minutes went by, the sounds of gunfire did not fade away or stop. The only noticeable change was the gunfire got louder and there seemed to be more of it. Just as Marctus looked through the scope again, he saw glowans walking across the bridge from the far end. There were so many that they took up the whole width of both bridges as they walked across it.

Marctus yelled down to Mendoza, "glowans coming across the bridge now!" Mendoza nodded and readied his soldiers and then ordered Marctus to start taking out as many as he could. Marctus aimed at one of his fellow glowans, put the crosshairs on his forehead and pulled the trigger. The gun kicked and Marctus watched as the glowan's head exploded into pieces. Birgue and Reol took out one each as well. Then as Marctus was about to fire at a second, the glowans started running toward their end of the bridge. Marctus, Birgue and Reol took out as many as they could. The enemy glowans reached the end of the bridge and met with the steel barricades that prevented them from going anywhere else.

Some of the glowans jumped off the bridge and into the water and Marctus could see them swimming back to the opposite shore. He shot a few of them in the water and returned his fire back to the bridge. The glowans could not get around the steel wall. They were shooting at it but nothing was happening. Then he saw that some of the glowans had started to climb up the suspension cables of the bridge. He, Birgue and Reol took them out and watched as they fell into the water or bounced off of other glowans, hopefully killing them too from falling from such a height.

Just as Marctus thought everything was going well and there was no way the glowans would be able to get on the other side of the wall, Marctus saw a large orange ball start floating across the bridge. He saw the glowans move aside for it and he told Birgue and Reol to start shooting it.

"Do you know what that is?" Marctus asked them.

"No idea Marctus," said Birgue.

"Our bullets don't seem to be doing anything to it either. It keeps moving and we can't use our guns on it because it's too far away," Reol added.

Marctus then focused his fire back to the glowans standing around the ball and took out as many as he could before the ball of light reached the steel wall. When he saw that the ball of light was at the wall he watched as the steel wall melted away like melted ice cream. When both of the walls were melted away, the light disappeared and the glowans started running off the bridge and up the road toward the soldiers below Marctus, firing their energy guns.

The soldiers returned fire and Marctus, Birgue and Reol shot down at them until the glowans below noticed their position. They then started shooting up at them as well. Because of the angle, Marctus had to retreat back downstairs to join the fight or be useless. Birgue and Reol followed Marctus down the stairs with their energy rifles drawn ready to fire. They exited the building and an energy ball barely missed Reol as she exited the building. They fell behind one of the overturned cars with Mendoza and started firing down at the advancing glowans.

The glowans were smart though. They had found a semi truck's trailer that looked like a big white rectangle and they were pushing it up the small road toward the troops' position. It was hard to hit the glowans behind it but they were able to take out a lot of the glowans running along the sides of it. Mendoza and some of the other soldiers threw grenades behind the trailer but all it did was kill the glowans currently pushing it. They were easily replaced by more glowans who continued to push it up the hill blocking the gunfire.

"All the damn RPG's are back with Carter so we have no way of taking it out," Mendoza said to Marctus who nodded but couldn't think of anything to say. Marctus looked back over the car and saw that the trailer had reached the top of the incline and was now just a few yards in front of them. Glowans still poured around the sides of it but the soldiers easily took them out. Then Marctus watched as the trailer tipped over on its side and watched as some human soldiers unable to get out of the way in time were squashed beneath it.

The glowans then pushed the trailer around which made a loud screeching noise so that the trailer was horizontal to the soldiers and Marctus, and then they began pushing again. The trailer was completely shredded by the bullets that had been piercing it and Marctus, Birgue and Reol were able to hit some of the glowans behind it. The glowans continued to push the trailer, which then worked as a scoop to pick up the sandbags and continued forward, backing the soldiers and Marctus into the streets behind them. As Marctus, Birgue, Reol and the soldiers reached the intersection behind them, Marctus realized what the glowans were doing all along.

When they had originally crossed the bridge they sent glowans around to flank from behind. They would have had to walk a few miles to be able to take a road to get here, but that was all the time the glowans needed to stall and push the trailer at them to force them back. Marctus and the remaining soldiers, which Marctus now realized were less than 30, were all grouped in a circle in the middle of a four-way intersection. Martcus saw glowans running in all directions, but they were not close enough yet to be shooting at Marctus and the troops.

As Marctus stood there, he thought about going invisible and running away to save himself, Birgue and Reol. Then he decided he would die fighting with the humans and would not run or show his fear. Just as he was settling on that decision, Mendoza grabbed him and demanded that he go invisible and head back to Times Square to hopefully help the soldiers there.

"I will not leave you!" Marctus shouted.

"It's not your choice! You're our only hope and if you die, then we have nothing to rally behind. Go now!" Mendoza yelled. Taken aback by the comment of 'nothing to rally behind' Marctus went invisible and told Birgue and Reol to follow him down a small alley toward Times Square.

As they ran Marctus heard the screams of humans and glowans, the continued gunfire of the fight raging on and hoped the humans were somehow winning. Then he remembered that Naivu was supposed to be setting Jayla free sometime during the invasion. He hadn't heard anything yet and, as he ran back toward Times Square, he tried to reach Naivu.

"Naivu can you hear me?" Marctus said jumping over abandoned cars. After a few minutes he got no reply and he began to panic. "Naivu are you there?" he repeated multiple times as they ran toward Times Square. Just as they reached Times Square and saw glowans and humans alike fighting, Marctus entered a building and once again asked for Naivu.

"I'm sure everything is fine, Marctus" Reol said. "I'm sure she got her out."

But Marctus always jumped to the worst possible scenario. He felt empty inside not knowing if Jayla was okay or if Naivu was able to free her. The feeling of not knowing was eating him inside and he felt sick to his stomach with worry.

"Marctus let's find Carter and see what we can do to help. Naivu will contact you soon with good news," Birgue said with a smile. Marctus nodded and stood up. Reol hugged him and said she was sure Jayla was fine. Marctus let the negative thoughts fade away, replacing them with positive images which gave him the motivation to head out of the building to find Carter.

Chapter 60

Jayla opened her eyes and looked around. She had landed on Earth and, from what Naivu said, she should be somewhere in New York City. The only thing she could see out of the see-through door was water. She undid the invisible seat belt and got up to open the door. Just as she was about to open it a glowan appeared on the other side. She screamed and jumped back begging for her life but then watched as the glowan took one look inside then walked away. At that moment she remembered she was invisible and the glowan wouldn't be able to see her unless it was wearing a suit like hers, which it wasn't.

She then opened the door and looked for the glowan. He was heading back toward a group of other glowans that were about to cross the Brooklyn Bridge. She grabbed her gun that fell off her back in the landing and noticed that it was broken in pieces and now felt completely defenseless. She then walked back out of the drop ship and looked up at the bridge. There were at least a couple hundred of them that were all gathered on the bridge walking toward the other side. She watched for a moment as they crossed and then heard gunfire. She thought there must be humans on the other side but she had no way of getting over there until the glowans were all across. She waited until all the glowans were either on the bridge or had crossed it before climbing up the hill to the road that led to the bridge.

She slowly walked between the abandoned cars behind the glowans, careful not to make any noise to draw attention to herself. Then something behind her made her jump and she almost screamed. A glowan was running toward her but she knew he couldn't see her because he wasn't wearing a suit. He had a small handgun that Jayla knew she could use to defend herself but she had no way of getting it. Just then she noticed a tire wrench lying on the street on the other side of an abandoned car that was missing a tire. She picked it up and waited for the glowan to get closer to her. When he was right in front of her she swung the tire iron with all her strength and hit him on the head. He fell to the ground twitching with blood flowing from his head.

Jayla picked up the gun and, when she held it, it felt like it was alive in her hand, like it was a part of her. It was light and when she fired it, there was no kick to it. It was unlike any handgun she had ever fired in her life. She looked for somewhere to holster it on her side but there was nowhere. She moved her hand across her body to the other side, dropping it by accident. The gun never hit the ground, instead it snapped to her side like a magnet. Satisfied, she continued across the bridge behind the glowans.

As she came close to the glowans, she walked behind a trailer that was shot to pieces and saw them walking up the street heading north toward Times Square. Jayla thought there was a possibility that was where Marctus was. As she walked up to an intersection she saw around 30 human bodies lying dead in pools of blood. She looked at the faces that were caved in on themselves and those that had exploded blood from every orifice and said a short prayer for them as she continued walking behind the glowans hoping that they would lead her to Marctus.

Chapter 61

Marctus, Birgue and Reol were following the sounds of gunfire that seemed to be coming from every street leading away from Times Square. When they had reached Times Square moments ago they found it filled with glowan and human bodies and realized that the humans must be retreating. Marctus, Birgue and Reol were still invisible and running as fast as they could to help the humans. They turned down a street that was empty but saw gunfire being traded across an intersection.

Approaching the intersection, Marctus slowly looked to his left and saw glowans approaching firing their weapons at human soldiers which were to his right. The soldiers were few in number and falling by the second as they were constantly pushed back. Unlike the glowans, the humans had to constantly reload their weapons. They didn't have a long lasting charge on them like the glowan weapons did, which was another disadvantage for humans.

After the glowans passed by Marctus, Birgue and Reol he followed them down the road and began shooting them in the back. They were able to take out quite a few before the glowans realized they were being attacked by an invisible force. They then turned around and began firing blindly hoping to hit whoever was taking them out. To Marctus' right was an entrance to a building that led to a roof that provided an excellent view of the street. He reached the roof and saw that there were only five humans left hiding behind an abandoned car and there were close to fifty glowans closing in on them. Marctus, Birgue and Reol began firing as fast as they could, taking out the glowans while they were invisible trying to help the humans. By the time the fifty or so glowans lay dead, the last surviving soldier was looking around trying to find his savior.

Marctus left the building and walked up to him and came out of invisibility. When he did, the human raised his weapon about to fire. Birgue grabbed it from him just in time and the bullet went straight into the air. Reol grabbed the human who then struggled to find what invisible force was holding him.

"Easy human we are your allies. I am Marctus," Marctus said to try and calm him down.

"Sorry, Marctus," the human said. "I couldn't be sure." He then stopped struggling and Reol released him and Birgue gave him back his weapon and the other two came out of invisibility.

"Where are you ordered to retreat to?" Marctus asked him after he caught his breath.

"The Museum of Natural History, it was our rendezvous point if we had to retreat. We had special defensive measures set up around it just in case. If anyone else is alive, they would be there," the soldier said.

"What's your name?" Birgue asked.

"Cortez. John Cortez, sir"

"John, guide us there. We will be behind you, invisible, and will cover you," Marctus said. John nodded and then started walking up the street headed north. Along the way the sounds of gunfire didn't stop. It seemed to be coming from all around them and at any moment there could be another fire fight.

"Where did all the glowans go John?" Marctus asked.

"No idea. At first they all ran out of the drop ship right at us. Probably around 1000 I would say. We were able to take a lot of them out while inside the bunkers, but when that sun ball came and destroyed the bunkers we started losing ground. I don't know how many of us in New York made it to the museum or if anyone did at all. Those 50 glowans you killed were just a break off from a larger group that headed east and west."

Marctus thought about where the larger group was going and why they would split up. Right now it was not a concern. The main goal right now was to get to the museum and find out what was going to happen next. If they needed to communicate, they had about 11 hours left before electronics would work again. If the mother ship fired another EMP blast, which Marctus was sure they would, the humans might only have seconds to communicate with anyone.

It was dark out when they reached Central Park and the museum was just ahead. The gunfire was very subtle in the distance but it was still audible. Marctus, Birgue and Reol all followed John as he made his way across the park staying hidden in the many trees and bushes along the way. After a few minutes they reached a small lake. John stayed put for a few moments surveying the area before making his way around the left side of the lake. Sprinting for a moment, he made his way up a small slope and was in front of the museum. It had large pillars but the top half of a statue had been destroyed so you couldn't make out what it was. There were glowan and human bodies all over the road and the front steps of the museum. Marctus looked up at the front door and saw it was shut.

"Do you think anyone is in there?" Marctus asked John.

"Don't know. When we were briefed about this safe zone we were told that there would be at least one other soldier outside as a lookout but seeing these bodies it may be the glowans found out about this place," John said looking up and down the road.

After a few moments he got up and said, "Let's check it out," and made his way across the street.

They reached the top of the stairs and John tried to open the door. It was locked. Checking that no one was behind them he knocked on the door three times. Nothing happened. After a few moments of waiting, the door slowly creaked open and a group of soldiers emerged with their rifles at the ready. They couldn't see Marctus, Birgue or Reol and asked John what his purpose was.

"I have Marctus with me," John said and at that point Marctus, Birgue and Reol came out of invisibility and the group of soldiers lowered their guns and ushered them inside. A couple of soldiers scanned the perimeter in front of the museum before finally coming in and closing the door.

"Are there any orders on where we are supposed to go or what we're supposed to do?" John asked the soldiers. Marctus counted about 30 soldiers around the empty entrance hall. They were all sitting down drinking water and splashing it on their faces from a huge round drum that was filled to the brim.

"None. We arrived about an hour before you did. Our best bet is to wait until the electronics are back up and then hope we receive orders before the aliens cut them out again," said the soldier who originally opened the door.

Marctus nodded and motioned for Birgue and Reol to follow. He stepped just outside the hall and tried to reach Naivu again. He waited ten minutes and still got no reply. Jayla was dead. That was the only thing going through Marctus' mind. There was no way she was still alive. If she were still alive Naivu would have told him. He also hoped Naivu was okay.

"I'm sure she's fine, "but Marctus cut Reol off before she could finish.

"Stop saying that. If she was fine we would have heard something by now. She's not fine. I don't know where she is or if she's even alive. But until I know for sure, I won't stop searching. We need to find a way up to the mother ship. That's the first step to finding her and also ending this war. Are you two with me?"

Birgue and Reol nodded and both said, "Of course," in unison. Marctus then returned to the other room with the soldiers and told them that he needed to leave. All the soldiers in the room looked at him with worry on their faces. John walked up to him and said, "But we need you here to help us fight." Around the room the other soldiers nodded in agreement.

"You don't understand. I need to find someone. I also need to try to end this war and I'm the only person besides Birgue and Reol here that can attempt that," Marctus said. John looked at him for a moment then said, "Well there's not much you can do tonight. Can you sleep on it?"

Marctus was tired and decided that he did need to rest. So did Birgue and Reol. He nodded to John and walked off to find somewhere to lie down. The soldiers had beds already set up along the wall in a room just to the right of the main entrance hall. Marctus laid down on one of the beds and shut his eyes.

Chapter 62

"We are defeating the humans around the world. Most of them have retreated and were slaughtered as they ran. We should have the planet secured within days," Captain Reath said to Admiral Schur in his quarters. They were sitting around the table that displayed the positions of the glowan forces on the ground.

"How much longer will the electronics be offline?" Admiral Schur asked.

"About eight more hours, sir" Captain Reath replied.

"Make sure we're ready to fire the moment they come back online. I want to keep their communications off as much as possible," Admiral Schur said zooming in on different spots of the table that displayed glowans walking, resting or performing other duties they were assigned.

Captain Reath nodded and watched as the Admiral continued looking at the table and bringing up holoscreens around the table and speaking commands in for different areas. Admiral Schur then focused in on New York City.

"Any sign of Marctus?" Admiral Schur asked.

"We have received a report that he is hold up in a building with few human soldiers," Captain Reath said to the admiral.

"I still want him brought here alive," Admiral Schur said. He brought up a holoscreen and started speaking a message and then it disappeared. "I am having groups surround the building until he is forced to come out. Have we found the female human that escaped?"

"Negative, sir," Captain Reath said. "We assume Naivu told her where Marctus would be and she would make her way to him, but we haven't had any reports of a sighting." Admiral Schur nodded and continued looking around the state of New York and across the rest of the US. He finally stood up.

"Good. See to it she is found and killed and Marctus is brought to me." The admiral then walked with the captain to the elevator to dismiss him. Before the elevator door shut, the admiral said, "I want him alive, captain. I want to show our race what happens to traitors." Admiral Schur then walked back to the command table as the elevator doors closed on Captain Reath.

Chapter 63

He needed to make sure he was invisible before heading down to the energy level of the mother ship. He stepped out of the room with the Elite space suit on and the invisibility activated. He was relieved it worked. Another glowan was walking right for him and he froze hoping he would not be seen. His fear was relieved as the glowan walked past him without any sign of seeing him. A voice then spoke in his earpiece.

"Sword, is everything a go?" the voice said.

"Affirmative," Sword said and made his way toward the elevator. Once inside, he located the button labeled "Energy Floor" and pressed it. Nothing happened for a moment and then a holoscreen appeared in front of the buttons asking for identification. Sword took out a severed hand from his bag and held it against the holoscreen. It scanned the hand, and then flashed blue and the elevator started to descend.

Sword exited the elevator and headed left down a long hallway that didn't seem to end. There was no one around so he decided to sprint down the hallway to get there quickly. When he reached the end, he turned right and saw his destination. In front of him was a very large window. Behind it, there was a huge spherical orange ball. It was similar to the many suns in the universe. This particular sun, though, was how the mother ship traveled, fired its main gun (including the EMP bursts), and other essential functions. Disabling this would render the mother ship useless until repaired.

"I'm in the main room looking at the energy sphere. What now?" Sword asked waiting to hear an answer from the glowan in charge. After a few moments the voice spoke, "Down the hall under the window is a holoscreen. Approach it and open it." Sword walked down the hall for a few minutes then arrived at the holoscreen. He opened it and again was asked for identification. He pulled the hand out of the bag once again and let the holoscreen scan it.

"Ok. I'm in," Sword said.

"Good. Now you're going to tell the sphere to stop working until you request it to start working again. Make sure you specify the individual whose hand you used," the voice said. Sword then pulled up a screen on the holoscreen that asked for a certain command. Sword typed in the command along with a bunch of override codes and also had to scan the hand two more times before the process was complete. Instantaneously, the orange sphere turned a very dark shade of blue and illuminated the area with blue light.

"It's done," Sword said.

"Good. Now burn the hand and get down here quick," said the voice again. Sword took the hand out, and sat it on the floor, took out his Adapt and pointed the laser at it and severed it into many pieces. He then took out a small device and shot a ball of fire at the pieces and burned them. The fire burned out quickly. He had done the same thing to the owner of the hand hours earlier.

Sword then ran back the way he had come and took the elevator up to the hangar of escape pods. He exited the elevator and ran to the nearest one. It was missing. Wondering who might have left the ship, he went to the next one, entered the pod and set his destination for New York City. He would fly it manually when he got into the Earth's atmosphere so he could land where he would not be seen, or so he hoped. He hit the button to detach from the mother ship and headed toward Earth.

Chapter 64

Marctus woke up to John's face as he shook him awake. "Marctus get up!" he said sounding alarmed. "What is it?" Marctus said. "Look outside," John replied. Marctus then shook Birgue and Reol awake and headed for one of the front windows. He looked out and saw something he hoped was not real. He hoped it was part of a dream he was in. There were at least a thousand glowans standing in front of the museum. They stood in the road and continued into the park. One glowan stood at the foot of the stairs to the museum not moving. He was dressed in a white space suit that was all too familiar to Marctus. It was an Elite.

Marctus removed himself from the window and put his helmet back on. "Has the Elite said anything since he's been standing there?" he asked the soldiers in the room. None of them said anything but John came to Marctus and said, "He said that if you surrender, we will all be sparred. If you surrender, no one here will die."

"Lies," Marctus said more to himself than anyone else. "How much time until the electronics should be back up?" John looked out the window at the sun and said, "I would say within the next thirty minutes. We're close." Marctus nodded and then told John what needed to happen if they were to survive this.

"When communications come back up we may only have a few seconds, or a few minutes. I'm just not sure. But we have to call in an airstrike of some sort. I know it's risky, but we need help or we are dead. That's the first thing that needs to be asked for when communications come back up," Marctus said and he again made sure John and the soldiers understood. When they all nodded at him and said they understood Marctus walked to the door and stared at it for a minute.

"I have to go out there and stall them. You two stay here. If anything happens to me, find Jayla," Marctus said to Birgue and Reol. "Marctus that's suicide don't be stupid!" Reol said but Marctus shook her off. "If we stay in here they will destroy the building and all of us inside it. We don't stand a chance against that number." Marctus then slowly opened the door and walked out. When he was outside, he noticed that many buildings in the distance were on fire. He also noticed it was eerily quiet. There was a light haze around the park. He also noticed most of the trees in the park were gone and glowans now stood where they once were. He glanced out over all the glowans in front of the building. Easily a thousand glowans stood before him all pointing energy rifles at him.

The Elite, however, was not pointing a gun at him or anything for that matter. He was simply staring at Marctus. After a few moments the Elite spoke in a calm voice. "Admiral Schur honors your dedication and commitment to the humans. He asks that you now surrender, revert to being part of your own race and show the same dedication and commitment you show now to these humans."

"You mean to say he doesn't plan to have me killed?" Marctus asked the Elite who he knew was lying. He knew the admiral was hoping he would come peacefully, and thinking he was going to be able to walk away from all that's happened. The Elite didn't respond for a moment and Marctus had the feeling he was communicating with Admiral Schur himself on what should be said next.

"There are no plans for your execution. Admiral Schur will discuss everything with you once you are back on board the mother ship," the Elite said. Marctus then looked up to the west and saw the mother ship still silhouetted in the sky. What he would give to be able to be on there looking out at Earth. But returning there would mean certain death.

"What is to happen to the humans inside this building if I come with you?" Marctus asked. He didn't know how long he had been outside, but he had to keep stalling in hopes of an airstrike or some sort of help. The Elite slowly started climbing the stairs toward him and began to answer Marctus' question.

"They will be the only surviving humans of their race and will be invited to colonize with us. More details will be finalized with Admiral Schur," the Elite said as he approached the last few stairs to where Marctus stood. Marctus nodded and didn't know what else he could say or do to stall. He would have to go with them and hopefully the humans would have a few more hours to live. Maybe they were smart enough to be running out the back of the museum right now. He hoped it had a back door.

Marctus dropped his gun on the ground and took a step toward the Elite. Just as he was about to let the Elite take him, he heard a loud screaming sound in the air as if the air itself was being sliced. Then he saw them. Six jets flying so fast they looked like a blur as they flew over the park. At first Marctus didn't understand why they flew by because nothing was happening. Then explosion after explosion struck the park and glowan bodies were sent airborne. The Elite had his back turned to Marctus and provided the perfect moment for Marctus to kick him down the stairs and retreat back inside.

"Marctus! The communications are still up! It's been about 10 minutes now," Birgue said as Marctus came inside. "Excellent! Is there any word about where any other groups of soldiers are located? Any information at all?" Marctus asked more to John than anyone else.

"Not yet. Units are still reporting in their locations and remaining soldiers from our squads," John said and continued to speak into the radio. Marctus then walked to the front of the entrance hall to address the rest of the soldiers. "We need to go outside and fight right now. The airstrike took out most of them but there are still glowans remaining and they will take this building unless we fight."

In unison all the soldiers got up and walked to the door. Marctus opened it and they ran outside and took cover behind anything they could find but mainly abandoned cars on the road. Glowans were coming up the small hill from the park and some of the glowans looked as if they had been caught in the bombing. They looked burned and some were missing limbs but they still fired their weapons and tried to run right at them. Marctus returned fire with the humans and watched as the glowans fell one by one. As Marctus was shooting he activated his invisibility and looked around for the Elite but he couldn't see where he had gone. He decided to remain in invisibility just in case he came back.

Marctus noticed that they had lost a few soldiers but were still killing more glowans than losing soldiers. If the glowans broke through their cover then they would be in serious trouble but for now everything was okay. Marctus and the humans continued to fight and even after thirty minutes the fighting still continued. The glowans would not stop coming over the hill. The airstrike took out most but there were still a lot to cope with. To Marctus' right, he saw glowans push a car over on top of the four soldiers that were behind it, forcing Marctus to retreat further back toward the door to the museum. He took cover behind the statue and watched as the glowans started to get the advantage. He saw that the thirty soldiers he started with were now down to about ten and they all huddled behind the pillars near the front door.

Then, to Marctus' right up the street a few yards, he heard a loud rumbling noise and watched as a tank came rolling down the street squashing cars and pushing others out of the way. The tank was firing at the glowans that continued to walk up the hill, raking them with a machine gun as the glowans tried to advance up the stairs to the museum. Marctus dropped as the gunfire hit the statue he was behind and destroyed it completely. When he got up, he saw that the last remaining glowans were retreating back into the park, running straight across it for cover. Some even dived into the lake. The tank continued to fire until they were out of range and then stopped.

The top hatch popped open and a soldier jumped out and walked toward the stairs. Marctus came out of invisibility and met him halfway. "Marctus! Pleasure to meet you. I was sent...." At that moment the soldier stopped talking and grabbed at his throat. The soldier was then lifted off his feet and seemed to be hanging in the air. Knowing what was happening; Marctus put his helmet back on, engaged the invisibility and saw that the Elite soldier he had been looking for was holding the human up choking him.

"Let him go! Now!" Marctus said aiming his gun at the Elite. He dared not fire for fear of hitting the human. "I will let go if you drop your weapon and come with me now," said the Elite. Marctus dropped his weapon and walked toward him coming out of invisibility with his hands up. The Elite too came out of invisibility but still held the human. The human's face was purple now and Marctus knew he would pass out and die any second.

Then something odd happened, a small orange ball hit the Elite in the head and, within seconds, the Elite's head caved in on itself and exploded. The human fell to the ground grabbing at his throat trying to get his breathe back. The Elite fell over obviously dead. Marctus looked around for who had fired that shot and down in front of the tank, right behind where the Elite had been, a glowan came out of invisibility and holstered the small energy gun to its side.

"Who are you?" Marctus yelled at the glowan. The glowan removed its helmet and long brown hair fell down on its shoulders and Marctus realized it wasn't a glowan at all. The human looked up at him with tears in her eyes and ran to Marctus. Marctus watched as Jayla jumped into his arms. She kissed him with such passion that Marctus felt the hair on his head stand on end and his stomach twirled with delight.

"How are you here?! What happened?!" Marctus said when they separated but he had so many other questions that he didn't know what to ask next. Jayla smiled at him with tears in her eyes and said, "Let's go inside and talk." She took his hand and they both walked inside the museum.

Chapter 65

Jayla was sitting on a bed that was brought into the main entrance hall for her by one of the soldiers. She was drinking a bottle of water that was also given to her and was trying to catch her breath from her tearful outburst after finally seeing Marctus. He sat next to her with his arm around her comforting her while she caught her breath and quenched her thirst. He rubbed where her arm had been severed and felt Jayla jerk away at the touch. He apologized and Jayla smiled at him.

"So what happened Jayla?" Marctus asked her again. "Tell me everything." So Jayla began with how Captain Reath had tortured her about what Marctus' plans were for resistance, among other things, and even though she told the truth he still tortured her and cut her arm off.

"After that I was simply an object. I was given very little food and water every other day and I felt I was dying. I can't explain it." Jayla stopped talking for a few moments and Marctus' hatred increased even more than he thought possible. Hearing Jayla describe it made it ten times worse and he wanted revenge.

"Then one day Naivu came and told me she was going to try to get me out of there, to be patient and hang in there. I couldn't see how I was going to stay alive and the next day the food and water I got was more than I had ever gotten. I don't know who brought it but I'm sure it was Naivu".

"Then the day came and she released me and brought me to a room to put this suit on and told me to stay invisible. By this time we were onboard the mother ship. We had landed there moments after it arrived. After I had this suit on we made our way down to the hangar room with many windows and where the escape pods are."

Jayla then got teary eyed again and had trouble finishing the story. "Then Naivu put me in the pod….and…and…she told me she was sending me to you but she couldn't come. Then she shut the door and was going to release me…but…but then the captain was there and told her that if she released me she would never be forgiven for betraying him….and she stood there for a long time and I thought she was going to give me up, but then she sent my pod toward Earth. As I floated away, I saw him shoot her and she died" Her sobs were harder than ever as she cried on Marctus' shoulder.

Marctus felt so much hatred that it made his eyes water with rage. Naivu was dead for trying to help him and when this was all over he would remember her. She's the reason Jayla and him were together now and he would not let Jayla be captured again. He would not let Naivu's sacrifice be for nothing. "How did you get here though after the pod landed?" Marctus then asked.

"Well, I landed right under the Brooklyn Bridge and saw an army of glowans crossing it. I followed them and they led me to Central Park. Some of their army went away and some stayed. When the army that split off returned, they actually had more glowans than when they had left. They all stood outside of this museum. It was night when this happened so I sat under a tree and slept until I heard you talking to the Elite. Then I woke up and watched what was happening. I moved closer so I could hear you better, then the airstrike happened, and now we're here," Jayla said.

Marctus nodded and said, "I'm glad you're here but I want you to remain invisible at all times and only come out of it when we are safe inside or unless I say so. Okay?"

"Okay," Jayla said and smiled at him.

Marctus then turned to John, "Are the electronics still up and running?"

"Oddly enough, yes, they don't seem to have shot us with another EMP blast," John said with a grin on his face. Marctus wondered why that would be and couldn't come to any conclusion. The humans could now use fighter jets and vehicles which meant that the glowans were sure to send in their types of aircraft which would out maneuver the humans' instantly. The humans were still at a disadvantage.

"Marctus you better hear this," John then said. Marctus walked over to him and listened to the radio. The president's voice was coming through it and Marctus walked in right in the middle of the speech.

"We will not give up. We will not surrender. I am ordering all our remaining forces to head to New York City for one last fight. Radio in for transports if you are hearing this and we will find you. God be with you." The voice ended and Marctus asked John what he meant by 'One last fight?'

"All over the country we've lost many civilians and soldiers. It seems that reports are coming in that all glowan forces are headed here. From what I've been able to gather, we don't know how many are left and our last chance is to stand together. I feel this may be our downfall," John's voice trailed away then he spoke up again. "We have electronics now and are able to use aircraft and vehicles but the aliens are just going to use theirs now and we will be doomed."

Marctus had no idea what to say to him. He was absolutely right. Their technology was so miniscule that it stood no chance against the glowans'. Marctus, Birgue, Reol and the humans were going to fight until they died. At any moment the next EMP blast would occur and the next wave of drop ships would come. Not to mention the remaining glowans stationed all over the rest of the country.

"MARCTUS!" a voice roared from outside. Jumping to his feet and telling Jayla to go invisible, Marctus made his way over to the front windows that had been shot out but boarded up. He peeked through a crack and saw a huge army of glowans out front. From what he could see, the army stretched clear across the park and was larger than before.

"MARCTUS!" the voice bellowed again. Marctus told John not to call in any airstrikes until Marctus came back inside or was killed. Marctus then walked to the door, opened it and stepped out past the pillars to better view the park. The army filled the entire park. There must have been thousands of glowans standing in front of him. The one glowan who he guessed was yelling his name was standing at the bottom of the stairs where the Elite had stood previously.

Marctus looked at him and the glowan smiled, "Have you figured out why there hasn't been another EMP blast yet?" Then in the air above the glowans, hundreds of glowan small air fighters came out of invisibility. The V shaped fighters hovered above and were facing in the direction of Marctus. As Marctus looked at the glowans in front of him he noticed that they were all wearing different suits. Suits he hadn't seen before. They were a dark blue instead of the black or white that he was used to.

Then the glowan at the bottom of the stairs said, "We fight for and with you Marctus."

Chapter 66

Marctus dropped to his knees in shock and awe of what he had just heard and what was in front of him. He heard the door behind him open and the human soldiers came out along with Jayla, Birgue and Reol. The humans too were in shock. John was immediately relaying information back to whoever gave orders for the humans. The glowan at the bottom of the stairs walked up to Marctus. Marctus got to his feet and faced him.

"My name is Dez. I saw your message back home before we were all gathered on board the mother ship. Everyone behind me also saw your message and wants to fight for you as well," Dez said smiling. Marctus was at a loss for words and was glad when Jayla spoke for him.

"How did you find Marctus and get here though?" she asked.

"I have eyes and ears all over that mother ship. How do you think the EMP blast was stopped?" Dez said. "A lot of us agree with you Marctus. We should be cooperating and colonizing with the humans, not exterminating them. Unfortunately, we had to reveal ourselves now or else risk being found out."

Marctus nodded and understood what Dez meant. If they would have shown any signs of showing themselves before they got here, they would have been killed. But how did they find and group together so quickly? Marctus asked him that exact question.

"Believe me…it was harder than it looks. When we were dropped off, we all ran from the fighting back to the areas that we designated for transport. Then we had a few pilots transport us all outside the city to rendezvous. When we were all accounted for we came here." Dez then looked around at all the bodies and then added, "I wish we could have gotten here sooner. For that I am truly sorry."

"It's understandable," Marctus said and Dez nodded that he understood Marctus' gratitude even though he didn't say it. Then Marctus heard John saying that the president was sending all fighter jets to this area to help, and made an announcement for humans not to shoot the glowans that wore dark blue uniforms. They are allies.

"Have you any thoughts on how to end this war?" Marctus asked Dez.

"Not the war, but the battle …Yes, I have one idea," Dez said. "I believe if we can either destroy the mother ship or force it to retreat, we will have time to build up an effective resistance."

"And how do you plan to destroy the mothership?" Marctus asked with doubt in his voice. From what Marctus remembered, there was no way to destroy that ship. It was so massive that any damages were easily repaired. Dez smiled and then started explaining to Marctus how to destroy it.

"The mother ship is powered by a large energy source in the shape of a sun," Dez said and pulled out a holoscreen that showed an image of a small sun. Marctus looked at the image with interest. "To destroy the mother ship we have to destroy this. The best way to do that is to plant energy explosions around that level of the ship and the upper levels as well. Once detonated, the explosions should produce enough momentum or force that the energy ball will implode, thus destroying the mother ship."

Dez finished and paused for a few moments before speaking again. "The other option is to wipe out enough of the army that they brought with them so they retreat back home to rearm and reinforce themselves."

"I think we need to do both," Marctus said. "Let's assemble a team to fly to the mother ship and plant the explosives while everyone else stays here and assists the humans. Do you know if the admiral is sending all of his remaining forces here?"

"Yes. He is having all forces in this country moved here. I don't know about the rest of the world, but there is still a significant force here. They will be here within the next few hours and will spread out everywhere. I am going to send my forces throughout the city to help defend the remaining humans in the city," Dez said then turned to John. "I need you to tell your leader to send humans to these positions to join with my glowan forces," and he showed John a number of different locations around New York City and surrounding boroughs. John nodded and relayed the information immediately.

"I don't know how long the EMP will be out, but until they can figure out how to fix it, the humans should have a little advantage," Dez said. Marctus then brought Birgue and Reol forward and told Dez that they were to be a part of his team to plant the explosives. "How many others will I need?"

"I think if you took 10 glowans you should be fine. I'll send six of my best, including myself. We should go after the battle commences, that way the admiral is preoccupied with giving his troops instructions as they try to break into the city and capture you."

"I don't think he's in it to capture me anymore," said Marctus. "I believe he will be throwing everything he has at the humans now. He wants Earth and wants all humans dead." Dez nodded and said he agreed with Marctus' assessment. "We'll give him one fight to remember then!" said Dez.

"Let's head inside and plan how we're going to get to the mother ship and plant the explosives," Marctus said. Dez nodded and then turned to his glowans that were in the park and gave a simple waive. They all dispersed and headed to their assigned areas. As the v-shaped ships flew off, Marctus asked how they were able to steal the Vipers in the first place. Seeing them in person was so much better than images he had seen throughout his years growing up.

"Just like the Elites, they are secret as you know. Once we were able to find where they were kept on the mother ship, we took them. They can fit 10 glowans on board and have a large energy gun for each glowan to fire. The pilot also has energy missiles available to him that he can fire. Amazing, really," Dez said watching them fly out to their positions. One Viper, though, landed in the park. "Shall we head inside?" Dez asked. Marctus, Brigue, Dez, Reol and six other glowans headed inside to discuss the plans for the mission. Jayla tagged along with Marctus to listen in. Marctus was introduced to the six glowans that would accompany them on the mission and thanked them for being part of the cause.

Their names were Poil, Gruz, Halum, Shale, Drang and Sword. Marctus learned that Sword had disabled the EMP hours ago and had just returned to Earth. He was eager to help anyway he could and jumped at the opportunity to be included on this mission. "Shall we begin?" Dez asked and opened a holoscreen that showed layouts of the different levels of the mother ship.

Chapter 67

Admiral Schur paced his room. He had just received word that a massive resistance group of glowans was now allied with the humans and preparing to fight. "Traitors," was the only thing he was saying to himself as he paced and considered what he could do. Should he just fire the main gun and wipe out Earth and wait for another planet to come along that has life? No. How long had it taken his race to find this one? He was not going to wait. He was taking this planet and nothing was going to stop him.

He opened his command table and saw that his forces were on their way to New York City where the humans and traitor glowans stood in defense. He would send all his forces there and eliminate them. Once they were gone, the planet was his. Once the EMP was operable he would fire it and the humans would once again be powerless. The only reasons the humans were even still alive was because of the traitors from his own race. He wouldn't fail this mission.

He ordered more glowans to guard all areas surrounding the energy sphere in case any more traitors tried to damage it. He also sent messages back to the home planet and commanded that new forces be ready for transport at a moment's notice. If worse came to worse, he would go back and pick up re-enforcements and return with a larger army.

"Admiral Schur," a voice spoke from the doorway into the room with the command table. Admiral Schur turned around startled at the surprise visitor and saw Captain Reath. He admired Captain Reath and thought he was the best captain he had ever had, not to mention how long the captain had been alive.

"Yes, captain? Please come in," the admiral said and motioned for the captain to join him at the command table. He sat down across from Captain Reath and waited for him to speak. Captain Reath then leaned toward the command table and zoomed out so that Earth was entirely visible. He then zoomed in above the state of New York and stopped.

"I've been thinking," the captain said before pausing for just a moment. "I've been thinking about advising you to fire the main gun at Earth." Admiral Schur looked at him for a long while before speaking. He knew that the captain knew that firing the main gun would make the planet uninhabitable and destroy everything on it. If they did this…there would be no point to being here in the first place. After he told the captain his thoughts, the captain pointed at the command table.

"We won't be firing it to destroy a whole planet. We will be firing it to destroy a certain area of a planet." Admiral Schur then looked at him seriously and said, "I'm listening." Captain Reath then zoomed out a little more so that New York and the surrounding states were visible as well.

"The main gun on this ship is powerful enough to take out an entire planet. That is true. However, if fired for only a moment, its effect can be less…catastrophic. What I am proposing Admiral, and something that would take the resistance by surprise with no way to stop it, is to fire the main gun right above New York. If we can fire it for just a moment, the blast radius will take out the entire state of New York and just a few hundred miles of the surrounding area."

Captain Reath stopped speaking and looked at the admiral. Admiral Schur ran this scenario over in his head many times, trying to find any negative side effects of doing this. It was true that that particular area would be uninhabitable and would have to be quarantined, but the rest of the world would be fine. The resistance and humans would all be grouped there and would be taken out. As for his glowans…they would have to make the sacrifice. But there was one problem…

"The resistance destroyed our energy sphere. We can't fire the main gun until it's fixed," Admiral Schur told the captain. He then noticed that the captain was smiling and, before he could even ask why, the captain said, "It has been repaired. We are ready to fire an EMP blast at your command, but if we do that, it will take longer to charge the main gun. On your orders, I will begin charging immediately."

"Are you positive this will work?" Admiral Schur asked the captain. Captain Reath nodded and said, "If it is fired correctly, it will do exactly as I said. I will even do the firing if you would like." Admiral Schur nodded and then thought for just a little longer, making sure this is what he wanted to do. He then made up his mind and relayed his orders to the captain.

"I want half of the forces I was sending to New York to retreat and back away from the firing area. The other half will be sacrificed and it will be for a good reason, but I do not want them to know we are firing the weapon. I will want you to be in charge of firing the weapon, as it has not been fired in my living memory. Lastly, start charging immediately. How long will the charge take?"

"If it hadn't been damaged, it would've only taken a few hours…Unfortunately, now it's going to take at least a day if not a little longer. I would say a day and a half at the most," Captain Reath said. Admiral Schur nodded and then said, "Good. Move the mother ship into position over New York City. We will give them something to worry about… and let me know when we are ready to fire."

Chapter 68

A day after Dez had explained the plan to the group and Marctus, Marctus continued to go over it in it his head until he could remember everything word for word. After they boarded the mother ship he would take Birgue and Reol outside the hangar door and kill the first glowan they saw. After doing that, they would need to cut off his hand and use it in order for the elevator to work. Dez had said the security there would be tough. After they did that, they were to go to the floor above the energy room and place the energy charges every 30 feet down the length of the hallway. At the end of the hallway, they were to place a larger energy charge on the floor so that the support of the upper levels would fall into the energy room below.

While Marctus, Birgue and Reol were doing that, the rest of the group were also divided and assigned different floors and areas to place the energy charges and to also keep watch. Dez would be with Sword in the Energy Room itself, placing the energy charges all along the transparent barrier that guarded the energy ball. The rest of the crew were to be on the floor below. Unfortunately, only Marctus, Reol, and Birgue would be invisible due to the special suits they had. After all the charges were placed, they were to meet back at the hangar they arrived in and leave. After they were a safe distance away, they would press the detonator. If anything went wrong with the plan, they were to meet back at the Viper and leave the mother ship or make it to the escape pods.

After running through the plan in his head again, Marctus looked outside at the massive army that was bunkered down outside. It was not as big as it was before Dez had sent all his glowans to areas around the city, but still it was big. These forces were just now being assigned locations to protect. The enemy glowans would be attacking by nightfall and the remaining human soldiers had just shown up this morning. It lifted the spirits of John and the other human soldiers that Marctus had been around the past few days when additional humans arrived. There were hundreds of them, but still not as many as Marctus had hoped for. John had said that there were still soldiers fighting across the United States that couldn't make it back here.

"We're to leave as soon as the glowans start attacking us," Dez said from behind Marctus. "If we leave when they start, everyone may be too occupied with the fighting on the ground and we should be able to slip away without much trouble." Marctus told him he agreed and said he would be ready. Birgue and Reol had been outside assigning the resistance glowans to certain places and Marctus told them when Dez wanted to leave. "Tonight it is! Can't wait! "Birgue said enthusiastically.

Marctus was now sitting on the end of Jayla's bed watching her sleep. He debated waking her to tell her when they were leaving but decided to let her sleep. She hadn't had any proper sleep since the night before the Elites attacked. But as he walked away, he heard her voice, "Leaving already are you?"

Marctus turned around and sat on her bed again and looked at her. "Tonight," he said. Jayla nodded and said, "I thought it would be soon. Who knows when they will get their power back up there and then wipe us out for good? The sooner the better...." She trailed off and looked at Marctus.

He knew what was coming even before she said it. "I still don't see why I can't come," Jayla said to him. They had debated this last night and it wasn't safe for her. Not to mention that Marctus didn't want her to get hurt by a glowan any more than she already had been. She would be better suited down here.

"You know I can fight. So what if I have one arm? I can manage," Jayla continued when Marctus didn't say anything. Marctus then lay down on the bed next to her so their faces were inches from each other. He could feel her warm breath on his face. "I don't want to risk you getting hurt," he said to her. "It's not safe up there." Jayla didn't say anything, just looked at him. After a moment, she said, "Can I please fight down here? It's my race and I want to be able to fight."

"I'm only asking that you not travel to the mother ship," Marctus said. "You can fight down here all you want. Just wear your suit so I can see where you are when I get back, in case I need to come searching for you." Jayla smiled at him and then rolled on top of him and started kissing him. He wrapped his arms around her as she lay on his chest kissing him. She was so warm on top of him that he didn't want to let go.

"Marctus we have a problem," Dez said from the doorway that led to the main entrance hall. Marctus looked up at Jayla and smiled and she rolled off of him and sat in bed next to Marctus. Marctus noticed that the sun was not shining through the windows anymore and wondered how the time had gotten away from him. "What is it?" Marctus asked. "Come look," Dez replied.

Marctus and Jayla got off the bed and followed Dez to the front doors of the museum. He opened them and Marctus and Jayla walked out to an eerie darkness around them. Marctus looked around at the glowans and humans that were in the park in front of him and noticed they were all looking up. Marctus then looked up and saw the mother ship was directly above them and it stretched across almost the entire sky.

"What does this mean?" he asked Dez. "They must have fixed it." Dez was nodding in his helmet and said, "Yes, I think they did. What's worse is I think they are preparing to fire the main gun. As for how much time we have, I can only guess but after the damage that the energy sphere suffered it would take at least a day if not more and that's also contingent on if they fire another EMP blast which they probably won't. Our mission needs to happen tonight."

"Marctus, are you seeing this?" Birgue said in his ear. "Yeah I am. You two ready?" he replied to Birgue. "Of course we are," they both replied. He smiled and then turned to Jayla. "Let's go find a good place for you to fight," he said to her. She went inside to grab her suit and then came out moments later. They set off toward the center of the park where one of the resistance glowans was assigning people to different areas.

"Marctus, it is very nice to meet you," said the glowan who introduced himself as Korce. "The pleasure is mine," Marctus said. "This is Jayla." He introduced Jayla, and Korce smiled and nodded at her. "Nice to meet you," Korce said. "Is there anywhere Jayla can help out? She wants to fight," Marctus asked Korce. Korce looked down at his holoscreen at where all the groups were surrounding the city and spread throughout the state. Finally he told them that a place a few miles north of here could use some extra help and she would be welcome there. "There is a Humvee heading there in a few minutes with some other soldiers. She can catch a ride with them," and he pointed over in the direction where a lot of Humvess were sitting.

Marctus thanked Korce and grabbed Jayla's hand and walked with her across the park to where the Humvees were parked. He wished they were walking through this park without a war going on. He wished the park looked like it did before the bombing and he and Jayla could just sit under a tree together all day and talk about how birds fly or something stupid. Doing anything with her made him feel warm inside and made his determination to end this war even greater so that maybe one day they could do stupid things together.

They reached the Humvees and Marctus walked her up to one of them and saw that the driver was just about to leave. He opened the back door for Jayla and she got in. He shut the door and she leaned out the window to say goodbye. "Make sure you stay invisible no matter what. I don't want to worry too much. If you see an Elite, keep your distance. He will be able to see you," Marctus said. Jayla just looked at him and smiled as he talked.

"Stop worrying about me. I will be fine. I promise. You just promise to come back to me," she said to him and Marctus leaned in to kiss her. He tried to remember every detail of kissing her. The warmth of her lips, the feel of her hair in his hands. He hoped he would be back to experience this again but just in case…he wanted to take it all in one last time. He backed away from the Humvee as it roared to life and said, "Be safe," before it drove off. He watched as the Humvee drove out of the park and down the road, then turned and was gone from sight.

Chapter 69

A few hours later when the sun was just about to set, Jayla was sitting up on top of a tower that had been recently put up by the resistance glowans. It was made of a transparent material of some sort so it almost looked like she was floating. They assured her though it was almost indestructible and she would be fine because she would be invisible on top of it shooting down at any approaching enemy glowans. When asked how she was supposed to shoot at them with one arm, the glowans chuckled and had her shoot the larger energy rifle. There was absolutely no kick as it fired off into the distance and it was very maneuverable with one arm. The glowans had mounted it on the tower to give her better stability as well.

Behind the tower stood a main road into the city surrounded by buildings and on each were human soldiers armed with sniper rifles. In front of the tower was a steel wall that the humans put up to prevent the glowans from running straight through. The tower was tall enough to see over the wall. Next to the steel wall were barbed wire and electrical fencing so that if the glowans tried to climb through it, they would die instantly. With the power back on, the humans felt they had multiple defenses at their disposal in order to prevent the glowans from getting through.

Back when Jayla was at the museum, Marctus had had one of the glowans install a com system in her helmet. Unfortunately, because she was human she couldn't get the earpiece system so she wouldn't be able to talk to Marctus. She would, however, be able to talk to any glowan in her vicinity. It came in handy when she was staring off down the road and saw a small blur moving closer. As they got closer she was able to see it was the glowans approaching. She told one of the resistance leaders what she saw and they immediately started taking defensive positions.

Jayla watched as they approached and she was given the all clear to fire when in sight. The range on the energy rifle was good if you could see far, and the helmet she wore helped her to see farther than she normally could. When the target got in range she started firing and watched as the glowans she hit toppled over exploding blood. Then she heard the sounds of the snipers behind her firing and the rest of the glowans that were placed just on the other side of the barbed wire, and electrical fence. The enemy was now running toward the wall and when they approached it and couldn't break it down, they tried to go around it through the barbed electrical fence. Jayla watched as many of the glowans got stuck and were electrocuted. They continued to take out the oncoming glowans until something odd happened.

A bright orange ball was approaching the wall now. Jayla watched as it moved right up to the steel wall and the wall started melting as if it were an ice cube. It pooled on the ground, then disappeared leaving a pool of melted steel which hardened instantly. The glowans now were coming through the wall shooting their energy guns at the resistance fighters and humans. Jayla watched as a few resistance glowans took bullets to the head and watched their heads cave in on themselves then explode. Then she saw one female resistance glowan die in the same way she saw Naivu die. Jayla took aim at the glowan that killed her and took him out watching his head cave in on itself.

The snipers behind Jayla were taking out the glowans almost as fast as they were coming through the wall. But then something happened that the resistance glowans didn't expect and Jayla knew it by the way the glowans were talking in her helmet. A glowan walked through where the wall once was and seemed to be holding a transparent shield. It was round and large enough to hide at least ten glowans behind it. From the talking in Jayla's helmet the glowans must have developed this after their first attack on the humans and finding a way to block their human bullets. As for the energy guns, the shield seemed to absorb the energy when hit.

"How do we take out that shield?" Jayla asked to any glowans listening. One glowan replied with, "You have to take out the glowan holding it. They are unique to the glowan and according to Dez not many glowans can do it." The glowan with the shield was now approaching through the wall and the glowans behind the shield were taking out resistance glowans easily because the shield was easy to hide behind. Jayla watched as the glowan continued walking and was almost directly underneath her. The glowan probably didn't even know she was up here and she should be able to aim down and shoot the glowan, putting an end to the shield. As the glowan approached though, Jayla saw him tilt the shield up so that she did not have a clear shot at him. Cursing to herself she decided she was going to do something risky.

She climbed down the ladder still invisible and was now a few yards behind the squad of glowans walking behind the shield. She ordered no one to fire so she could take them out. She started firing and hit six of the glowans behind the shield who fell over with surprised looks on their bloody faces. Seeing what was happening, the other glowans turned around and started firing blindly behind them. Jayla was able to dodge all of the energy shots and take the remaining glowans out, finally taking the shield glowan down just before their group was able to gain any more ground. She heard compliments in her helmet about what she'd just done and was making her way back up the tower. But now the glowans were flowing in through the wall like water over a dam and she had to weave through the glowans in order not to get caught in any crossfire or to cause any unwanted attention.

"Marctus would have told you that that was reckless," said a glowan in her ear. "Marctus doesn't have to know," she replied back with a smile on her face. She reached the top of the tower and was safely out of the way…although she did think Marctus would've thought that was awesome in a way. She then started firing again at the glowans below her taking them out as they flooded underneath her. Finally, one glowan reached the bottom of the tower and looked up toward the top and seemed to be looking right at Jayla. Jayla knew she was invisible but maybe the glowan noticed the energy balls appearing out of nowhere and knew someone was up there. Jayla watched as the glowan fired a few pulses up at her and she quickly dodged back away from them. Then a couple of glowans started climbing the tower toward Jayla.

Jayla aimed down and took the first two out who fell from the ladder on top of the others, but they still continued to climb. Then one of the glowans shot up at her and hit her gun. When the energy ball hit her gun, it exploded in on itself leaving her defenseless.

"I need help at the tower my gun was destroyed," she said to any of the surrounding glowans. She then saw a bunch of energy balls hit the glowans climbing the ladder and they fell off just like the first two had. She then decided it wasn't safe and started to climb down just as another glowan was climbing up but a resistance glowan had made another accurate shot and took him out before Jayla reached the bottom. Jayla then grabbed one of the guns that the glowans dropped and ran back toward the buildings.

"We're retreating back toward the city Jayla hurry up!" one of the glowans in her helmet yelled. "Where should I go?" she asked in return. She kept running through the army of glowans shooting them in the back as she went until she reached the foot of the first building into the city. She went inside and watched as the enemy filled the streets and headed toward the main city.

"Head to the roof and we'll pick you up," the voice said. She did as she was told and took the elevator up to the roof where she met up with a couple other humans who were busy shooting at the glowans as they made their way through the streets. She came out of invisibility and startled them, but let them know that a transport was coming. "Awesome," said one of the soldiers who continued firing.

Moments later a Viper hovered above the roof and Jayla wondered how they were supposed to get into the ship. As soon as she thought this though, she saw that a section of the ship was lowering itself to the roof. The section that lowered had three individual seats and when Jayla and the two soldiers sat in them they were lifted back up into the ship. "Wow, that was cool!" one of the soldiers said as they were now flying over New York toward Central Park.

Chapter 70

Marctus was on the Viper in space just a few thousand miles away from the mother ship. They were waiting for the all clear from a source inside the ship to signal all was clear to land. After a few moments, Dez received the signal and they sped off toward the ship. Entering one of the lower hangars, Marctus quickly looked around and saw no one was in there. Good start so far.

Marctus and the glowans all exited the Viper and headed for the hangar door. The hangar door opened and Dez walked a few steps out to see if there were any glowans in the vicinity. When all was clear he motioned for them all to follow and they headed up the long, dark and tall hallway toward the elevators. "Where is everyone?" Birgue asked more to himself than anyone.

Finally they came to the first elevator. They still needed identification and if they tried using themselves, they were at risk of revealing that they were there. Dez then divided up the team and sent the group who was headed toward the floor below the energy room to the next available elevator which was down the hall and around multiple turns. Marctus then heard a door shut down toward where they had come from and knew it was not one of them. Quickly, they hid down the hall behind a turn and peeked to see a few glowans walking their way.

Signaling to Dez that there were glowans walking toward them, Dez nodded and signaled for Marctus to tell him when to dive out and fire. Marctus nodded and aimed his gun around the corner and took out one, Dez then rolled onto his knees and took out the next, Birgue then fired and took out the third. Poil, Gruz, and Birgue grabbed the bodies and dragged them through a doorway off the hall that was used for storage thereby hiding them. They removed their hands before they closed the door on them. Birgue handed Marctus a hand and they all made for the elevator again.

Marctus, Birgue, Reol, Sword, Dez, Shale and Drang all got in the elevator. First stop was going to be the energy room floor where Sword and Dez needed to be. Marctus said that they would help them clear the area outside the elevator before leaving. Dez nodded and, as the elevator came to a stop, the door opened to the hallway beyond. Peeking out, Dez saw no one and motioned for them to follow. The whole length of the hallway was empty. No one was here.

"This is not what I expected. It's almost too unexpected. Be on your guard," Dez said to Marctus, Birgue, and Reol and then bid them good luck as they ran down the hall and left Marctus, Birgue, and Reol to go to the floor above them. As they reached the floor above, Marctus peeked out and once again saw no one. They've been invisible this whole time so if the enemy glowans were invisible they would've seen them by now but no one was in sight.

The elevator door shut behind them and they made their way right down a hallway. At the first intersection, Marctus began placing the energy charges along the wall. He pulled them out of the bag he was wearing over his shoulder and was throwing them to Birgue to place further down the hall. Reol was watching their backs scanning the hallways looking for any enemy glowans. After placing charges down the entire hallway, Marctus found the last intersection for where they were to place the energy charges on the floor. He placed them as Dez had said and then headed back to the elevator.

"Dez we are done up here and heading back to the Viper now," Marctus said but after a few moments with no reply, he then tried to reach Shale or Drang who were on the floor below the energy room and got no reply from them either. "Should we go check on them?" Reol asked. "Would they do the same for us?" Birgue answered Reol. Marctus knew Dez would leave them if he had too, but Marctus was not Dez and didn't want to leave anyone behind. "Let's find them," he said to Birgue and Reol who nodded and all three of them stepped into the elevator.

As the elevator stopped, Marctus peeked out and saw nothing. He made his way left down the hall and after a few minutes of jogging to reach the end of the long hall he saw that the hall turned right. As he turned right he quickly dodged back behind the wall from the sight that was in front of him. He peeked around the corner and on their knees in front of a large window with the large orange energy ball behind it knelt Dez, Sword, Shale, Drang, Poil, Gruz, and Halman. Behind them Captain Reath had a gun to their heads and seemed to have been waiting for Marctus.

Then Marctus saw glowans running down the hallway he had just come from. He was trapped. They were all trapped. He dropped his gun and walked around the corner with his hands up. The glowans behind Marctus, Birgue and Reol pushed them forward until they were just a few feet away from the captain.

Captain Reath had the gun to Drang's head and was looking at Marctus with a hungry look on his face. Marctus didn't say anything but stared right back into the captain's eyes. The captain then said, "We have a lot to talk about Marctus," and then shot Drang in the head. Within the small confined room Marctus heard every bone in his head break and explode.

Chapter 71

Jayla was now manning a gun on the Viper that had picked her up. It was easy to use this large energy gun with only one hand because all she had to do was move her body and the gun would swerve left to right, up to down, wherever she needed to aim. The Viper was flying low enough to take out glowans approaching Central Park but the resistance was holding them off pretty well. So far there were only a few streets that the enemy glowans were able to get past and needed assistance. Other than that, the other areas were doing fine holding them off…for now.

After what seemed like hours of Jayla firing down at enemy glowans, she received word from one of the resistance commanders named Hogart that air support was needed. "What happened to the fighter jets?" Jayla asked. "Human pilots are not as skilled as we are and, unfortunately, were taken out as well as most of the tanks and Humvees. The Vipers are really all that's left now," Hogart replied. Jayla thought to herself that after hours of fighting the humans' technology was almost completely taken out. Humans never really stood a chance Jayla thought to herself as she waited for the Viper to reach the air support area. If it wasn't for the resistance the human race would be gone by now…. Jayla then hoped that, if they were to win this battle, perhaps humans could use the glowan technology and make their own technology better.

They finally reached the area that needed air support and she saw why. The glowans had started climbing over the artificial walls that were put up and also seemed to have melted all the steel walls and bunkers that were placed here. Not to mention that Jayla also saw five invisible figures down on the ground but knew no one else could see them. "There are five Elites down there. I'm going to try and take them out first," she said to any glowans listening below or nearby. She easily took out three before the other two ran inside of the buildings. The Viper pulled up as high as one of the tallest skyscrapers and sat there hovering about the battle field. Jayla was able to zoom in and see what was going on and noticed that the resistance on the ground was losing. Why did the Viper pull up?

"Why did you pull up? Go back down so I can help!" Jayla said. The pilot then responded with, "Not until those Elites are in sight. Remember, they can jump higher than a normal glowan and I don't want them to board us." Jayla said she understood and then saw one of the Elites leaving the building to join the fight. The pilot must have seen the Elite as well because he lowered the Viper back down for Jayla to start shooting. But just as Jayla started shooting, the Elite jumped from the ground and grabbed hold of the Viper from underneath. Then from the window of one of the buildings to the left, the other Elite jumped on top of the Viper and both started shooting their energy guns into the controls of the ship.

The Viper then started spinning out of control and Jayla felt like she was on a roller coaster as the Viper went into a fast and steep dive toward the battle field below. As it was falling Jayla felt an invisible force come over her like there was a seat belt tightening around her and when she collided with the ground, she didn't move an inch and was perfectly okay. The seat belt released her and she got out of the Viper and saw the two dead Elites next to her. She then looked for the pilot and saw he had been shot by the Elites when they had boarded mid-air and lay dead in the wreckage as well.

Looking around she didn't know exactly where she was but did see resistance glowans fighting up ahead of her and made her way over to them. "Where do you need me?" she asked one of them as she approached. The glowan told her to flank behind them and take out as many as she could. She said okay and picked up an energy rifle off the ground and ran behind the oncoming enemy glowans. She wrapped around one building and finally was behind the group. There were only a few hundred or so left in front of her.

She started shooting them in the back once again while invisible and then something unexpected happened. One glowan in front of her realized that someone invisible behind them was shooting and turned around so quick that Jayla missed her shot at him and hit the glowan's gun instead. The glowan then whipped out an Adapt and had the laser extended out to try and hit the invisible being. Jayla put her arm up in reflex to block the laser and felt the beam burn into her arm. She pulled her arm back quickly and inspected the wound which was just a small cut but most importantly, she realized it had burned through the part on her arm that activated and deactivated the invisibility. She was now visible and the glowans turned to look at her. The glowan that had revealed her yelled something inaudible but Jayla knew it meant attack her. The glowans all turned to look at her and, right before they were going to fire, another Viper came falling from the sky and took out all the glowans in front of Jayla with a few energy missiles. The Viper landed next to Jayla and a resistance glowan said, "We received the distress signal from Dez, get in we could use one more fighter."

Chapter 72

Marctus was now on his knees in front of the group of candidates that knelt facing him. Behind him were at least ten glowans with energy rifles pointed at him should he try to make a move. Behind the candidates in front of him were ten more glowans along with Captain Reath. Of the nine resistance glowans Marctus came with, five lay dead in pools of blood created by Captain Reath. Dez, Sword, Birgue and Reol were all still alive. But Drang, Poil, Gruz, Shale, and Halman all lay face down, dead.

Hours ago, minutes ago, or what seemed like minutes to Marctus, Captain Reath began telling Marctus what he was going to do to end this resistance and if he complied his comrades would be forgiven and allowed to live. The glowans in front of him told Marctus to do no such thing and that was when Gruz was killed. Moments later for no reason at all, the captain killed Poil. Captain Reath then had asked Marctus to surrender again and when Marctus did not answer he killed Halman. After Halman was killed, Shale tried to get up and fight the captain but was shot before she got to her feet and was killed.

Now the captain had the gun pointed at Reol's head and Marctus could see she was crying. Reol had helped him so many times he did not want to watch her die. He finally blurted out, "What do you want?! Don't kill her!" and the captain lowered his weapon. "I want you to end this resistance. Tell the resistance on Earth to join us once again and wipe out the humans so we may colonize this planet for the benefit of our race," the captain said to Marctus.

"How am I supposed to do that when I am up here?" Marctus said to the captain.

"We will send you down to Earth with our glowans to deliver the news to your resistance," the captain replied. "If they don't accept the terms of the surrender, then we will kill you and then the rest of them." Marctus nodded and the captain motioned for them to get on their feet. The captain then ordered the ten glowans behind him to leave to prepare the transport for Marctus.

"Your friends will stay here until the task is complete. If you fail, they will die as well," the captain added before telling the remaining glowans behind Marctus to escort him to a hanger. As Marctus walked up the long hallway toward the elevator he had entered from, he tried to think of a plan to escape this, help his friends and also to set the rest of the charges to destroy this ship; however, with the number of glowans behind him watching him, he would never make it out alive. Sure he may take down one or two but he would be killed in the end as well as Birgue, Reol, Dez and Sword and eventually Jayla as well as the human race.

As the glowans called the elevator down to them, half of the group walked further down the hall and turned a corner, vanishing from sight. The remaining five still stood behind Marctus waiting for the elevator. Still at a disadvantage, Marctus decided not to try anything stupid here either. The elevator had arrived and Marctus was right in front of the door. When the door opened there was a glowan in a dark blue suit that told him to drop. Marctus did as instructed and dropped to the ground and the glowan in the elevator took out a couple of the guards behind Marctus. Marctus then picked up one of the rifles that was dropped and took out the remaining three who were too stunned to comprehend what was going on.

The resistance glowan helped Marctus to his feet and Marctus told him to help him free his friends down the hall. Marctus sprinted back toward the energy sphere and when he got there the captain and glowans were gone. He ran the length of the transparent window which took a few minutes then came to the other elevator on the floor. He saw it was going up and Marctus knew for sure it was going to the captain's quarters where he would hold Birgue, Reol, Dez and Sword. Marctus turned to the resistance glowan and thanked him for saving him and asked his name. "Achile," the glowan said and Marctus then asked how he got here.

"We received a distress signal from Dez that he was in trouble. He ordered us to come here should we receive the signal so we did," Achile said.

"How many of you are here?" Marctus asked knowing that a Viper could only fit ten people on board.

"There are five of us including me," Achile said. Marctus didn't like the numbers but, then again, he trusted that the resistance glowans were better fighters and were fighting for a better cause and could handle being outnumbered. Marctus pressed the button for the elevator so he could take it up and free his friends. "Where is the rest of your crew?" Marctus asked.

"They are finishing planting the energy charges on the floor below. Our mission is to complete placing the charges and get out of here," Achile said and that's when Marctus noticed he had a bag over his shoulder that carried energy charges. "Are you not here to save us then?" Marctus asked not wanting to know the answer.

"Our orders are to finish placing the charges and if it seems possible to save anyone, then we will try," Achile replied to Marctus. Marctus then nodded and remembered that this level had no charges placed on it. Dez had been captured before the charges were placed. "Hand me some charges and let's finish placing them around here," Marctus said.

Marctus placed one right next to the elevator then told Achile to finish the hallway while he was going back and place them all along the transparent window. When Marctus reached the energy sphere, he began placing the charges in sections along the window. Then, because he could not get to the top of the large window, he took out a small device that launched the energy chargers. When they were all stuck on the window, Marctus thought he had close to a hundred charges in this area and knew that should be enough.

He then finished placing charges through half of the hallway he had entered through and met Achile by the elevator he had rescued him at. "Is it possible to rescue my friends?" Marctus asked and Achile then spoke to who Marctus assumed were other resistance glowans and said, "The charges have all been placed. We can attempt to rescue your friends but if it's too risky, we will leave." Marctus nodded that he understood the orders and when the elevator arrived he got in it and ascended toward the floor where the captain was holding his friends hostage.

Chapter 73

Jayla had exited the Viper and followed the four glowans through a series of hallways and doors before they reached an elevator and split up. She went with another resistance glowan and the other three went somewhere she didn't know. As she followed the resistance glowan she told him she shouldn't be here and the glowan asked why. She saw an empty room and pulled the glowan inside and took her helmet off.

"Jayla! We thought you were just another glowan," said the resistance glowan frantically. Jayla asked his name and learned that he went by the name of Dagor. "Dagor, it's okay I want to help but I need to be invisible," Jayla said to him.

"Of course, of course. Follow me," Dagor said and he left the small room they were hiding in and ran down the hallway. Dagor made a quick left at a narrow hallway and then a right into a large room containing space suits. Jayla grabbed one of the female Elite suits and put it on then went back into invisibility. "Much better," Jayla said to herself. Dagor then nodded and motioned for her to follow.

"Where are we going?" Jayla asked as Dagor led her through a maze of hallways. If Dagor lost her on this ship, she would be lost forever. "We're headed to place charges in the control room of the ship. It was not in the original plan, but in case of an emergency like this, it had been ordered by Dez to do," Dagor said then stopped just outside a large door.

Dagor pressed a small switch on the wall that Jayla didn't see until Dagor had pressed it and the door opened. Dagor signaled for her to stay back and Jayla heard voices from inside. "Who opened the door?" one of the voices said. "I don't know go check it out," said another.

A glowan then emerged from the door and, when he exited, Dagor shut the door behind him and then shot him. Dagor dragged his lifeless body to the side and put it in a side room and then opened the door again and walked in. He fired at everyone in the room and hit every single glowan behind the ship's controls. When all were dead, he told Jayla to place the charges around the room and then meet him back at the door. When she had finished, she was back at the door and saw a group of glowans running toward her and the control room.

"We got company," Jayla said to Dagor across the room and Dagor told her to run but she wouldn't let him be killed. She let the group of glowans run pass her into the control room and then she started shooting them in the back. When the surviving glowans turned around to see where the shots were coming from, Dagor took out the rest of them.

"Smart plan," Dagor said and motioned for Jayla to follow him back out into the hallway. He led her into a room and told her to wait. "What are we waiting for?" Jayla asked. "Where are Marctus and the others being held?"

"I'm not sure. I'm waiting for orders," Dagor replied. Jayla and Dagor sat there for a few minutes before Dagor received any news. "We are going to try and rescue your friends now. Marctus seems to be fine but some of the others were captured and they are headed up to the captain's quarters where Marctus thinks they are being held. They're headed there now." Dagor then left the room and started up a hallway with Jayla behind him.

"Can you tell whoever is with Marctus that I am here?" Jayla asked him. "Yes, I suppose I ..."but at that moment Dagor's face exploded blood and Jayla saw that a glowan had spotted him and had shot him. Jayla tried not to scream and was able to hold it in and returned fire at the glowan that killed Dagor. She went over and checked the body and found an Adapt on the glowan and decided to take it just in case she needed to use it. Jayla was now completely lost and had no way of finding her way back. She took Dagor's helmet and tried talking into it but nothing happened. She tried to talk to any glowans near her but couldn't hear anybody. The glowans she was with must be using a different form of communication because nothing was working.

Scared and alone, Jayla walked through the maze of hallways trying to find her way back to one of the resistance glowans. She had to find either the hangar with the Viper, or she needed to find an elevator and then find which floor the captain's quarters were on in hopes of finding Marctus. She decided on the latter and continued trying to find her way through the many dark hallways.

Chapter 74

Marctus and Achile exited the elevator, looked left, and noticed that the hallway they stood in was different from the rest of the ship. It wasn't dark and certainly wasn't as tall as the other hallways. Marctus could actually see the ceiling and lights illuminated the length of the hallway that was before them. There was no hallway behind them only a solid wall and this elevator seemed to be the only elevator in the hall.

Marctus and Achile made their way down the hallway slowly toward a door that stood open at the far end. Halfway through the hallway Marctus heard the elevator behind them open again and saw two glowans exit and run toward Achile and Marctus. As he was about to fire, Achile pushed his gun down and said they were resistance.

"Achile, glad we found you here our communications went out for some reason," said one of the glowans known as Ferce. Achile nodded then told him to be quiet as they were sneaking up to the door to see what was beyond it and didn't want to draw attention to themselves. Marctus led the way and when he reached the door he stood to the side of it and just peeked in to see what he could see. Through the small window of the door he saw Dez, Birgue, Reol and Sword all on their knees in a large empty room but Marctus couldn't see anyone else in the room.

He told Achile, Ferce and the other resistance glowan named Hilek what he saw. "Let's go in," said Achile. But Marctus thought this seemed odd. If they were in there and no one else was, then what was the captain playing at? "Should we just run in there and try and take out anyone we see?" Ferce asked looking at

Marctus. Marctus thought for a moment for a different alternative but none came to mind.

"Let's go in. Be careful not to hit Dez, Sword, Birgue or Reol," Marctus said and then moved to the other side of the door and placed his hand on the switch that would open it. He held up three fingers and lowered them one at a time and when he lowered the last one he opened the door and ran in behind Achile, Ferce and Hilek. As Marctus entered the room he noticed no one was in there. It was definitely the captain's quarters because it was decorated with pictures of the captain from the first years of finding Earth and with all his medals and accommodations. He also noticed that Dez, Sword, Birgue and Reol did not look up as they entered. He walked over to them and put a hand on Birgue's shoulder and watched his hand fall through it. It was a holoscreen projecting them into the room.

"Get out of here!" Marctus yelled and as he turned toward the door he knew it was too late. Two glowans had already flanked behind them and had killed Achile, Ferce and Hilek who now lay on the ground dead. Marctus held his rifle up pointing at the two glowans wanting to fire but before he could make up his mind the captain walked in. Captain Reath had the small energy gun that an Adapt turned into and was pointing it at Marctus.

"Did you really think that I would keep them up here?" Captain Reath asked Marctus smiling. "I knew you weren't serious about surrendering. I knew you had some sort of plan to get out of this." Captain Reath then changed the gun into the laser and walked over in front of Marctus who still had his gun up and pointed at the captain's head.

"Lower your weapon Marctus," the captain said and Marctus ignored him. He wanted to fire at him but knew that doing so meant the death of his friends. When Marctus didn't drop the gun, the captain very swiftly kicked it out of his hands and then kicked Marctus in the face sending Marctus back across the floor, blood pouring from his nose.

"Did your human friend ever tell you how I tortured her?" Captain Reath asked him and then motioned for the two glowans to stand guard by the door. "She begged me to stop before I cut her arm off. But what use is it to a human that was going to die anyways I asked myself." Captain Reath then walked to Marctus and picked him up by his hair and had him kneel on the floor.

"I'm not going to let you walk away this time. I'm going to kill you myself and your whole resistance army is going see their leader die in the most painful way imaginable," Captain Reath said. He then ripped the suit and under clothing off of Marctus and forced him back into a kneeling position completely nude. "What should we start with?" Captain Reath asked more to himself than to Marctus.

He then punched Marctus in the face and Marctus fell over backwards onto the floor. Captain Reath then sat on top of him immobilizing him and used the laser to start carving something from Marctus' face down his neck and onto his chest. Marctus had never felt so much pain in his life and he screamed louder than he ever thought possible. He could smell the scent of his burnt skin and when the captain got off of him he looked down at his chest and saw that the captain had put one of the worst symbols imaginable on his chest.

It covered his entire chest and was in the shape of a diamond. In the diamond was a symbol that was branded on glowans who were sentenced for death. Marctus saw the streams of blood running from the wounds on his chest but they weren't life threatening. It hurt to move his chest or to even move at all. He just wanted to die now. Then the captain grabbed his hair and pulled him to his knees again. Marctus' breathing was heavy and he coughed up a lot of blood. He felt around his mouth with his tongue and noticed he had missing teeth and he was sure his nose was broken.

Marctus wasn't going to die without a fight. He stood up and lunged at the captain but he was very slow and the captain side stepped and let Marctus fall back onto the ground. Marctus got back up again and tried to punch the captain, grab the captain, or do anything to the captain, but the captain simply stepped aside each time and, on Marctus' last attempt, the captain elbowed him in the nose again and Marctus fell over and his vision blurred.

He slowly regained focus and saw that the captain was standing over him looking down at him. "You could have avoided all of this if you would have just done what you were ordered to do," he said. He grabbed Marctus by the hair once again but Marctus could feel no more pain. Everything hurt so badly that nothing the captain did could make the pain worse. Not the cuts to his arms, not the cuts to his legs, nothing. Marctus lay there in a small pool of his own blood and was sure he was going to die any second. His vision was blurry, and he had trouble breathing through all the blood in his nose and mouth.

Then the captain crouched down next to him. He took a long look at Marctus then said, "Any last words for your traitor friends Marctus? Or the human female who I will be sure to tear apart piece by piece?" Marctus conjured up all the strength he could and sat up just enough to spit as much blood as he could in the captain's face. The captain stepped back and wiped his face off then looked back down at Marctus. "So be it," he said.

The captain then had the laser at Marctus' neck. Marctus closed his eyes and hoped his death would be quick. Then, Marctus heard a scream. He didn't feel the pain or even feel himself scream but knew it must have been him. He opened his eyes and still saw the room in front of him. He turned over to his left where the captain was standing and, after letting his eyesight come back to him for a moment, saw that the captain was now kneeling down looking for something on the ground.

Marctus' vision then came back in full and he saw the captain's left arm had been cut off. Had he cut it off himself? The captain then picked up the Adapt in his right hand and lunged for Marctus but before he got to him his right arm was severed from his body as well. Screaming in pain the captain told the guards to help but Marctus looked over at the guards and saw that they were both lying dead. Marctus then focused his attention back to the captain and at what was happening to him.

The captain was kneeling; blood was oozing from where his arms had been removed from his body. He was looking around the room for whoever was doing it. Then Marctus saw an Elite come out of invisibility in front of the captain. The Elite removed its helmet and long brown hair fell down onto its shoulders. Marctus realized that it was Jayla.

"You pathetic human," the captain spat at her. "You have to fight me invisible in order to win." Jayla then walked behind him and said, "At least you had control of your body," and then with one quick movement she sliced off the captain's head and Marctus watched as a pool of blood began forming underneath the captain's body.

Coughing up blood and with tears running down his face Marctus tried to say Jayla's name but couldn't. She ran over to him and placed a soft cushion of some sort under his head and then yelled to someone, "In here!" Moments later, Marctus saw Birgue, Reol, Dez, and Sword walk through the door and gather around Marctus.

"He's going to need a medical bay but we need to get back to Earth. We have one there and there is no time to go to the one here," Dez said. Jayla took a blanket of some sort from the captain's furniture and placed it over Marctus's chest. Birgue grabbed Marctus' shoulders, Sword grabbed his feet, and they carried him out of the room to the elevator. Before Marctus passed out he remembered seeing Jayla's face in front of his telling him he would be alright and that was enough for him to finally give in to the exhaustion and pain and pass out.

Chapter 75

Jayla was running alongside Marctus' body that Birgue and Sword were carrying through the halls of the mother ship. Dez was leading them back to the hangar where a Viper was waiting for them. "Have all the charges been placed?" Sword asked mainly of Dez but to everyone in general. Jayla told him about how she and Dagor placed them in the control room. Dez then said, "I trust that my backup crew placed the charges for us when we couldn't. It was their main mission when they received the distress call."

"Do you have the detonator?" Reol asked Dez.

"I do," Dez replied and stopped just outside the hangar door. Jayla peeked in and saw that there were glowans around their Viper. She counted at least ten but couldn't be sure. "Let me go in there and take them out. I'm the only one that can go invisible," she said to the group. Dez nodded and opened the hangar door for her. The glowans all looked over but when they saw that no one was entering, they shrugged and went back to talking to each other.

Jayla snuck up behind every one of them and fired as fast as she could to kill them all before they realized what was happening. Dez then came in to kill a few that were hiding from her and then signaled for the rest of the group to come in. They carefully loaded Marctus into the Viper and secured him in. Then they all got in and Dez piloted the Viper out of the hangar and into open space. Once they were far away, Dez let the Viper float and they all looked at the mother ship.

"Who wants to detonate it?" Dez asked.

"I do!" Jayla said and grabbed the small round disc that Dez was holding. When she grabbed it a holoscreen opened up in front of her and she clicked on the blue button which turned a bright shade of green then back to blue. "Now any second here…," Dez said watching the mother ship.

After a moment, explosion after explosion appeared on the end of the mother ship where the energy sphere was located. Jayla watched as the vacuum of space tore apart the ship from the inside out and watched as the force of the explosions sent the mother ship flying away from the Earth. Jayla then saw some of the ship get sucked into a large yellow ball which she assumed was the energy sphere, and after the ship got sucked in, it seemed to explode outward and the yellow energy sphere disappeared. Pieces of the mothership were flying into Earth's orbit as well as out into space.

Jayla could only imagine what the humans down on Earth were doing right now. She herself wanted to scream at the top of her lungs because it was all over. The ship was destroyed and anyone on it was soon to be gone as well. Dez, Sword, Birgue and Reol were all cheering and hugging each other in their seats and Jayla looked down at Marctus and put a hand on his chest where the mark was. "You did it," she said and kissed his forehead. "Shall we return to Earth?" asked Dez and he turned the Viper and headed down to Earth.

Chapter 76

Alarms were sounding throughout the ship. Admiral Schur had no idea what was going on other than that, moments ago, the whole ship shook and he heard loud explosions. He tried contacting Captain Reath but got no answer. Then one of his guards came to tell him that it seemed the resistance had placed charges throughout the ship, had detonated them and now the mother ship was floating out into space uncontrollable.

"We need to get off the ship, sir," one his guards said. Admiral Schur was angrier than he had ever been. How could this have happened? Captain Reath had told him that he captured Marctus on board and everything was taken care of. "No, I want a ship down to Earth. I'll kill every last one of the traitors!" he yelled at his guard.

"But, sir, if you don't evacuate now and regroup back home then you're just wasting your life. Come back when we're stronger," said the guard. Admiral Schur knew the guard was right and that his army was now doomed, but he still had an army back home he could bring here when the time was right. The thing was, he didn't care. He had never lost a battle or anything similar in his life and he felt ashamed. He let his race down. "Lead me to my ship," he said to the guard and the guard sprinted from the room with the admiral behind him.

They reached the hangar with the escape pods and Admiral Schur got into one along with the other four of his glowan guards. They detached from the mother ship and, as they moved away from it, Admiral Schur looked at the mother ship and never thought he would see this ship destroyed. "They will pay," he thought to himself and moments later the escape pod went into the wormhole and traveled into the emptiness of space away from the Earth.

Chapter 77

Marctus woke up inside a large tent-like structure. He tried to sit up but a sharp pain hit him originating from his chest and forced him to lie back down. He then remembered what had happened to him before he passed out and felt around his mouth with his tongue. His missing teeth were now back and when he reached up to feel his nose it didn't really hurt and didn't feel broken anymore. He felt his face and noticed the scar that ran down to his chest.

He then threw the blanket that was on top of him off and looked down at his chest. The symbol that Captain Reath had burned on him was still visible as a red scar but at least it wasn't bleeding. The cuts on his arms and legs were also gone and didn't seem to have scarred as badly as the symbol on his chest did. He looked around the room and noticed it was empty except for him and a couple guards standing at the front. One of the glowan guards looked back and saw Marctus awake and alert and then notified someone that Marctus was awake.

Moments later a group of glowans came in. Dez came in first followed by Birgue, Reol and Sword. They gathered around Marctus and said they were glad he was awake and Birgue said he thought he might not ever wake up.

"How long have I been out?" Marctus asked.

"About three days," Dez said. From your injuries I'm surprised it wasn't longer. We healed you up as best we could with what we had and we even used some human technology as well. When he said human Marctus then thought of Jayla.

"Where's Jayla? Is she okay?" Marctus said trying to sit up again. Reol pushed him back down and said, "Relax Marctus, she's fine. She's been by your side for the past two days and is finally sleeping." Marctus nodded and was glad she was resting. Then he looked over at Dez and asked, "What happened after you guys found me? I don't remember."

"Well, Jayla is really the hero here," Birgue cut in before Dez could speak, and Dez then told Birgue to tell the story. "We were being held a few floors above you in some conference room. The captain had them set up a holoscreen and had the holoscreen in his room transmit our images into there so you would think he was holding us there."

"After kneeling for what felt like hours, the guards that were around us all of a sudden fell over dead. We all looked up to try and see who killed them and that's when Jayla came out of invisibility and helped us," Birgue said. Marctus cut in and asked, "But how did Jayla get up there?"

Dez spoke up, "From what I gathered she was fighting with some resistance troops in a Viper. Then some Elites had crashed the Viper she was on and she was then on the ground flanking the oncoming enemy glowans. Somehow her invisibility was damaged and she was about to be killed or taken hostage, but a group of resistance glowans in another Viper helped her thinking she was another glowan and told her they needed assistance because of the distress call. I'm sure if they would have known it was Jayla they wouldn't have asked her to come," Dez finished explaining. Marctus understood though and right now was glad Jayla did come.

"So then," Birgue began speaking again, "Jayla told us you might have been headed up to the captain's office 'cause a glowan she was with told her that might be where you were headed before he was killed. When we got up there, Jayla heard you screaming and went invisible and killed the two glowans guarding the door before walking in. I believe you saw what happened then right?"

"Yeah. I did. So how did you get me out of there?" Marctus asked.

"Right…so now after you had passed out, Sword and I carried you back to the elevator and down to the hangar with the Viper in it. Jayla again took out more glowans in the hangar to clear the way for you and then we boarded and sped away from the mother ship," Birgue said.

"The charges!" Marctus said suddenly. "I finished placing charges in the main energy room! Were you able to detonate them?"

Dez smiled then showed Marctus a video on a holoscreen that was recorded from the Viper. Marctus watched as the mother ship blew apart and was floating away from the Earth. "If you go look outside you can still see it but it is now smaller in the sky and getting smaller every day."

Marctus smiled and laughed. "What's so funny?" Reol asked him.

"I honestly never thought we would win this," Marctus said and it was true. He was ready to die with the humans and he can't believe that it is all over. This brought up a few more questions he needed answers to.

"So what happened to all the glowans when they saw the mother ship explode?" he asked.

"Most of them continued to fight because they were 100% loyal to our race. The others came to our side and are now being processed and evaluated. We have sent glowans all over the world to help destroy the remaining forces. We also have groups all over the country gathering information on whether any humans are alive and other details," Dez said.

Marctus hoped that not a lot of humans were killed. Hopefully they would be able to re-build with the glowans and live together peacefully. He then thought of that small group of humans that had almost killed him back when the battle was just starting and hoped that the humans would be a little nicer now since they had been saved. One more question popped in his head though.

"Was Admiral Schur killed?" he asked to the group.

"We don't know for sure," Dez said. "He was definitely on board but there were a few escape pods that left the mother ship and it's possible he was on one. I currently have glowans trying to find the answer to that question. If he *is* alive, I'm afraid this war is not over just yet."

Marctus understood and knew in his heart that Admiral Schur was still alive. Once he was healed and back on his feet, they would have to start preparing for the next fight. This would mean getting the humans upgraded on their technology so they stood a better chance, not to mention training them on their race's technology efficiently.

Marctus then heard the door of the tent open and saw Jayla standing there. He sat up so fast that the pain that came from his chest didn't bother him. He swung his legs off the bed and Jayla ran into his arms and he felt her hug him so tight. It was the best – but terribly painful - feeling he had ever felt. She looked up at him and kissed him.

"Get a room," Birgue said smiling as he left the tent with Reol, Sword and Dez.

Marctus smiled but continued kissing her then broke away and said, "Thanks for everything." She smiled and said, "I still kicked ass even with one arm."

"Yes you did," Marctus said laughing and then collapsed back down on the bed. Jayla pulled up a chair and sat next to him and explained everything Birgue had moments earlier. Even though Marctus had been unconscious for three days, he felt tired by the time the sun set and told Jayla he was going to get some sleep. She climbed in bed with him and they both slept.

Chapter 78

A week later, Marctus was able to do everything normally again. No pain prevented him from doing the things he wanted and he was able to go as he pleased. For the past week as he was recovering, he was informed that the human population all over the world was better than the glowans originally thought. The humans appeared to have descended into underground bunkers and emerged when they heard the mother ship had been destroyed. Unfortunately, not every human was able to make it and their deaths would be honored.

The other good news that Marctus was informed about was that the glowans were now sharing their technology with the humans and helping to apply it to almost every single human built object. The humans now had electronics that ran on glowan technology so that EMP blasts would do no harm. They updated their medical equipment and the humans were able to cure many cancers and diseases that they had previously struggled with, and at the moment there were a lot of other things in the works.

Marctus was walking with Jayla in Central Park. The trees were all dead, or burned, or uprooted but Marctus and Jayla made the best of what would normally be a beautiful walk. They walked hand in hand and talked about a lot of things. Jayla wanted to hear all about Marctus' home planet and he described it as best he could but vowed to one day take her there and show it to her in person.

"Do you think that day will ever happen?" she asked him.

"It's hard to tell. Maybe if we win this war, yes," he replied truthfully. He knew that a bigger fight was coming and that the glowan army was larger than the resistance and humans combined.

But he also knew that they had better fighters and now that the humans had access to their technology, they stood a chance.

They approached a medical tent which is where Marctus was leading her all along and when he stopped outside of it she looked at him confused. "Why are we here?" she asked. He didn't say anything but pulled her into the tent with him instead. He greeted the doctors standing before them.

"Is everything ready?" Marctus asked one of the lead doctors named Dr. Jira.

"Yes, Marctus. Is she ready?" Dr. Jira replied. Jayla then let go of Marctus' hand and became scared and asked, "Am I ready for what?" Marctus grabbed her hand again and said "Are you ready to have your arm back?" and smiled. Jayla's eyes grew wide and tears appeared in her eyes. She nodded her head vigorously and Dr. Jira walked her over to a chair.

"Jayla please remove just your top layer clothing," Dr. Jira said and Jayla took her sweater off leaving her in just her sports bra. Dr. Jira then brought over a clear sphere similar to the one Marctus saw Dr. Symborg use to make the clones. Dr. Jira put the sphere, which was about the size of a basketball, up on her shoulder. The sphere seemed to swallow her shoulder and it looked like half her shoulder was in a bubble.

Dr. Jira then opened a holoscreen from it and entered a series of commands. The sphere glowed a bright blue, then began to shake and moved very slowly off her shoulder. As it moved off of her shoulder though, Marctus saw something appear behind the sphere attached to her shoulder. As the sphere moved outwards the object got longer. Finally, the sphere reached its end and glowed green. Dr. Jira then grasped the sphere and moved it aside. Now, protruding from Jayla's shoulder was an arm.

The main difference was that the arm was transparent. Marctus could see through it but the objects behind were blurry. Jayla looked at it with tears running down her face. Dr. Jira then took another device and rubbed it over her arm. The arm glowed blue as he rubbed and, finally, when the doctor was done, the arm glowed green then fell to Jayla's side. She lifted it up and moved it as if it was a normal arm.

She looked at Dr. Jira but couldn't find the words so hugged him instead. She then hugged Marctus and put her shirt back on. Marctus thanked the doctor and the two of them walked out of the tent hand in hand. Jayla held it up to her face the whole time they walked, examining it. "It feels normal but it doesn't look normal," she finally said.

Marctus laughed and said, "We were going to do it before the battle started but we didn't have enough time." Jayla smiled and nodded and said, "I didn't even think I would ever get my arm back or anything. I thought I might have to get a robotic arm or something."

"You'd be surprised what technology you can create when you've been around as long as the glowans have been," Marctus said and they sat down beneath one of the very few trees that still looked somewhat normal. They looked up at the now very tiny mother ship in the sky and Marctus leaned in and kissed her. He kissed her warm lips and thought of nothing else, putting all his thoughts for her into the kiss and she did the same.

"Didn't I tell you guys to get a room?" Birgue said from behind them making Jayla jump from the sudden interruption. Birgue was walking hand in hand with Reol. Marctus had known there was something between them all along. He then put his arm around Jayla and continued looking up at the darkening sky.

"Are you ready?" Marctus asked her when the sun had finally set.

"Ready for what?" Jayla replied looking confused.

"The coming fight," Marctus said. "Could be days from now, months, or even years. But, are you ready?"

"Of course I'm not ready," Jayla said. "But as long as I'm with you, I know we will win".

Epilogue

Admiral Schur was looking at the sky. The new mother ship would be completed in a few months' time. At that time the army would be boarded and ready for travel back to Earth. When Admiral Schur returned home three years ago, defeated, he initiated a training program for all of the future soldiers that would make them the best and deadliest ever. With Dr. Symborgs studies about humans, he was able to implement a program that will make the glowans better than they already were.

When Leader Kune had learned about the defeat at Earth, Admiral Schur was close to being killed for failing. But when Leader Kune learned about the resistance and the numerous traitors on board that prevented the war from ending quickly, he gave Admiral Schur the benefit of the doubt. With this second opportunity, Admiral Schur would not fail Leader Kune.

"Admiral Schur you have a message from Leader Kune," a glowan said behind him bringing the admiral out of his thoughts. Wondering what Leader Kune wanted now, he headed back into his quarters and opened the holoscreen.

"Leader Kune," Admiral Schur said and bowed slightly. Leader Kune appeared in front of him.

"Admiral Schur, we have a new development in the mission regarding Earth and it could benefit us or it could hurt us," Leader Kune said.

"What is it Leader?" Admiral Schur asked, and for the first time in a while he was confused as to what this 'development' could be.

"We've found another planet with life on it" Leader Kune said.

About the Author

Brian Shostak is the author of his first self-published book "The Candidate". He is a retired competitive e-sports player and now spends his time writing, gaming with friends, exercising, and spending time with his family. He currently resides in Utah with his daughter Lily.

Stay Connected with Brian:

facebook.com/brianshostak

Twitter- @BrianShostak

Snapchat- bshostak

Instagram- BrianShostak

www.ingramcontent.com/pod-product-compliance
Lightning Source LLC
Chambersburg PA
CBHW030031180626
46810CB00001B/316